TO THE MOON AND BACK

Jean Nicole Rivers

To Lauder,

I love you to the moon and back.

Come to the Dark Side

Go to http://eepurl.com/bUiLp9 to join my email

network and be the first to get FREE short stories,

news on beta reading opportunities, availability of

new ARCs, and much more.

Enhance your experience with the curated playlist and

Pinterest page for this novel.

https://amzn.to/3bZsEhx

https://www.pinterest.com/jeannicole19/to-the-

moon-and-back/

If necessary, please see the TRIGGER WARNING

in the back matter.

Everyone is a moon, and has a dark side which he never shows to anybody. —

Mark Twain

Prologue

◆—◆—◆

Glowing beams from boys' flashlights bounced aimlessly along the gnarled web of tree branches overhead as Timrek Grant finished his story. "Because he was pissed that the townspeople would not pay him what they owed, he used his magical flute to lure all their children into the dark forest. And none of them were ever seen or heard from again."

Skepticism crept into the faces of the four boys. The summer tradition of telling scary stories in Jayden's back yard had made them jaded authorities on what passed for a good one.

"That's lame! A fairy tale. Fairy tales aren't scary, and they're for girls." Russie Cunningham grunted, breaking the silence. He lifted himself and sat crisscrossed, his round belly giving him the appearance of a dollar store Buddha. The effort alone left him breathing hard. *For girls,* Jayden noticed, was becoming the catch phrase for them as they all moved into double-digit ages.

"Well, you got something better, Russie?" Timrek asked, digging his finger into the mahogany waves on his head to reach a deep itch.

"I do," Damien Reed said. At once, he laid flat on his back, gazing at the moon so splendid in its fullness, it seemed to demand the worship of the stars gathered tightly around it. The other boys grew still, waiting for him to speak again. Damien was a veteran member of the group but one of its more silent partners.

Cameron Landis interjected, "Well, if Damien has a story, it must be good. Shit, I've only ever heard him say three words: nope, basketball, and burger."

Everyone laughed except Jayden, whose tense expression was marked with the concern that his father might overhear some of the curse words that had crept into Cameron's vocabulary during the summer.

"Never mind. It'd be way too scary for you guys, anyway. Probably would need to sleep with your mamas tonight because it ain't no fairy tale," Damien cautioned, turning his gaze skyward as the boys' uproarious laughter collapsed into awkward silence. "It's all the way real life, and it happened right here in Black Water."

Jayden steeled himself as a rare breeze that signaled the end of summer pressed through the trees. "Well … let's hear it, Crypt Keeper." His words joked, but cautiously, as if he were carefully removing the lid of a cursed tomb.

Satisfied, Damien sat his flashlight on the blanket and raised onto his elbow into what Jayden assumed was a better storytelling position.

"You know the old, white house off Maple Road? The one almost surrounded by Langford Woods."

"Yeah, yeah, we all know that one," Russie stated mockingly. "The Sandman lives there, and he comes and gets you if you stay up, blah, blah, blah. Just a story our mothers tell us to get us to go to sleep."

"Yeah, Damien." Jayden slumped over to plop his chin into his hands. "He puts sand in your eyes. We know all this stuff."

"Sand?" Timrek's eyes bulged. New to Black Water, he wasn't yet familiar with all its more unsavory legends. There were many.

"Razor-sharp sand that makes your eyes bleed," Cameron taunted.

Timrek cringed.

"That's the legend, alright," Damien said coolly. "But do you know where the legend came from? Why we all know the Sandman lives in that house? How it all started?"

Gazing around the circle, their eyes met in obvious defeat. None of them knew the origin of the beast who, for years, had been the object of their bedtime Black Water nightmares.

Damien smirked. "I heard my mom talking to Mrs. Grant last night, telling her all about it. A long time ago, a family lived there, and the Sandman, with his pointed ears and huge snout, murdered them. One. By. One."

Timrek ducked frantically as a bird took flight from one of the low-hanging tree branches. The other boys broke into soft laughter.

"It was just a bird," Cameron joked, prolonging the giggles.

Damien then returned to his story, and the group mirth crumbled into dead, cold silence.

"One night under a full, orange moon, some raging beast's howls came from the forest and through the walls of the house off Maple Road where two little girls were up late, talking about the day's adventure, which had sent the older sister to the ER and left her with a fresh ankle cast. Earlier that night, their mother had warned them to be quiet and go to sleep, but they didn't listen and paid the ultimate price."

"Into the house, he crept, ducking into the shadows and watching the family from dark corners with glowing, yellow eyes. First, he slipped into the nursery where a baby boy watched his mobile made of tiny, blue teddy bears turn in the moonlight. The Sandman sprinkled some glittering sand and snatched him from his crib, whisking him into the darkness and returning with only the boy's eyes. By this time, the two girls' heads were beginning to nod, but they weren't yet asleep when they heard the noise. The older one sent her little sister to her own room for bed. Then, she limped into the dim hallway where something floated across her face. She waved and knocked the small thing to the floor. Bending over, she saw a bright, red butterfly now dying. Down the darkened hallway, a door creaked. 'Mom?' she called out. 'Dad?' No answer."

"The Sandman slinked along the wall and into the study where the father was working. Grabbing him from behind, the Sandman cut deeply into his throat, spraying the wood-paneled walls red. Into Dad's eyes, the Sandman sprinkled his sand and took what now belonged to him."

"Up the stairs, he continued, all the while humming a soft lullaby. From her hiding place, the older sister recognized the tune but stayed quiet. The Sandman entered her room, but she was not in bed. He looked underneath it, but she was not there either. He rose and turned, locking his gaze on the closet door. When it swung open, she screamed, but he was on her in seconds, and she felt the sharpness of the blade sinking into her over and over. When she was finally silent, with the help of his sand, he took her eyes too."

"In the next room over, he looked for the youngest daughter, but she wasn't there. Under the bed and in the closet, he found nothing. All through the house he searched, ripping open cabinet doors and peeking behind furniture. He looked and looked, but she hid good."

"When the police finally came, they found the mom dead at the bottom of the stairs. The only one left was the youngest daughter who had called them, and all she could say was, 'The Sandman.'"

After a long silence, Russie spoke, a slight quiver in his voice. "Bull!"

"You calling my mom a liar?" Damien retorted.

Timrek shook his head. "What a wacko. That little girl killed her whole family. Didn't she?"

"That's the thing." Damien sneered. "Some people thought that at first, but no kid could do that kind of damage. Besides, there was hardly any blood on her pajamas; that's what my mom said."

The circle of boys went quiet until Mr. Guillory's amiable voice crackled through Jayden's walkie-talkie, startling them. "It's getting late, Jayden. Let's wrap up, kiddo." A directive that was secretly a relief to them all.

Jayden awakened from a light sleep, his throat scratchy from a full evening of talking and teasing. His nightstand held only his alarm clock and the walkie-talkie. He sighed, realizing his mother had forgotten to leave his glass of water at his bedside, a chore she completed most nights without fail.

An unfamiliar creak from the hallway froze Jayden in place; his breath caught in his chest. Listening closely, he waited to hear it again, but he heard only the distant chatter of the television from his parents' bedroom. After the evening's ghost stories, Jayden was terrified to get out of bed. He lay back down, pulling his covers to his chin as he stared out his door into the unlit hallway. After only a few seconds, the difficulty swallowing made it clear he couldn't ignore his nagging thirst for the rest of the night. Cursed with a dry throat, Jayden threw back his blue-and-black-checkered comforter and placed his bare feet on the carpet. As he tiptoed to the door, an alarmed squawk startled him. "Man down, man down. In need of immediate assistance!"

Jayden's heart pounded as he followed the pleading voice to the floor where he spotted one of his toy soldiers.

"Man down—" the action figure began again.

Jayden grabbed the toy and slammed it against his bookshelf until it was quiet. Peering down the hallway in both directions, he ensured he had not stirred his parents. On second thought, he wanted nothing more than to wake them. He dreamed of running down the hallway and bursting into his parents' room, crying. Through sobs, he would tell his mother she had forgotten his bedside water and insist he was much too scared to go to the kitchen alone. But he thought better of it—he was not a baby anymore, and he knew ghosts were not real—not even the Sandman. Besides, a couple weekends before when Jayden begged to sleep with his parents, his father threatened to end the Friday night gatherings if Jayden could not handle them.

The petrified boy took a moment at the top of the stairs like a child walking to the edge of a high-dive pool platform for the first time—frightened to go forward and just as frightened to go back. Down the stairs, his shadow, commanded by the hallway nightlight, followed menacingly, but to his relief, his heart rate slowed as he entered the kitchen. Even under the thick cloak of night, he realized the haunting shapes and shadows at first glance were nothing more than a mundane medley of familiar family possessions. This was his home; he knew every corner and crevice, and he felt a deep comfort in his propensity to walk it blind. Regardless of the many creaks in the floor or objects that made for easy accidents, the kitchen still preserved a slight aroma of the lasagna his mother had baked for dinner, and his little sister's handcrafted paper flowers stuck to the window over the sink. He knew the way.

Jayden pulled a plastic cup from the cabinet and filled it with water, reflecting on the silliness of his fervid imagination and the maturation that had seemed to engulf him during the last weeks as he transitioned from boyhood. *What monsters?*

Two deep gulps almost finished the cup, but he froze just before quaffing down the last swallow. *What monsters?* he thought again, trying to dislodge the feeling of the presence behind him. The tremble he saw first then felt in his hand served as accelerant to the fear that initiated it, and at once, he was plunged into a self-induced cycle of fear over which he swiftly lost control. As he turned, time seem to slow at first sight of the imposing figure. His breath now caught in his throat and grew like expanding foam, working wildly to sever any supply of oxygen to his chest. Even in the dim light, Jayden could discern the two sharp ears growing pointedly from the top of its head, the beast's bulbous eyes cutting through him in a jaundiced glare. With his free hand, Jayden slapped his palm to his chest to keep his frenzied heart in place.

It's him. He's here. The Sandman.

Clawed paws reached for the boy's bourbon-brown eyes. "Jayden …" His name was thick on the beast's tongue before melting into the most familiar pitch.

A salvaging light filled the room, pulling Jayden's hand from his heart to his blinded eyes. His vision strained between the cracks of his fingers, revealing a fragmented image of his mother, her hand on the light switch, her floral-printed robe cinched tightly at her waist with her reading glasses perched perfectly on her nose and two rollers sitting clumsily atop her head.

"What are you doing?" she asked through a yawn as she rolled her neck from side to side.

It took every ounce of restraint Jayden possessed not to collapse onto the floor as he exhaled with such gravity it pained his chest. "Just getting water, Mom. You forgot."

She took the cup from his hand, washed it, and placed it on the dish mat—maternal groan included. "Back to bed. Now."

With an obedient nod, he raced up the stairs, jumped into bed, and buried himself under his comforter in a seamless sequence of movement. From beneath the cover, his hand appeared, searching the nightstand until he located the walkie-talkie.

"J-Man to D-One, you there?" A noisy crackling prompted Jayden to adjust the volume. "J-Man to D-One, come in."

From the home on the other side of the fence, Damien's voice sleepily snapped through. "D-One, here. What's up?"

"I-I was just wondering … What ever happened to the girl?" Jayden swallowed hard.

"What girl?" Damien's annoyance was apparent.

"The one from your story. Do you know what happened to her?"

"*Go to sleep!*" his mother yelled as she passed his room.

"Yes, Mom," he responded just as her bedroom door closed.

"Negatory." Damien's voice filtered through with a soft crackle.

Shoving the walkie-talkie under his pillow, Jayden flipped onto his back and tried to resolve himself to the unsatisfying conclusion to Damien's tale, but within seconds, he could no longer fight the fatigue from the day, and his eyes fluttered to a close. Brilliant moonlight flooded the room and the hallway just outside Jayden's bedroom door where a peculiar shape slid along the angles of the silvery light before vanishing into the home's otherwise dull darkness.

Chapter 1

—◆—◆—◆—

Behind the black eye holes of a new bunny mask, Jada Parker squinted. Aaliyah glanced up from the honey-colored sunflower on her sketch pad, playful specs of sunlight hopping along the twisted ropes of her brown hair.

"Maybe if you took off that stupid thing, you could see better," Aaliyah said flatly, her attention drawn to the sprawling trees that streamed by the truck window at such speed that at times, the landscape appeared an endless abstract of sage and walnut watercolors.

"I can see just fine," eight-year-old Jada snapped, the triumph of the speedy comeback short lived since not only could she *not* see, but now she was lying about it—and Jada Parker disliked lies even more than she disliked not being able to see straight.

Through the rearview mirror, Mack Parker narrowed his eyes at his daughters before interjecting, "Girls." Not that it did much good. Aaliyah and Jada respected their father, sure, but he could never correct them with a look as did their mother. The fault was in his eyes; they were too kind, especially when set on his family.

"Fine. I can't see," Jada mumbled to no one in particular, exhaling in relief at her reclaimed record of honesty.

With eyes pressed shut, Simone Parker stirred gently in the passenger seat, contemplating whether to emerge from her feigned sleep and join her husband's efforts to wrangle their daughters. Each of

Simone's limbs were heavy from the move. Even her mouth seemed weighted and hesitant to speak, but it was Mack who had done most of the moving and most of the driving; the least she could do was keep the girls on their best behavior as they neared the end of their long road trip. For the most part, her daughters occupied themselves quite maturely for much of the drive time. Restlessness was rightfully setting in as they approached their fifth hour as prisoners of the tightly packed pickup truck, restrained within its taut belts.

Not a moment after Simone blinked her eyes open, Aaliyah pounced with a whine. "Mom, did you have to buy Jada those stupid masks?"

"They're adorable," Simone said with a yawn.

"Yep, they're adorable," Jada parroted, snaking her head toward her sister. Just below the mask that covered her eyes and nose, profound Cabbage Patch Kid-like dimples surfaced on her rounded and richly bronzed-colored cheeks as she smiled.

"They're creepy," Aaliyah said in a sneer.

Jada chirped with a giggle. "Adorable!"

"You got your sketchpad and pencils," Simone interjected, her patience wearing thin. "Your sister wanted those masks and the book, so everyone is happy, right?"

"They are a *little* creepy," Mack added just as the car quieted.

"Daddy!" Jada cried playfully.

A thin smile curled Simone's lip, and she whispered, "Instigator."

"Thank you, Daddy," Aaliyah said smugly before an infectious laugh escaped her and swept through the truck.

Simone pulled her homemade smoothie from the cup holder and took the last sip, raising her eyebrows at the intensely fresh flavor. This far into the new pregnancy regimen, she should have been used to it, but every so often she tried a new recipe, and this morning's spinach-based concoction was what Simone could only imagine was like eating newly mowed grass.

In the back seat, Jada's eyelids grew heavy, blinking until they consumed her consciousness.

Earbuds in, Aaliyah retreated into her self-contained, pre-teen reality, with her focus on whatever image she was now sketching.

As Mack pressed the button at his left side to crack the window, Simone read the stern expression sculpted by her husband's furrowed eyebrows and tight lips. She wished it were as simple to examine his inner thoughts as it was the distorted aesthetic that was the result.

"Everything will be okay," Simone assured her husband, squeezing his hand.

He was the spitting image of his father, the man a car accident took when Mack was barely eight years old. Studying his profile, she marveled at his strong nose, his artfully engineered jawline, and the heartbreaker smile that refused to age no matter how many years passed.

Mack kissed his wife's hand before placing his on her rounded belly. "I know." He glanced in her direction without making eye contact.

A face created of symmetrical shapes and clean lines that met upon Simone's smooth skin always confirmed her attractiveness, but her reflection never betrayed her with illusions of supreme beauty, which occasionally caused her curiosity on her merit for Mack's choosing. Once before, in a rare moment of raw vulnerability, Mack confided in her that it was her permanence and strength that drew him. Glamorous it was not, but also not easily imitated, and Simone took the practical singularity that captured her man's adoration as a compliment.

"You know I'm not completely thrilled about this move, but I think it's good and necessary. The house is paid off and in good shape. The"

"We've spent the last of our savings," Mack reminded her in a hushed tone likely meant to ensure the girls did not hear. Indeed, it was a startling notion. The unpredictability of uprooting one's family and moving them to start a new business and a new life almost required narcotics to cope.

With the death of Mack's father—the dissevering of a most smoothly operating unit—his mother was destroyed, yet that insistent sorrow of singleness thrust her into the clutches of one uneasy relationship after another. Each breakup launching her into an emotional volatility that made her unrecognizable to her young son who developed a stutter as a result of the inherited stress—a flaw of the troubled childhood Mack worked tirelessly to correct as an adult.

Without hesitation, he loved his mother, especially the improved version who had grown from her eventual second marriage, but alone, she never had the penchant for emotional endurance that made it safe for a child to trust. Simone craved maintaining her post upon that pedestal of sturdiness in her husband's life.

"We didn't spend it. We invested it … in a shop … for you. Instantly, you go from out-of-work mechanic to finally owning your own place. Things will be a little tight, but it'll work."

He smiled, a gesture that made him a twin of the father-in-law Simone only knew through photographs. Mack *was* her rock, just as his father had been to his mother. Over the years, Simone had heard the stories more than once. Every evening, a brawny Mr. Parker would fumble his keys in the front door lock. Every other Friday afternoon, he would relinquish his check to his wife to ensure every bill was paid, and every Friday evening when he traipsed to the local hole in the wall with his weekly allowance—which would be well spent watering him to a maudlin state—he would once again walk through the front door no later than 11 p.m. Even if Mack forgot every trivial detail of his father's life, he could never lose the fact he was always lovingly present.

"You should be resting, not working." Mack caressed his wife's stomach.

"I have a whole month and a half to go and sitting at a computer is hardly strenuous. Besides, the money is good for this project, and I need the insurance for now. Honestly, this is everything we've always wanted—to get away from the city, to have our own business, room for the girls to run—only difference is it just kind of happened instead of us planning it," Simone said.

"It just happened so fast, and you hate the house—"

"Whoa! I don't *hate* my house." She was offended despite the dimensions of accuracy.

"Simone, you hate coming here when we have to do maintenance and repairs on the place. You make sure we leave Black Water almost as soon as we arrive, and you never want to stay in the house."

"Mack, my entire family was killed in that house." Simone's whisper took on a shrieking quality.

"I *know*." Mack stroked his wife's forearm. "That's why I don't get why you want to go back. I don't blame you for not wanting to stay there.

I can live with it because I wasn't there, the guy is locked up, and we haven't ever had a single incident in the house. But, if I were you, I just don't think I could do it."

"Well, you're not me." Simone settled in her seat.

"Sorry, babe. I'm not trying to fight."

Simone rested her head on her seat and exhaled. "This thing has defined my entire life, and I'm ready to be done with it. I want my house back. I want my memories back." Simone's voice broke. "I want my family back."

Mack massaged his wife's neck. "Okay, then I'm gonna support you one hundred percent. I want you to be able to have all of that."

"As long as we're together, I'm happy."

Mack leaned sideways and softly kissed his wife, then grimaced. "Spinach in the smoothie? What happened to the fruit?"

Simone sniggered. "You don't like it?"

"Here." Mack redirected her attention to a familiar highway sign.

Welcome to Black Water: You'll never want to leave.

Chapter 2

———◆—◆—◆———

hrough the inhospitable tangle of trees, Simone glimpsed what was left of the Grammercy Bridge; its rusted metal arches seemed strained while the deck had completely relinquished maintaining a full set of planks and resolved itself to picturesque imperfection. Years ago, it was a popular site for teen make-out sessions on warm, spring evenings.

Reminiscing in silence, Simone considered a certainty she had struggled to circumvent. Months ago, when they last made repairs to the house and Mack joked about the for-sale sign on Watkins Auto—*"We should buy it"*—the curse had barely crossed her mind. Before Simone revisited the idea after another few weeks of Mack's unavailing job search, she denied its influence, even doubted its existence. As the brawny men pushed boxes into the moving truck, packing pedants, bickering over proper placement, her mind raced to keep it out altogether. But, as her family coasted along the highway into town, she knew it was true—for her, at least.

For all those born in her hometown, all roads—no matter how long or winding—invariably led back to Black Water.

From the trees, a town emerged. Oakley High School, which sat in a comatose state that signaled summer, had not changed from Simone's time as a student.

"So relaxing," Mack remarked, marveling at the Stepford-like order and tranquility as he did each time they visited.

The town square was as it had always been—treelined streets through which peeked classic, brick storefronts. Packs of lackadaisical shoppers looked more cheerfully deranged than happy, like characters from 1950's marketing ads, wide smiles plastered across their otherwise expressionless faces. A parade of stunning Victorian, Tudor, and Colonial homes marched passed the car windows as they drove through the wide, shady streets. How cunning a lure beauty could be when enticing one to the most perilous of things.

It was about ten minutes before the buildings and quaintly grouped houses faded from sight, pushing them to the peripheries of the other side of town.

"Mom?" Jada croaked as the truck bounced from Maple Road unto the long, gravel drive that mapped an easy curve to the house.

"Yes, sweetie?" Simone answered, never averting her eyes from the path ahead as she waited anxiously for her home to come into full view.

"Why do all of these stories end with, *They all lived happily ever after?*" Jada asked, examining her book.

"Because they are fairy tales, Jada Boo. Don't all good stories end with happily ever after?"

"No," Aaliyah interrupted.

As they approached the curve, the moving truck came into clear view, and Simone was grateful for Mack's foresight to leave a key so the movers could start upon arrival.

Mack jumped from the truck with the girls on his heels. "How long ya'll been here?" Simone heard him bellow before closing the door, man-talk for *Sorry, I'm a little late.*

The home gleamed under a sun that seemed could be no warmer anywhere in the world than the Midwest on a summer day. From afar, the face was flawless except for a single black shutter that hung off its hinge next to one of the five second-story windows. Paint peeled from each of the seven beams that decorated the spacious front porch, which only added to the home's rustic charm. Butterscotch-hued light bathed the front yard, lending a shimmery glow as if the sky had recently rained gold glitter. Lush lawn flanked every side of the home in generous volume before hitting the perimeter of trees that led into Langford Woods. These trees were a second home to Simone and her sister, Ella, in their youth. As soon as they could walk, their mother, Dorothy Ann, would take them for long strolls on the trails, picnics under the canopies, games of tag along its hills, and hide and seek in its hollows. There were days when they wandered barefoot because, *Sometimes you just need to feel the freedom of dirt under your feet,* Dorothy would say.

It was not as if the Mills home were a disgraced acquaintance dismissed long ago for some heinous transgression. When the walls needed painting, the floors needed replacing, or the drapes needed steaming, Simone submitted to the call of duty, but it was the ephemeral nature of the tasks that made them feasible. It was a practical estrangement, an adult child nursing an ailing and abusive parent. On previous visits, Simone insisted they stay at one of the three local lodgings in town and rarely brought the girls on site if it could be avoided.

Never had she been ready to exhume the roots that fastened her to these four walls. Perhaps it was the finality in the last swell of her belly or the alignment of opportunity and distance in the rearview, but things were different. For months, the gestation of her child worked in complement with another process that prescribed the expulsion of the shadows, the ghosts, and the Sandman from her rightful home.

"You coming?" Mack asked as he opened the passenger door.

"I'm coming," Simone responded, wondering how long she had been sitting.

Using the truck for support, Simone steeled herself against the warm air and the otherwise charming fragrance of earth and grass that her pregnant senses suddenly perceived as pungent. Her smoothie threatened a disastrous comeback.

Simone followed her husband as he grabbed a big box from the truck bed and marched toward the house.

On the first step of the porch, she noticed a fluttering. A flamboyant butterfly landed on the rail near her hand, its wide wingspan flushed in scarlet and edged with a black the color of a moonless midnight. After a few seconds of rest, it took flight toward the forest. The tingle of discomfort in Simone mounted as the little creature became lost behind the trees that beckoned anything that got too close.

As she stepped into the foyer, it seemed altered even from a few weeks ago—softer, more enthralling. To her left, the living room was filled with boxes and, most importantly, a recliner she had purchased for Mack a few Christmases back. It purposely resembled one her own father had owned and made the room feel complete. On the other side of the living room was the sunroom—a room of windows that made for an ideal painting studio, and Simone could easily see her mother's easel and stool there again. In the dining room to Simone's right, Dorothy Ann was setting the table, swaying lazily to the bluesy notes from the stereo. Through the dining room, in the kitchen, a pot of something delicious bubbled on the stove.

Just in front of her to the right were the stairs and, to the left, a hallway that tunneled farther along the ground floor of the Mills home, leading to a closet, a bathroom, and what had once been her father, Daniel's, study. Light from the room made a butter-colored square on the hardwood floor that looked more like a stain than anything else. For the first time in a long time, the house conjured no sentiments of anxiety. There was no obligation, no cold exchanges over plumbing or wiring. The rooms and corridors seemed to be in a suspended state of lightness, like an unruly child home from military school full of promise to behave.

It felt like … a home.

Standing in front of the oversized, oval, hallway mirror, Simone studied herself—her average height, her head full of thick black waves of hair and eyes that glittered a spectrum of browns when caught in an ideal slant of light. In their early phases of dating—as Simone had teetered on whether to fall in love with the broad man whose quiet laugh at his own silliness had always infected her, launching her into her own irrepressible chuckle in otherwise quiet bookstores, the man who had asked her penetrating questions from across the table in romantic restaurants—it was the eyes that were decisive. Not his, as beautiful as they were, but her own. Mack had insisted he would marry her, if for no other reason than he wanted his children to have *those* eyes—her eyes.

Turning to view her profile in the mirror, she pulled her loose shirt snug against her belly so that she could survey its growth.

There was a crash on the second floor, and Simone turned to the landing at the top of the stairs. She gasped at the sight of her sister, Ella, who cradled baby Charlie, in her arms. In Ella's face, a smile began to bloom just before her features drew back in fear as snarling, salivating breaths erupted from the vast darkness at Ella's back.

"You're not real," Simone murmured, closing her eyes and reopening them to discover a place she barely recognized. The room disintegrated into decay. Memories of the good times receded into a decrepit darkness that spread over the home like mold, slowing her mother's mournful music to a dreadful crawl.

It wasn't real—none of it was real, she knew, but she had to touch it. The pulsating black sludge that covered the banister reached to her almost as much she stretched her hand to it. Only inches from the oddity, she shook when she felt someone grab her from behind. Turning, she found herself securely wrapped in her husband's arms, returned to her home in its expected state. The bannister was clean, and the landing at the top of the stairs was empty except for the sunlight that poured into the hallway from the bedroom windows.

Aaliyah and Jada appeared briefly, lost in giggles as they galloped from one side of the upstairs through the landing to the other side, exploring each new corner, the sound like bells driving out the darkness.

"Mom!" Aaliyah called. "There's a hole in the floor."

"What?" Mack shouted. "Where?" He started for the stairs.

"In the hallway closet."

Simone grabbed her husband's hand with a gentle squeeze. "It's the laundry chute."

Mack exhaled before marching back out the door to grab the last of the boxes from the moving truck.

"The *what?*" Jada sang.

"The laundry chute. You put your dirty clothes in there, and they fall into the basement near the washer and dryer."

The girls engaged in some excited exchange over the domestic peculiarity before chasing one another down the stairs and through the dining room.

"No running," Simone commanded, but it was too late. The girls had blown through the kitchen, leaving only the resounding clang of the back-screen door in their wake.

Mack barreled through the front door with an oversized box labeled KITCHEN in black permanent marker, and Simone trailed to start unpacking what he brought in, at least what they needed to eat.

"*Mom!*" Aaliyah screamed from the back yard, her panic-ridden voice piercing a stake of ghastly maternal intuition through Simone.

"Aaliyah!" Simone yelled as she galloped through the back door with Mack close behind.

In deep silence, both girls stood in the center of the lawn, staring at the back of the house.

Slowly approaching them, Simone and Mack turned to follow their daughters' gazes. The back wall of their home had been spray painted with towering red letters that read, STAY AWAY SANDMAN.

"Go inside, girls," Simone instructed.

"Who's Sandman?" Jada asked, still rooted in place.

"Go!" The tone of Mack's voice warned the girls that they were rapidly wearing out their margin of acceptable rebellion.

As the girls scrambled inside, Mack put his arm around his wife, pulled her close, and pressed his soft lips to her temple.

Welcome home, Simone thought.

Chapter 3

Radiating orange light from the downing sun illuminated each of the squiggly words tagged across the back of the house. Simone examined each letter, her eyes darting rapidly between them.

"Mr. Parker, we're done in here!" one of the movers called from somewhere inside the house.

"You okay?" Mack asked.

A diffident nod dismissed her husband into the house to excuse the movers. Simone walked closer until she could smell the paint, then she rubbed her fingers into the word *Sandman*, the scarlet residue reminding her of a potentially harsh new reality. Harsh, at least until she could harness the past into something manageable, something digestible.

By the time Simone finished unpacking the kitchen, the entire town was gradually unwinding under the honey hues of dusk. Many of the windows had been opened earlier to air out the house, and Simone, with shaded spots of moisture at the armpits of her shirt, closed her eyes and savored one of the most emblematic scents of all-American summer— barbeque grilling somewhere in the distance.

Something heavy thudded to the floor just as Simone stepped into the foyer. Aaliyah yelped, a familiar but faint sound that never failed to startle her mother. With a giggle, Jada emerged from the closet in her bunny mask. Aaliyah was right, Simone realized. The masks, despite their wholesome intentions, were hideous—rudimentary moldings of animal faces with gapping eye holes and bold features that put one in the mind of sixties Halloween costumes, unintentionally unrealistic to the point that they would later be appraised as peak horror in celebration of the holiday.

"*Mom!* These masks!" Aaliyah moaned as she knelt to collect some of the scattered clothing that had fallen from the box she was carrying.

"Stop scaring your sister," Simone fussed as she passed Jada, sauntering down the hallway. "We still have a ton of unpacking to do, and you two are playing."

Aaliyah's eyes widened. "*I'm* not playing. Besides, she's not scaring me; she's *annoying* me."

"Jada, stop annoying your sister," Mack called from the living room.

"Thank you, Daddy," Aaliyah said before shooting her mother a flippant look filled with those muted arrows that every daughter knows strikes their mother directly in the chest. She turned and continued up the stairs, wobbling under the weight of her box.

"Ever the good guy," Simone whispered to herself as she opened the door to her soon-to-be office. Through the window at the far end of the room, Simone could see the last illuminating ambers of evening giving way to night. Soon the glow of the lighting bugs would dot the blocks of dark all around them, as if God had lowered the celestial landscape to a level in line with the universe's human underlings, if just for an evening.

The movers had perfectly centered her desk in front of the window facing the door. To her left, boxes were stacked in front of the fireplace where Simone and her sister, Ella, had spent many winter evenings flipping through magazines in front of the crackling fire while their dad worked, read, researched, and wrote. Always warm, his office was inviting, except when he had a patient, at which point it transformed into a noir-filtered parallel universe—a narrow but bottomless chasm where the sphere of reality could never quite close to create that protective seal of relative balance. Whenever her father was with a patient, he would tie a shamrock-colored ribbon around the doorknob—a sign for Simone, Ella, and Dorothy Ann to stay away, an unnegotiable practice they must stringently obey.

Wiping a thin layer of dust from the mantel, Simone studied the artwork above it, one Simone had insisted Mack hang as soon as the movers had departed. While another had hung in the living room as long as Simone could remember—none of the renters had ever taken it down or requested its removal—the one here above the fireplace was one she had taken with her from the house many years ago. Seteh—as Simone sometimes liked to call her—was a colorful, feminine abstract that hung in almost every place she had ever lived. Centered in the off-white canvas was a portrait of a woman. Black spirals of hair were pinned to the top of her head, high above stiff and slightly hunched shoulders, within a circular outline where the structural features of identity should have been neatly composed was a mangled rainbow of colors thickly swirled in seemingly haphazard strokes, some of which barely resembled eyes, a nose, and a mouth. Even without eyes, Seteh was endowed with a piercing focus that commenced an unescapable mutual gaze with every woman who passed her.

On the other side of the room, a built-in floor-to-ceiling bookcase was empty except for a dilapidated copy of the Bible with a textured red cover, a book of fairy tales, and an old edition of *The American Journal of Psychiatry.*

"These go in here?"

Simone turned to find her husband standing in the doorway, carrying a box full of overstuffed manila folders.

"Yes, please. We can share this as an office if you'd like."

"Nah, you got it. I'll probably just keep my office at the garage. There's that small room for it," Mack reminded her.

"Oh, okay." Simone scanned the floor as she moved to a box near the bookshelf to transfer more books unto the shelf.

Mack dropped the box on her desk and crossed the room to stand near his wife. "Was this your dad's? I thought your family wasn't religious." He flipped through the Bible, noting several highlighted passages.

"Doubtful. Maybe the Jacksons missed it when packing. We *weren't* religious," Simone responded.

After dropping the Bible, Mack picked up the medical journal. "Psychiatry ... pretty strange stuff."

"Not really, but I suppose it can be. Most of my father's patients were run-of-the-mill—mild depression, anxiety attacks—but he had a few who were more interesting," Simone explained as she filled the shelf.

"I'm listening." Mack fell into the chair and propped his feet onto the desk.

Simone removed his shoes and massaged his toes through the thick, cotton socks. "Well, this girl, Rose Medrano, was probably about fourteen or fifteen. She could move things with her mind."

"Bullshit." Mack snorted; the corners of his mouth lifted in an exaggerated Joker-like smile.

"Not bullshit. I found her mesmerizing. I didn't even realize a psychiatrist could have patients so young. Another was a young man named Marcus who was part wolf. I met *him* for myself. And last, a woman—Betty—she was dead but still walking around, living and breathing."

Mack rolled his eyes. "What's the joke?"

Simone smiled. "No jokes. As a kid, they haunted me because I believed their psychosis were real. They were real, even if they were not based in a reality the rest of us could experience. It was real for his patients, and I never could fully forget them. Once, after a session with Marcus, I went into my father's office to look for a notebook, and I found his medical journal open to a page full of highlights on a condition called clinical lycanthropy. Basically, he thought he was transforming into an animal—in his case, a wolf. Betty Gerard, the woman who thought her skin was rotting because she was dead, was likely a victim of an illness called Cotard delusion, probably brought on by deep depression from the long, painful cancer that eventually took her twenty-one-year-old son. Once I was older, I researched that one myself—just my amateur diagnoses."

"And these are real diseases?" Mack's features displayed a formation of disbelief.

"Very real. The girl who moved things with her mind, Rose, had a severe form of PTSD after an accident where her six-year-old sister became pinned under a car her father had been working on in their garage. Rose lifted it. After that, even though doctors relegated the incident to some rare surge of adrenaline, she got it in her head that she could move things with her mind. I heard my father discussing it on the phone. I remember seeing a picture of her in the paper when it happened. She must have been so frightened. What I remember most were her bloodied knees from where they had dug into the coarse cement as she lifted that car just enough so the little neighbor boy could pull out her sister." Simone eyed Mack who listened in wide-eyed silence. "Nothing too magical. All well-documented physiological and psychological phenomenon."

"You would have made a great psychiatrist—if only you could have gotten passed the calculus," Mack said, finally exhaling.

"Well, I guess a law degree was the next best thing. No math there," Simone joked.

Mack gave a sardonic hoot. "Seriously though, sounds like scary stuff."

"It was, a little. Back then, we believed in the magic and fairy tale to an extent. Often, it was the only way to digest some of the hard truths that came with growing up. Once, when my father had Rose in for a session, he stepped out to take a call. I had come in from the back yard, playing with a soccer ball. Just as I noticed the green ribbon on the doorknob, I lost control of the ball, and it bounced down the hallway and stopped right inside his office door." Simone swallowed hard. "I knew I wasn't supposed to be near my dad's office when he had a patient, but technically, I wasn't. I was just going by the door, right? So, I tiptoed down the hallway, trying hard not to disturb anyone, and just as I approached the threshold of the door, I locked eyes with Rose for just a second before the ball wafted into the hallway and the door waltzed to a gentle close as if under the influence of some invisible hand. I know it was probably the wind from an open window or the air conditioning kicking on, but the point is I believed. That was just one of a few incidents that scared the crap out of me," Simone finished as the doorbell rang.

"Pizza!" Mack jumped from the chair, kissed his wife, and jogged out the door.

Simone surveyed the reassembling of the room, locking eyes with Seteh once more before following her husband. In the hallway, she almost tripped over Jada who was sprawled on the floor, close to the office door, reading one of her books. "C'mon, Jada Boo. Time for dinner!"

Her husband took the pizzas into the dining room.

"Aaliyah?" Simone called up the stairs.

"In here, Mom!"

Simone jumped at her daughter's voice from the dim living room where she rocked in the recliner while admiring the painting on the main wall.

"Grandma painted this?" Aaliyah asked, never removing her eyes from the canvas. It was a wash of broadly stroked charcoals, silvers, and ivories that formed a midnight landscape of dense trees not unlike the ones surrounding their home. Against the slate-colored sky, a circular moon radiated, anointing everything it touched with a divine glow. Dead center at the base of the forest, the painting took on an impressive three-dimensional quality, opening to a trail that led into the deepest cavity of the woods where the besieging beams of blackness converged in an abyss that sheltered the tiniest point. Not visible at first glance—only if the viewer studied it more than once, only if they got up close—there, in the center, they could discern the vibrant spec of blue.

"Yes. She was talented."

"Where is this place?" Aaliyah asked.

"I don't know. It could be anywhere or no place at all, completely made up." Simone caressed her daughter's hair. "I wish you could have known her."

"It's weird, but now I kind of feel like I *do* know her," Aaliyah said just before fleeing in response to her father's bellowing declaration that pizza was being served.

After dinner, Simone sent the girls to get ready for bed as she and Mack cleaned the table. Simone sifted through boxes for five minutes before she located the Ziplock bags and loaded leftover pizza squares into one. She yanked at the refrigerator door three times before it opened with a jerk. "Honey, this door is sticking."

Mack stopped pinning something on the wall by the phone and narrowed his eyes at the malfunctioning appliance. "I'll fix it."

"What is that?"

"A calendar with all the local events and businesses. It was in the drawer."

The current month featured a full-page photo of a blonde woman.

"That's Dr. Penny," Simone said.

"I knew she looked familiar." Mack pretended to recognize the woman in the white coat.

"She told me to call to book my appointment as soon as we got settled."

"You should do that tomorrow." Mack lifted the calendar pages. "This is cool. They're having a summer-closing evening picnic with fireworks in a couple weeks."

"Yay. All the hometown favorites," Simone croaked just before palming her lower belly. "Ow."

Mack jumped to his wife. "You okay?"

Simone cupped his concerned face with a smile. "I think that was my first Braxton Hicks." Her eyes lit in excitement. "We're well on our way."

"But you're okay though?"

"Yes, but that reminds me." Simone retrieved a folded piece of paper from her purse on the counter.

Mack recognized it immediately as he had been forced to review it repetitiously until each of its points were seared into him as much as the statement, *I will not hit others* was embedded into the memory of a schoolboy forced to write it one hundred times after an elementary incident.

"The birth plan," the couple said simultaneously.

Simone pinned the paper to the fridge door under a magnet.

Name:Simone Parker

Partner's name: Mack Parker

Doctor's name: Dr. Jessica Penny

Hospital Name: Gateway Community Hospital

My delivery is planned as unmedicated vaginal.

I'd like my husband, Mack Parker, present before, during, and after labor.

During labor, *I would like the following:*

1. *Medical intervention limited to only necessary/emergency procedures.*

2. *Freedom to move around/deliver in any position I feel most comfortable.*

3. *Music played (I will provide).*

4. *Not to be offered pain medication. I will request if I feel it necessary.*

5. *The lights dimmed.*

6. *The room as quiet as possible.*

7. *As few interruptions as possible.*

8. *As few vaginal exams as possible.*

Postpartum, *I would like the following:*

1. *Skin-to-skin contact immediately with myself or with my husband, if for whatever reason I am unable.*

2. *Delayed cord clamping*

3. *My husband to cut the umbilical cord*

4. *No immediate bath for baby. Vernix should remain.*

5. *No pacifier to be given to baby.*

6. *Baby to remain in the room with myself and my husband.*

7. *If my baby needs medical attention that requires him to be separated from me, I would like for my husband to accompany him.*

8. *I plan to breastfeed exclusively.*

"I've already submitted a copy to Dr. Penny's office, and I will put one in the hospital bag," Simone explained.

"I didn't even know people did this until you got pregnant with Aaliyah." Mack slid his arms around his wife from behind, planting his large hands at the base of her belly, and nuzzled his nose into her neck.

"Me either," Simone admitted.

"Can I say something without you getting mad?"

Simone stared at him blankly.

He started with a snicker. "I love this whole birth plan thing. I really do, but doesn't it seem a little …"

"Audacious?" Simone interjected.

Mack nodded.

"Of course, but why shouldn't we determine how we want to bring our child into the world? We're paying for a service and the expertise of the medical staff, honestly, only if a problem arises. Remember that time you ran to Aaliyah's school to fight them wanting to put her in a remedial math class? We're bold on behalf of our children every day once they're born. Why not be the same about the conditions of their birth?"

In feigned defense, Mack raised his hands. "I'm on your side. It's just sometimes things don't go as planned, you know?"

"I know," Simone said, contemplating the plan, conceived not in refutation of flexibility but in longing for solidity. "I know."

"Everything will be good." Mack drew in Simone once again.

She allowed herself to be guided into the comforting firmness of her husband's chest as she reached to flip the light switch, blending their intertwined silhouette into the tableau of quotidian shadows.

Chapter 4

———◆—◆—◆———

Above Aaliyah's head, the light sputtered, creating a recurring pattern in which the walls seemed to hemorrhage bursts of darkness before allowing the hallway to recover to its original dim state. She brought her knees to her chest and wrapped herself tight as she strained to catch every word of the bedtime story her mother read at Jada's bedside.

"All magic comes at a price, dearie…" her mother's voice sang.

Down the hallway, a flutter caught Aaliyah's eye—movement of a figure dipping into her room.

Mack emerged from his bedroom in shorts and t-shirt, drying the back of his neck with an oversized towel. The hallway light flickered. "What are you doing out here?" He took a crate from against the wall and stood on it to tighten the bulb in the ceiling light fixture.

"Nothing," Aaliyah responded blankly.

Mack's gaze went to the low, rumbling giggles from Jada's room, then back to his oldest daughter. "C'mon, I'll tuck you in."

Right outside her door, Aaliyah stopped short when she spotted it. On the floor was a black butterfly. Its rather large wings sported six purple spots so bright, they seemed iridescent.

"What is it?" her father asked.

"A butterfly." She realized it must have been the movement she had spotted earlier, the fluttering about that had created the choppy shape of something dancing into her room. "It's dead."

With a yawn, Simone closed the book and placed it on Jada's nightstand. "The end."

"Who's Sandman?" Jada asked abruptly.

"The Sandman …" Simone repeated thoughtfully. Knowing this question was coming, she was still unprepared.

Jada nodded eagerly.

"Well … the Sandman is a magical type creature. He comes to little children who can't sleep, and he sprinkles glittery sand into their eyes which makes them fall into a deep, deep sleep." Simone's voice was purposely thick and soothing, like salve to a wound. "When I was little, my mom used to sing me a song about him." Simone began to hum, hesitated, then started again in song as her memory jogged. "Hush, little baby, don't you cry. Here comes the Sandman, close your eyes."

Jada smiled.

"I love you," Simone said.

"I love you more." Jada's voice was reduced to a whisper as her eyed closed.

"I love you four." Simone kissed the dozing girl's forehead.

As she turned off the light before entering the hallway, Jada was suddenly reawakened. "Mom?"

"Yes?" Simone turned.

"What's he look like?" Jada asked with wide eyes.

"Who?"

"The Sandman."

Tilting her head, Simone took a moment. "I think the point is for you to sleep, so you never find out."

Disappointed but secretly grateful at not receiving a disturbing physical description of this foreign night creature, Jada resettled in her bed, pulling the covers tightly around her neck.

"Close your eyes," Simone warned with a soft grin.

Halfway down the hallway, Simone stopped to close the door to the linen closet and noticed a light glowing at the bottom of the laundry chute in the basement. Something moved; a slight shadow across the cement floor made Simone flinch. Bending, she moved her ear closer to the opening but gasped as a figure came into view. "Mack! You scared the shit out of me."

Her husband dropped the basket from his hand at the sound of his wife's voice. He looked around, then finally up. "You scared me! I was just bringing down some clothes."

"Use the chute!" Simone pointed to the tunnel through which she was speaking.

"I forget about that thing."

Simone rested her hand on her head before speaking. "Honey, just leave the basket, and I'll wash it in the morning. I'm gonna tuck Aaliyah in, and I'll be to bed."

Little had changed in Ella's old room; the base of the wallpaper was cream with enormous ochre-colored flowers spotting almost every inch. The baby chandelier in the ceiling—their mother used to insist was an antique—was missing a few of its hanging crystals but still in good condition. The turquoise paint that covered the wrought iron frame of Aaliyah's timeworn bed was chipping and revealing a burnt orange rust that only lent to the room's warm, throwback feel. Likely just her imagination, but Simone would swear the room even smelled of the sweet bubblegum her sister had kept in stock. For Simone, even more than her own room, stepping into this room to say goodnight to Aaliyah felt like stepping back in time. The crux of something being yours was that you came to know it so well you didn't know it at all. After a while, the eye for subtleties was lost, and things changed in such minute increments that one day you looked, and what you thought you knew was now strange and unfamiliar, like a sixteen-year-old girl waking one morning in a room she suddenly realized was for that of a child. This room revived Simone's senses of reminiscence.

"This was your Aunt Ella's room," Simone announced as she approached Aaliyah, who was already in bed.

The girl set aside her sketchpad, removed her earbuds, and met her mother's eyes in question.

"This was your Aunt Ella's room," Simone repeated while taking notice of the impressive amount of unpacking her daughter had done. She noticed a photograph that leaned against a candle on the dresser. At once, Simone grabbed the picture. "Where did you get this?"

"That's you, isn't it? In the middle?"

"Yes," Simone muttered as she studied her childhood image and those of her sister, Ella, and their neighbor, Myeisha, the rich greens and browns of the forest ever the backdrop of their adventurous childhoods at their backs.

"Jada found it in the basement inside a box. Who are the other girls?"

Even further into her own thoughts now, Simone could hardly hear her daughter's voice through the wind tunnel of memories that drove her to some obscure place between the photo and Ella's room. The room pulled away from Simone, fading into a distant blur. The aroma of freshly wet dirt invaded her nose as she beheld the scene of encircling greenery. A young Simone stared directly into the camera, the wind blowing her raven-colored curls in a way that veiled part of her face. She wore a bohemian-looking blue and white frock with a green cardigan, and, on her head, a feathered headdress made by her sister. To her left, Ella stood a few inches taller, two cornrow braids crowning her head. Frocked in a loose-fitting scarlet dress and a ratty fur coat that had once belonged to a single, childless, more sophisticated version of their mother, Ella posed with her hands clasped in front of her. A thin fox mask rested atop her head as she stared off camera into the distance. On the other end was Myeisha; a full bun sat atop her head; her flawlessly freckled face covered with a white, sheep mask—another of Ella's creations.

With almost pristine clarity, Simone recalled the overcast sky being only a trivial deterrent to that one of many forest adventures the trio had set upon throughout the years. Looking back, she wished she could have somehow intuited that day would be different. Only hours from the time of that snapshot, their lives would be forever altered in tragedy that defied their full comprehension. By night's end, Ella would have a broken foot, a result of her fall from the butterfly tree, and an inevitable darkness said to have been birthed in the depths of the trees would follow them home.

"Mom?" Aaliyah called, summoning her mother back to the emotional safety of the present, an extraction for which Simone was grateful. "Who are the other girls?"

Simone gently returned the photograph to its place before turning to her daughter. "Uh … on the right is an old friend, Myeisha McDonald. Her family lives about a half a mile through the trees west of the house. On the left is your Aunt Ella."

"That's Aunt Ella?"

"Yeah, that's her. She made those masks and that headdress for us. She was a young artist. She got that from your grandma." Simone sat in bed beside her daughter.

"What did you get from Grandma?"

Simone faltered. "I don't know. I'll have to think about that one. Time for bed."

"Can we finish reading *Alice in Wonderland?*"

Simone checked her watch. "Aaliyah, it's getting late, and we've had a long day. We'll read tomorrow. Deal?"

Aaliyah's eyes dropped. "That's because you spent so much time tucking in Jada."

Pressing her fingertips into her eyes, Simone sighed. "I'm sorry, sweetie. You know, I used to love all those fairy tales when I was a kid. Your grandmother would read them to Ella and me. Sometimes she would even make up her own. Hey, maybe that's what I got from her, my love of fairy tales." Simone finished by tenderly tapping the tip of her daughter's nose. "Thank you for reminding me of that."

"What was your favorite story?" Aaliyah wanted to know as she scooted underneath the white lace cover that Simone was pulling to her chin.

Simone thought for a moment. "*Where the Wild Things Are.*"

"That was my favorite when I was little too!" Aaliyah's eyes widened in delight.

"I know." Smiling, Simone kissed her daughter's forehead and started for the door. She noticed Aaliyah scanning the room. "What's wrong?"

"I just don't know how much I like the new house."

"Why?"

"It's just weird. It makes a lot of noises."

"Well, it's not actually a *new* house. It's a very old house, which is why it makes so much noise."

Aaliyah huffed.

"What is it?" Simone shifted, resting her hand on her hip

At that moment, a shuffling in the closet startled them both.

"What was that?" Aaliyah asked, her voice barely audible.

"Nothing, I'm sure." Simone crossed the room toward the closet door. Standing just before it, her heart thundered, pumping terror through every part of her body. Though she knew nothing was in the closet now, once ... something gruesome had been crumpled in one of its corners. Simone opened the door to blackness. The small space illuminated with her pull of a thin metal cord revealing little more than clothes hanging lazily and a few boxes along the back wall. On the floor near the front, a heap of sweaters lay scattered. Simone's eyes panned from the high shelf to the floor. "You stacked these sweaters too high. They just fell. That's all."

Aaliyah continued clutching her pillow.

"One sec." Simone raised a single finger before disappearing out the door. In the hallway, she prodded through a couple boxes before locating the object of her search. In a triumphant burst, Simone reappeared in Aaliyah's room, holding up a small item.

"I'm too old for a nightlight, Mom," the girl complained, but not so much that her mother abandoned her task.

"Well, you're still *my* baby." Simone plugged the light into the wall outlet. "I love you, and I'll never let anything happen to you." She turned off the light and slipped out.

The faint aromatic residue of her mother's perfume wafted through Aaliyah's room, now saturated in the artificial tangerine light. Aaliyah lay in bed, monitoring the cavernous strip of darkness that was the slight opening in her closet door. She silently waited for what she knew, despite her mother's ramblings of reason, was coming.

Chapter 5

---◆---◆---◆---

Warm water lapped over Simone's belly as she relished in the evening quiet that would soon be only a distant memory. Babies had a way of sucking the silence from a household as greedily as they chewed at the breast. Unsure of whether she was even supposed to be taking a bath, she resolved herself to the philosophy that after submitting to the babies' unnatural demand for oversized chili dogs—a food she hadn't eaten since childhood—giving up lunch meat and caffeine for the first trimester and alcohol altogether, that she deserved the occasional and modest luxury. The compromise was its brevity, and she pulled the plug almost as soon as the tub filled with the near-scalding water, just how she liked it.

After two kids, she should have known, but with the volume of varying information between friends, doctors, relatives, and the internet, she was still unsure about soaking in the tub—something about not heating the baby ... brain development. *No, that's just during the first trimester*, she quarreled with herself before altogether plunging the thoughts into the bottomless pool of maternal mental anguish many mothers found themselves drowning in if they were not careful.

Vanity was never a gripping vice for Simone, but she loved her body and took what she knew was a foolish pride in not yet having a single stretch mark. Removing the lid from the homemade concoction of vitamin E oil, cocoa butter, olive oil, and a few other ingredients, she admired her divine and stretched form before slathering the greasy mix into her breasts and belly. "I can't wait to meet you, Baby Trace," she said to herself with a smile before slipping on her husband's oversized t-shirt.

"What did you say?" Mack called.

"Nothing. Just talking to myself," Simone responded as she crawled into bed and melded herself into the slopes and curves of her husband's form.

Mack clicked away at the keys of his laptop before shutting it and placing it on the nightstand. "I heard you putting Jada to bed."

"And …?" Something more was coming, she knew.

He hesitated before speaking in a huff. "What's the deal with this Sandman stuff?"

"We've been over this, Mack." Simone rolled her eyes.

"I know, but we're actually living in this house now, so I think that calls for us to discuss it again. Jada is worrying about this Sandman. It's spray painted on our house, and Aaliyah is …"

"What?" Simone pushed.

"Uncomfortable. She thought she saw something."

"It's an old house, Mack. I told her the same thing. There will be strange noises and such. She's just needing some extra attention right now."

"She didn't say she heard something, she said she saw something."

"Saw what?"

"I don't know," Mack responded, the pitch and length of his words transforming to reveal that seductively confident East Coast accent she only heard when he was angry.

"Honey, the Sandman and the story about my family is just an old wives' tale. The guy who did it—his last name was Sanden—sounds like Sandman, right? Throughout the years, especially with the influence of my father having his patients in the house and other aspects, the story became creepy, and the rumor developed that it was *The Sandman*. It's a small town, Mack. This is how small towns work. Kids and adults alike have nothing better to do, so they make up stories, sometimes scary ones."

"What *other aspects*?" Mack asked, zeroing in on the most dubious piece of Simone's monologue.

Simone hesitated. "What?"

"You said, 'And other aspects helped the rumor develop.' What other aspects?" Mack nudged.

Simone's body sank. "Mack ..."

"You know you can talk to me. Why are you trying to hide things?"

"*I'm not*"—Simone heard the shrill pitch of her own voice and stopped to calm herself— "... hiding things from you. It's just difficult." She let her face fall into her palms.

Mack tenderly lifted his wife's chin. "I want to know. I need to know."

"One other thing. I never told you this part because I hate thinking about it." Simone stiffened. "Their eyes, after he killed them, he took ... their ... their eyes." She snapped her own eyes closed, as if trying to save them.

It was Mack's recoil in that moment that Simone was always afraid of. That profound knotting of the brows that twisted Mack's forehead now, as if he were trying to decipher some foreign language, was what

Simone hated. Just being a part of such a grisly affair bestowed some inherent degree of guilt, even unto innocent, unwilling participants.

We're just so glad you survived, was correct but little more than a shabby disguise for, *How did she make it out alive?* Then, *Isn't that strange?* And last, *Something isn't right.* Soon the curiosities and questions infer that a fundamental element of your mere existence is at least partly the cause for the tragedy in the first place. In a lone survivor of the most horrendous of tragedies, a pariah is born.

"Their *eyes?*" He repeated before swallowing deeply, as if to get rid of the sick words that rotted inside his mouth.

"There's an alternate version of the Sandman, a dark version. A hideous monster. He lives on the moon, and he comes down into the woods to prey on people, mostly children, who won't sleep. He sprinkles sharp sand into their eyes so that he can remove them."

"How could you not have told me this?" Mack stood, his athletic build causing the floor to creak under his bare feet.

"Because I don't particularly enjoy telling people that my family's eyes were plucked out by a maniac. What difference would it have made, anyway? It's a ghost story mixed with a tragedy to make an urban legend and at my expense. I never told you because I *never* wanted to have this conversation," Simone croaked, her eyes filling with tears.

Mack got back into bed and pulled his wife close. "I'm sorry," he whispered into her ear. "I know it hurts you, and I'm here for you, but do you think it's a good idea to be telling the girls about this stuff?"

"They both saw the graffiti, Mack. When Jada asked me who he was, not telling her would have only made her more curious. Besides, the Sandman is supposed to be a good guy whose magic sends children off to a peaceful sleep. My mother used to tell me and my sister stories about him all the time. He was not a boogieman at first, and I don't want my children to fear something that isn't real. I don't want them to be afraid. It's not reality. The tales about the Sandman and my family are all just children's rumors. Part of my reasoning for moving back into this house is to dispel some of these old ghosts so neither I, nor my family, is ever haunted by them again. I want my girls to know when tragedies happen, you can't run away from them because they follow you wherever you go. I've learned that. You face your fears head on; that's the only way," Simone said as the last of her tears dried in steely determination.

"Okay."

"I'm tired, and I just want to rest now."

"Okay," Mack responded again without argument as he nuzzled his wife in one arm and rubbed her belly with his free hand until she half slept, sure that his most vital role now was not investigator or instigator but repository for the barrage of emotions his family was filtering through at this tangential time in their lives. One day, he would be the narrator of their family history, and he relished in the thought of such a substantial role, but he now knew not all the stories would be easy.

"Mack?" Simone called as they both floated somewhere along the boundaries of consciousness.

"Yeah?"

"Did your parents ever tell you any fairy tales?"

He snickered. "The only thing like a fairy tale I remember was my father telling me he was going to see a man about a dog whenever he would leave on Friday nights for the local tavern. I believed him too."

"I remember that one. Did he ever come back with that dog?"

"Neva," Mack said, his response sending them both off to sleep.

Chapter 6

———————◆—◆—◆———————

The late afternoon air was moist from earlier rain as Simone, Ella, and Myeisha stood for the photo Daniel Mills snapped.

"Can we go for a hike, Daddy?" Ella asked.

Over their heads, he peered into the woods as if the trees would provide an answer. "It's getting late, girls, and you know how your mother feels about—"

Simone twisted her face in a pout. "Daddy, please! We'll be fine. We've hiked these woods a million and one times."

"We won't be long, Mr. Mills," Myeisha added.

Daniel had always appreciated the sensibility of his daughters' friend. A functional alcoholic was the way Daniel's family had heard him describe Myeisha's mother on several occasions, after which he noted that children—especially female children—of afflicted mothers often developed a strong sense of responsibility. *If she's functioning, what's the problem?* Dorothy Ann would ask. *The problem,* Daniel always responded, *is you're functioning until you're not.*

"One hour and …" He stated firmly, knowing the girls would double whatever time he allotted, but they were almost completely obscured within the trees before he could finish his thought.

Langford Woods had long been a place of solace for the girls. In its hills, brush, and shade, the girls would spend hours. Climbing trees, chasing squirrels, and playing hide and seek were favorites, but some days, they simply laid on their backs and watched the sky, followed birds, or traced the clouds with their fingers. Here they lived imagined lives in deeply spun worlds of make believe that consisted of such profound detail and conjured such raw emotion that Myeisha had trouble keeping up and often grew frustrated with their elaborate play and shared sisterly intuition.

"How is it having a new little baby brother?" Myeisha asked as they navigated through the light fog.

Simone stopped to collect a leaf with a peculiar pattern. "Okay, I guess. He's cute and all, but he cries."

"*A lot,*" Ella added.

"Hope he doesn't steal all your parents' attention," Myeisha stated, bringing the adolescent cavalcade to a halt.

"What do you mean?" Simone asked.

"When a new baby comes, your parents hardly pay attention to you anymore. Especially if it's a baby boy. At least, that's what Cynthia Reed said. We've already been out here for more than an hour. Ya'll ready to go in?" Myeisha asked, always the first to say they should head back.

Simone and Ella were rarely ready at her first request, offering only desultory responses as they wandered farther into the comforts of the woods' wide hollows and deep trenches.

"I'm going to try to climb the butterfly tree," Ella stated, jogging ahead.

"Again?" Myeisha whined. "It's getting late."

"It's way too high," Simone said. "None of us have ever gotten passed the first branch."

"Well, I'm older than you two. Bigger and stronger," Ella stated with a smile as they all looked up the side of what they concluded was the tallest tree in the forest. On one side of the tree sat several butterflies, their outstretched cobalt wings overlapping one another to create a brilliant patch of colorful life.

"Climb up over there." Simone pointed to the bare side of the tree. "Don't bother the butterflies."

"I am!" Ella snapped, finding her first good footing a little above the base of the tree. At first, it came easy, the first couple of feet, but her climb grew difficult as the nooks into which she could dig her hands and feet became sparse as she reached the middle section of the trunk. Searching the mass like an ambitious explorer, Ella discovered a small knob. She pushed herself unto her tiptoes and reached for it. Ella's hand grasped the nodule, and she tried to pull up but failed in firming her grip.

"You can do it!" Myeisha yelped with a jump.

Simone kept a transfixed eye on the butterflies, the mass of cerulean wings fluttering intermittently and imputing upon their congregation the look of a singular breathing creature.

Well above the butterflies, Ella drifted to the other side of the tree where she found more prominent bulges of wood with which to catapult herself upward. Ella's hand shot up in wild search of the tree branch she knew was just above her head, and there she found the steadiness to launch herself farther into the orange sky.

Down below, Simone and Myeisha cheered as she reached new heights.

Ella stopped to catch her breath.

"Come down now, Ella. We gotta start back," Myeisha instructed.

"Just one more branch. I've come this far."

Myeisha rolled her eyes. "One more, Ella."

"Be careful of the butterflies," Simone warned.

"I'm trying, but this is the only place I can climb!" Ella yelled, her breath now short. Extending her hand one last time, Ella tried to grasp the branch above her that was just out of reach. Not quite as high as the branch, a sturdy piece of tree bark protruded. Gripping it, Ella strained to pull her weight upon it. A bloodcurdling crack sent her stomach into her chest as the bark split from the tree. The woodland world around her zipped into the sky as she plummeted.

Another crackle and Simone's hand gripped her own mouth as Ella's ankle crashed into a branch, shuddering the mass of butterflies from an adjacent area of tree trunk into a frantic fleeing. Lost in the raucous sapphire cloud, Simone's attention did not return to earth until she heard the thud of her sister's body hit the soft ground.

As if a loud noise within the now hushed home had woken her, Simone's eyes popped open. Burrowed deeply into her side, she found Jada. After positioning Jada closer to her father, Simone tried to get comfortable. She thought of what woke her. There's no more abrupt awakening than one that rips you open from the inside out, self-originating. Simone often wondered about those occurrences. Were they nothing more than a real-world, physical reaction to a dream action? An instinctual gift warning you to survey your surroundings when you would otherwise be deep in a blind slumber? Perhaps your unconscious mind registered some subliminal stimuli and knocked you from your dormant state just as a prowler eyed your home and, unbeknownst to you, the light you turned on as you then skulked about serves to deter an unimaginable, incoming hell.

In the convoluted bog of witching hour thoughts, Simone was blissfully sinking back into the murk of unconsciousness when she heard it again. A tapping sound roused her. She was sure it was the same beat to which she had originally woke. Sitting upright, she eyed the bedroom's double doors, anxiously awaiting the next calling.

"Aaliyah?" she whispered as she pulled back the covers and got to her feet. At Aaliyah's door, Simone took the mellow drum of her daughter's snoring as a sign that she didn't need to uncover the huddled mass. Back in her room, Simone began to slide into bed when another round of tapping froze her. Turning, she focused on the en suite bathroom.

Like walking on a frozen lake, the bathroom tile was icy under her toes. Nothing was out of place, and for a moment, she thought there must be rats in the walls, though the sounds of their rituals leaned more toward scratching. Tiptoeing thru, Simone peered into the porcelain enameled expanse of the clawfoot tub.

Tap, tap, tap.

Whipping around, she gasped at the reflection of her childhood self in the mirror. Moving closer, Simone studied herself standing just outside of Langford Woods, complete with blue bohemian frock, just as the girl studied her adult image with as much confusion from the other side.

Simone tried to touch the reflection, and just as her shaking fingertips brushed the mirror's surface, she yelped at the flutter of an onyx butterfly floating through the mirror. It was followed by a swarm that engulfed the room at once, violently flapping their black wings and herding Simone to a fall into the bottomless tub, crashing her down into a leaden abyss.

Chapter 7

O f course, Simone should have been at least a little nervous, but she felt eerily calm. Mothers are so very instinctual when it comes to the wellbeing of their children. Like those in confessional sessions of reenactment crime shows who reveal with stony accuracy how they *knew he (their son) was gone or were wrenched from sleep at the precise moment she (their daughter) was believed to have died.* Simone sensed that Baby Trace was not at all in distress.

While focusing on the pregnancy and birth poster that was standard décor in any self-respecting OB/GYN's exam room, Simone felt Dr. Penny's hand fondle her uterus, and she realized that almost everything about this miraculous process was reduced to infographic austerity. Everything was the doctor's levels, numbers, and measurements, which made Simone feel less like the divine mother than the anatomically equipped but soulless female illustration staring back at her from the wall. Surely something more seraphic than mammary glands made us fit to mother.

Dr. Penny popped the latex glove from her hand. "Everything feels fine. Baby hasn't turned down yet, but we still have some time for that."

"I read in a blog that putting an ice pack where the baby's head is may help him turn."

"I … don't object to you trying that if you think it will help." Her face lifted as if with forceps in an expression that openly revealed her skepticism—same as her previous OB/GYN had reacted to Simone's collected blog tips. "So, you say you had a fall?"

"I woke up on the floor in the bathroom. I'm not sure if it was a fall exactly. I don't have any pain or anything. I remember going to the bathroom last night. I think I was dreaming. With the move, the new business, and trying to get the girls settled and ready for school, it has been a lot."

"I see. I'll have my nurse come in with the fetal monitor so that we can listen to baby's heartbeat to ensure he's not in distress. Sound good?" Dr. Penny proffered her hand to shake. "Have you thought about scheduling your induction?"

Cursed with a willful face that refused to veil her true feelings, Simone's expression scrunched. "My induction? You think I need to be induced?"

"Not necessarily at this time, but I don't like to let my patients get too far past due."

"Did you have a chance to review my birth plan?"

Dr. Penny stopped and rolled her eyes slightly into her head, giving the impression of reflection. "Ah, yes. I recall now. And you still plan to move forward unmedicated?"

"I do."

"Have any of your previous births been unmedicated?"

"No."

An almost imperceptible glint of satisfaction swept the doctor's face. "Uh-huh. Well, that is your choice, Mrs. Parker."

As the nameless nurse strapped on the fetal monitor, Simone twisted with the same notions of finding another doctor, perhaps even a midwife—especially after her first appointment with Dr. Penny when Simone had asked if she were aware of racial disparities in pregnancy-related deaths and how she combated bias to which her answer was not a clear, *Yes, I'm aware, and this is how I handle,* despite Simone's desperate wish for such lucidity. It was some slang-ish babble Simone tried hard to forget, though a phrase from the conversation—*Don't hate on the white girls*—had somehow gotten seared into her memory. It was too late. Too late to find another doctor and too late to find a midwife. Besides, the pickings were slim in Black Water, and Dr. Penny had come on a personal recommendation from her previous doctor. The only thing that scared Simone more than the certainty of the things she did not like about Dr. Penny was the uncertainty about the things she would dislike in the next doctor and with so little time left in her pregnancy.

Years ago, when she learned she was pregnant with Aaliyah, she knew little more about pregnancy than her stomach would grow for nine months, and then a baby would come out. After reading books upon books about pregnancy and birth, she learned she was entitled to some say in how her baby entered the world, and while she wasn't ready to buck the system entirely, she had mustered the courage to present her doctor with a birth plan. With Jada, she wanted a doula, midwife, maybe even a home birth—something Mack was hardly comfortable with—but early complications in pregnancy forced her back unto the supercilious medical path. And now with Trace, the life-changing move had made it difficult to comfortably take full control of her birthing approach.

As she figured, Baby Trace's heartbeat was normal. They were both fine. Leaving the office in perfect condition, well on her way to delivering a healthy baby boy, she should have felt joy and appreciation, but instead, she felt like the compilation of terms, facts, and illustrations that made the birth and pregnancy poster ... cold.

Chapter 8

———◆◆◆———

S unlight streamed through the age-hazed glass of the windows, waking each part of the house on Maple Road at its own pace. In the kitchen, Simone hovered over the warming coffee maker, trying to ignore the faucet's maddening drip. All the mommy blogs insisted that one caffeinated drink per day wouldn't hurt. She was a veteran as she approached the birth of baby number three, but new studies came out every year, and she committed to staying on trend when it came to what was best for her children. An anxious Simone adjusted her coffee mug to ensure it was directly under the spout from which her black gold would shortly spew. When the Ready to Brew sign appeared and the blessed blue buttons illuminated, she pressed the one for the largest cup and rubbed her belly with a satisfied grin.

Bags had emerged under Simone's eyes, giving her otherwise sweet and symmetrical face a hint of the haggard. A week of unpacking, helping to launch a new business, and preparing children for school—all while carrying around thirty pounds of extra weight—could do that to a person. The expected bumps in the night from an old house were not helping and had led to a regression of sorts that created an uncomfortable and crowded family bed with Jada squirrelling under their covers every night and even Aaliyah once. It took Simone back with thoughts of the complete lack of sleep the first weeks, even months, after each of her girls were born.

In those times, her daily life was a draining cycle of breastfeeding and pumping—a constant percolator of life's milk to the lips of her babies. *Sleep when the baby sleeps,* she recalled that piece of incessant and often unsolicited advice. The zest for which she planned to apply it after Aaliyah was born was laughable. Once the baby is down for one of the many catnaps they indulge in during the day or night, one must pump, clean the pump so it is ready for the next round, put a load of the baby's laundry in the wash, perhaps shower, and maybe even eat a little something if the duration of the child's slumber permits. *Sleep when the baby sleeps* was nothing more than a deranged male fantasy meant as an attempt to dictate a woman's actions for their own benefit, like the slow-motion sequence of teenage girls pillow fighting in skimpy pajamas at a slumber party. If women slept when the baby did, they would be relaxed and happy and somehow dinner would get made and the towels would fold themselves, but girls don't do that at slumber parties, and moms don't sleep when the baby sleeps. Mothers were the ringleaders of a sleep deprivation circus where they also walked the tightrope, tamed danger, and juggled fire, all while basking in the sated coos of their happy, healthy children. Admittedly, it was worth it.

Shutting her eyes, Simone took a deep gulp of the dark roast coffee even before adding creamer and tried to repress the sound of the drip from the faucet. Whipping around, she thrust down the faucet handle as far as it would go. The drip persisted.

Through the window, her eyes caught movement in the yard. Moving closer, she discerned her husband's figure on a ladder. He was painting over the red letters on the back of the house, his muscles visible through the t-shirt that clung to him as he stretched to reach the eaves with his brush. Simone recognized the deficiency in her gestalt vision of this return home bringing her family immediately closer, like those in coffee commercials as they held hands over a steaming cup. Like any journey—glamorized at the offset by a series of neat expectations and soon weighted by inconvenient actualities—she had given little thought to the possibility of a return to the family bed or the long hours Mack would be at the shop. She missed him more than ever.

After brewing a second cup, Simone headed outside. "Thank you for getting this done." Simone lifted the coffee to him on the ladder. "With so much going on, I didn't think you would get to it so soon."

Mack guzzled the hot coffee in three swigs before handing the cup back to his wife without smiling. "That's what I'm here for." The rising sun highlighted the angle of his strong jawline.

Simone's expectation of intimacy with her husband was increasingly dwindling. He always kissed her in the morning, even if it meant fully descending a ladder. *An irresistible temptation,* he used to say.

"I'm going to the store to pick up a few things. Do you need anything?" Simone finally spoke after a few more smooth strokes of Mack's brush.

"No, I don't think so." Mack applied another coat of paint to the ancient siding. "This is almost a perfect match. Can't even tell the difference." Mack spoke to himself in rugged awe.

"Okay. I'm going to leave the girls. They're still sleeping." Simone watched the last of the spray paint that had dried to a rich maroon shade disappear under the almost perfect chiffon.

"Yep," Mack chirped.

With rolled-down windows to take in the fresh air, Simone cruised through town, internalizing every element. Full overarching trees lined the streets, leaving hardly a single space for the sun to beat down unfiltered. A model sum of modest but proud churches dotted its area, enough that one assumed the townspeople shared a sufficient sense of morality but not so numerous that more secular folks were dispirited by the potential for Byzantine religious protocol. Often the recurring breeze carried the fragrance of sweet-smelling laundry detergent from line-hanged clothes, and almost every lawn bloomed in flamboyant garden-of-the-month flawlessness. In other words, by all appearances, Black Water was the stuff of all-American wet dreams.

At a familiar intersection, Simone spotted her elementary school. She could hear the lively jingle of the ice cream truck that waited for them in the street daily upon the ringing of the school's final bell. The doors of the quaint, brick building swung open, and children burst onto the cement steps—Ella and herself always at the center of the joyful tableau in fits of laughter. As she studied her younger self and her older sister, the buzzing of the bell continued. Soon, the bang in her ear became painful. Squinting in a futile attempt to block the noise, she realized it was not coming from the school. In a car behind her, the driver was laying on their horn. Simone blinked, clearing her vision. No children were on the steps of the slumbering school, and no one was at the intersection except her and the irritated driver in her rearview. Raising her hand in line with apologetic motorist manners, Simone checked the intersection again before pulling through.

At a stop sign a few blocks down, Simone studied Woodcutter Park—the only playground she had ever known to have an authentic carousel. Only illuminated and open for rides on Sunday evenings, it became a traditional rendezvous for child-toting husbands of wives who needed a little recovery time before another Monday. They would discuss the pressures of work and occasionally banter over potential partnership in entrepreneurial endeavors that would never materialize, tuning out the squawks of the children spinning round and round. Admittedly, there was rarely a need to intervene, but once, as Simone rode blissfully insulated in the nauseating overwhelm of gleeful music and twinkling lights, she noticed a girl become visibly sick. As the girl's father exchanged sports highlights with another dad, he failed to notice his daughter stumbling through the moving horses, toothy smiles molded across their wild, plastic faces. At the edge of the carousel's spinning saucer, she faltered before swooning into the dirt, an action that seemed to gain the attention of the fathers who guarded the perimeter. It was the first time Simone saw an ambulance take anyone away; it would not be the last. Now the ride appeared completely out of commission, remaining only as a tarnished tribute to the childhood joy of the town's elder millennials. The morning grew dark, and leaves rustled at the ride's base as the nearby swings did a ghostly sway under the invisible hands of the now chilly wind.

Simone rolled up her windows. Fall always tried to come early in Black Water.

Chapter 9

———◆—◆—◆———

Taking her time, Simone cruised the freshly stocked aisles under the piss-colored lighting. Seventies-inspired melodies that were meant to be cheerful but were overwhelmingly depressing blasted from the overhead speakers so loudly, she wondered more than once if anyone else was bothered. All ladies who once shared a body with another human—the most natural, unnatural performance ever created—knew you could love your family fiercely and still revel in the spa-like quiet and indulgence that came with grocery shopping alone. Just as she was leaving the house, she had heard her girls wake, which downgraded her strides to a creep that carried her silently down the stairs and out the door.

In the magazine section, she stopped and rifled through a couple pages of a home and garden spread. Next, she taste-tested the bagels and cream cheese an older woman in the grocery store uniform had offered, and before she realized it, her list of a few items kissed the lip of the cart.

She'd hoped the trip would pass without her recognizing anyone and with everyone extending the same courtesy by overlooking her. There was no longing to reminisce or rekindle as it always came back to him—the Sandman. Just as she finished lining her items on the conveyor belt, she lifted her eyes and tried to hide her surprise at the familiar face.

Keon Louis was in the cashier's nook, already swiping her toilet paper and cans of soup across the scanner—perhaps a manager, as his fern-colored apron differed from the rest that were brown. Throughout school, Simone had been classmates with Keon and his twin brother, Deon. Their uncle had raised the quiet pair in a large Victorian just above Huntsman's Bluff, a popular point for Black Water stargazing. It was rumored that the two shared telekinetic powers. More than likely, the whispers were originally based on nothing more than humdrum twinhood superstition, but Simone was lettered in the ways in which rumor and superstition materialized into distorted reality. What happened their senior year of high school when Deon Louis drove his 1975 Chevy Malibu off Huntman's Bluff to his death illustrated that mutation impeccably.

The brothers had been the primary candidates for a basketball scholarship that could have catapulted either of them out of Black Water forever when Deon had decided to better his chances by having his girlfriend, Selma, publicly accuse his stronger, older brother—by two minutes—of trying to force himself on her. Not even a full day after Selma's stoic confession to the school counselor, Keon had become the target of a vicious campaign that concluded with him losing his place on the basketball team and any opportunity for a scholarship, even if there wasn't enough evidence to arrest him.

On the last day of school, Deon and Selma had parked at Huntsman's Bluff where Selma claimed that Deon had abruptly began choking. Selma always claimed she had tried to help, but he was thrashing and clawing at some invisible restriction of his airways so violently, her petite form was useless. When the whites of Deon's eyes had flooded his sockets, Selma crawled from the car to get help. As she had started to run for the road, she stopped at the startling growl of the engine waking.

Deon's body had laid limp inside as the car revved forward into the already failing, metal median. Selma had watched in a paralyzed state as the car reversed and rammed forward again, bending the barrier under its hulking steel. It had taken only three ramming crashes before the car had cleared the path to sail into the wide-open sky before crashing into the rocky gorge, Deon's lifeless body thrashing around inside. Selma's uncontrollable shrieks had grown in fury at the site of Keon standing above her on a higher peak.

Or at least that was Selma's story, Simone thought. Keon's uncle had sworn his nephew had been home all evening, and even if he had not, Selma was clear he had been nowhere near the car. The accusations had earned her some at-first-doubtful, then sorrowful, glances. *First, Keon assaulted you, and now he murdered his brother by invisibly rocketing his car over a bluff … yeah, right,* summarized the susurrus town consensus. For a while, Sheriff Handow had suspected Selma—but again, no evidence. Only days later, the medical examiner had ruled Deon's death a suicide, and Selma had recanted her story about Keon—both, not that it mattered. Destiny had now deigned Keon to middle aged grocery store clerk.

Head down, Simone paid for her groceries, her silence made more inconspicuous with the bookends of a short *good morning* and *goodbye* before pushing her heavy cart through the automatic double doors and into the now gloomy morning.

As she closed in on her maroon minivan, the sound of someone saying her name startled Simone. With a quick roll of the eyes, she turned to spot an older woman approaching with the wide, elegant strides of a royal. Around her, the woman carried a golden silhouette that broke up the atmospheric gray around them that now threatened rain.

"Simone Mills, is that you?" The woman's honeyed voice sounded like a blanket cloaked around them, drawing them close in a warm dialogue that pushed the rest of the parking lot into the distance. At every point on her face, the skin drooped just slightly off the bone. Around the left corner of her hairline, a patch of silver blotted her tightly curled, ebony mane. On her left cheek, a faint brown beauty mark at the midpoint of the angle between the corner of her mouth and her eye alluded to a starlet despite its wilting canvas.

Different but the same, Simone recognized her immediately. "Dr. Duran," Simone greeted the woman her father, Daniel Mills, had hired long ago to work alongside him.

"Call me Candace." The woman hauled in Simone for as tight a hug as Simone's belly would allow. "I wasn't sure if that was you."

"It's me," Simone said, her orderly white teeth making a brief appearance from behind weakly drawn lips. "How are you?"

The last time she had seen Dr. Duran in her official capacity was around the time Simone entered high school. After the death of her parents, the family of Simone's best friend at the time, Myeisha McDonald, had taken her in, and she had become Dr. Duran's patient. Against the doctor's advice, Simone had decided to stop seeing her as she started high school. The rumor-fueled biosphere of hierarchical archetypes that was high school would have been difficult enough to navigate for a girl with no family, like a lone surviving astronaut, crash landed on a distant planet with no communication to Mother Earth. Having a reputation for seeing a shrink against the backdrop of an already notorious family tragedy could have only made things worse. Initially, her visits with Dr. Duran had proved comforting—laying on her couch and unpacking the horrific memories, sometimes under hypnosis. But, at some point, Simone had desired normalcy over comfort, even if her normal was abstract at best.

"I'm well, darling. The better question is, how are you?" Dr. Duran cupped Simone's stomach with her mature hands.

"Fine. I'm fine."

"When is this little one due?"

"About another month." Simone sighed with a chuckle.

"Wonderful. Is this your first?"

"My third and last."

"Amazing. What are you doing in Black Water?" Her hands were still planted firmly on Simone's stomach.

"I moved back with my family. My husband is a mechanic. We bought Mr. Watson's shop on Poppy Road, and I work from home as a contract attorney."

Dr. Duran nodded thoughtfully. "Where are you staying?"

A knot twisted in Simone's throat. "We're ... uh ... at the old house."

Candace's face swam into that faint expression of condescending concern that psychiatrists seemed required to master before earning their degree. "How is that going?"

"It'll take some getting used to, but I think it'll be fine. And it really is the best move for my family," Simone said brightly, then took a beat to realize she was being analyzed in a grocery store parking lot.

Perhaps perceiving her previous patient's cues, Dr. Duran concluded, "We should get together for lunch soon, or if you need to, you could just lay on my couch. I'm serious."

"As enticing as that sounds, with the new business just starting and me working contract, my insurance situation isn't the best right now, so …"

Lowering her chin, Dr. Duran spoke sternly. "I would never charge you a dime. Understand?"

"Sure." Simone nodded in agreement.

Dr. Duran started away, then stopped. "I do have to ask. Did you ever work through what you saw that night?"

Stress coursed through Simone's body in fractals, a panicked reaction to loss of oxygen. "What do you mean?" Simone silently reminded herself to breathe. Struggling to dam the memories of him, she blinked hard to clear him from her mind.

The creaking of her bedroom door as it swayed open in the middle of the night made her tremble even now as an adult. Under the covers, she waited as he crossed the room, his sluggish gait leaving dirty prints on the wood floor until he was standing over her, exhaling his foul breath down in thick huffs. Never would she pull the comforter down because she knew if she saw his face, she would never recover. Looking upon the glowing orbs dotted black in the middle that rolled around inside the cavernous eye sockets of the hard, skeletal face that peeked out from the matted locks of hair would surely usurp her breath. His protruding, tooth-filled snout would open wide, and his gnarled claws would extend toward her, digging out her precious umber eyes.

He's not real, Simone coached herself, mentally pushing him back and away from the memories of her bedside, out the door and into the hallway, until she was returned to the safety of the parking lot.

"Never mind." Dr. Duran started away again, her jade earrings jangling at her sudden movement.

"No, please, I want to know. Being back here comes with the fact I must have some hard conversations."

After a brief hesitation, Dr. Duran continued, "When I was treating you, you insisted the Sandman was responsible for what happened. Is that still what you think?"

Momentary overwhelm engulfed Simone. After she had left Black Water, all the evil had faded into a discombobulated collage of, at best, uncomfortable memories. It was like watching a frightening film in the theater that kept one up all night, listening for strange noises and watching for sinister shadows, the recollections of which dulled with each passing evening until the once petrifying reel amounted to nothing more than a few innocuous images. Before, in the city, it was all just something in her head—a compartmentalized part of her past that belonged to her alone. In Black Water, it was different; everyone knew something, but no one knew everything. Its legends were the hard-earned birthright of its natives and just as much what held them together as what kept them isolated. Indeed, like those of Keon Louis and Grady Thompson, the shared tragedy was Black Water communion—flesh torn from one to keep the others alive. It made all its residents vulnerable as individuals but durable as a community. Simone was home now, stronger than the fear that fed the haunt and ready to face anything that would not be forgotten.

"I didn't see his face, but of course, I know the Sandman is not real."

Even after the commotion ceased, Simone remained under her parents' bed, waiting without a clue as to what was coming. Then, there it was; a butterfly with golden wings that seemed to radiate light flew into the tight space under the bed and landed on her finger, instantly relieving her terror. It lifted, hovering in her face before flying back into the openness of the room. A young Simone followed obediently as it flapped into the hallway where she could now hear the low humming of the tape player that expelled the familiar sounds of a woman droning on about the color of her true love's hair. Under the amber hues of the dim hallway light, the mint-colored dinosaurs on her favorite pajamas seemed to glow. As Simone moved through the hallway, pressing one small foot in front of the other, the Sandman came into view.

Chest heaving under his black cloak, he stood at the top of the stairs about to descend.

Simone stopped.

He turned. The elongated bone that spread across his brow was thick and arched in an eternally ravenous expression. A snarl revealed his yellowed, canine teeth. As if he had been waiting for her, he lowered himself to a squat and opened his arms wide in summons for Simone to fall into them.

Simone gripped her belly and moaned through a cramp after which she found herself facing the older woman once again.

"You okay?" Dr. Duran asked.

"Yes, just Braxton Hicks."

Dr. Duran pursed her lips. "Let's get together soon." She turned and crossed through a labyrinth of cars, fading into the clouded light of the morning sun.

71

Chapter 10

————⟢—⟡—⟣————

B y the time Simone emerged from her office, it was late afternoon. With Jada napping, Mack off at the shop, and Aaliyah entertaining herself with her sketches, Simone was feeling satisfied with the few hours of work she could complete. There had even been time to put a chicken in the oven and launder a load of clothes that was now causing the timer on the dryer to squawk. As Simone crossed through the foyer, she caught a glimpse of a man standing just at her property's tree line. At second glance, he was gone, but his crisp, white collar shirt and pressed khaki pants were still blazing in her memory. Simone changed directions and moved deeper into the living room until she stood at the sunroom's threshold. Scanning the perimeter, she confirmed there was no one.

"Oh, Reverend Cramer, have you come to haunt as well?" she whispered to herself before returning her attention to the shrieking dryer in the basement.

Just enough light from the retiring sun stretched into the tiny ground windows to keep Simone from yanking the string for the single artificial bulb in the ceiling. A new pile of clothes lay in the center of the cement basement floor under the laundry chute her family had taken to all too well. After throwing the girls' warm and freshly laundered colors in a basket, she transferred the wet towels to the dryer. Just as she pressed the start button, as if activating her own sickness, nausea and vertigo swept her in a wave. With her previous pregnancies, morning sickness had been somewhat neat and had the decency to strike as its name described, but after some self-assessing research, she now knew morning sickness was common for some women in their last few weeks of pregnancy and, of all of the inhumanities, could attack at any time of day. Lately, keeping down anything was a masterful feat as a variety of even the most subtle smells tested her gag reflexes, and the lingering flavors of reluctant meals coated her throat and held her on the constant verge of vomiting.

"Don't be so hard on your mama," Simone purred with a belly rub as she sat on a flipped plastic milk crate. Filled with forgotten pieces of furniture shrouded in dusty sheets and cobwebs occupying each corner, Simone was reminded of all the tall cleaning that was still necessary once Baby Trace finally decided to make his debut.

A smile lit Simone's face as she fantasized about her son's appearance. Bulbous cheeks that made it appear he was squirreling away food in them was the first feature she created. Round, dark eyes inherited from his father would blink sleepily at her in the evening under lamplight as she plucked her empty breast from his mouth, and his laugh would be an uncontrollable uproar that would shake his body with glee.

Mommy's here, Simone thought to herself as she caressed his gingerbread-colored skin with her mind's eye. With a deep inhale, she devoured his sweet, milky scent.

Almost doubling her over, a violent gag erupted from her mouth at the stench of decay that snuck through her nose and burrowed into the soft tissue of her throat. Simone scanned the basement. Surely an overlooked bag of trash had been left behind, or perhaps a hidden rodent lay dead amongst the abandoned artifacts.

Triggered, the stink forced her to a time when the basement had other occupants. Dorothy Ann Mills had stood in the same spot, her face twisted in a failing attempt to process the origin of the odor. As she scouted the obscure space, she spotted a patch of distinct darkness in a corner.

Dorothy Ann dropped the seafoam-colored laundry basket with a yelp at the sight of Betty Gerard. Draped in the black mourning dress that she had barely removed since her son's funeral, Betty seemed to float toward Dorothy Ann.

"Mom?" a young Ella called as she and Simone descended the stairs. "Are you okay?"

Dorothy Ann steadied her breath before speaking. "I'm fine, sweetheart. I ju … I just need you to get your father, okay? Get your father now!" Her cracking voice shot Ella upstairs like a rocket.

Through Betty's thin veil, Dorothy connected with the beady eyes that dwelled far back in the pronounced sockets.

"You can't see me. I'm dead," the emaciated woman wheezed.

"No …" It was the only word Dorothy could muster through her horror as she noticed untreated—and likely self-inflicted —wounds on Betty's forearms that made a comfortable home for the start of infection.

"I'm dead." Betty's singsong words were less of an assurance than a constant intonation whose consistency made it so. "I'm rotting from the inside."

"How long have you been down here?" Dorothy's alarm turned to annoyance as the woman's uninvited presence suddenly explained days of odd noises and odors from the basement. Dorothy pushed down a gag; Betty smelled as if she hadn't bathed in weeks, and her gown, even in black, struggled to hide the layers of filth.

The thought of her husband's patients lurking in her home with her children erupted her anxiety. Only a few were this extreme, but *why did he have to have them here?* It was a fight she had fought with her husband more than once.

Betty approached Dorothy who protectively grabbed her pregnant belly.

Ella burst out the basement door right into her oncoming father's arms, making her wonder if he had a sixth sense about the trouble inside his own house.

"Betty!" Daniel called with hypnotic calm as he descended the basement steps in shadow.

Betty's neck gave a sickening crack as her head angled on her stiff neck toward Dr. Mills' voice.

"Help me, I'm dead," the woman rasped, like dust from the barely moving mouth of an old ventriloquist's dummy.

"You're not dead, Betty. I can see you and hear you. You can't see dead people." Dr. Mills nodded slightly to his wife.

"I can see you," Betty retorted as Dorothy shuffled her daughters up the stairs.

"Of course, you can, Betty. I'm not dead."

"Not yet." Betty sang the last words Simone heard before her mother pushed her and Ella into the kitchen.

The torn cloth curtain that dressed the concrete shower fluttered, extracting Simone from her memories. Her eyes searched the ceiling for the vent which she spotted on the right side of the basement.

Lifting herself from the crate, she noticed the flit of movement in the curtain once more. *Perhaps a possum or, God forbid, a rat,* Simone thought as she crossed the cool cement. In front of the shower, she stood for a moment before throwing open the curtain and gasping in horror. Simone stumbled backward at the sight of Betty Gerard, her matted black hair growing from beneath her veil unto her shoulders like strangling vines. The impenetrable stink of rotting flesh overpowered her as the inured, little woman lunged forward, her black clawed hands reaching for Simone's throat. Squeezing her eyes shut tightly, Simone felt her backside collide with the wall behind her. With no room to retreat farther, she waited to feel Betty's chokehold. It never came.

First, she opened one eye, then the other and found herself staring at a still configuration covered in the black sheet. With a Scooby Doo villain reveal aplomb, she pulled at the sheet and discovered another of her mother's paintings nestled on an easel.

Partially draped in an olive-colored robe at the chest, a sea of sienna skin was exposed as the woman transfixed on something at a low angle. The skin underneath her eyes was thin and textured, like over-tenderized raw meat, and just along the southern edge of the canvas was something else just out of sight.

On the floor of the shower was a cardboard box. The opening of its ragged flaps revealed a chest of sentimental treasures—old albums from celebrated women jazz singers over which her mother fawned, ornate costume jewelry, and a few extravagant dresses purchased without

Daniel's permission that always, eventually, caused friction. At the bottom of the box was Dorothy's black, smock jumpsuit which she would wear when she painted. It was speckled with brick reds, burnt oranges, and a wild splatter of emerald green right across the chest.

Maybe this was the reason Dr. Duran was concerned. Physically, it was a house, a place for her to live with her family, but metaphorically, it was a home; it belonged to her and she to it with such great volume of roots and tendons that she could never be free outside it, only inside. The risk came in knowing that if she could not feel safe in her own home, then no place in the world could ever hope to offer protection. Dr. Duran's hesitations were Simone's provocations, and she anticipated these opportunities to clear her home.

Simone was startled at the voice of someone behind her. "Mom?"

Aaliyah stood on the stairs with Jada bending on the next step up, trying to see her mother through the eyeholes of a crooked bunny mask. "We found you!"

"Yes, you did. You found me." Simone handed the painting to Aaliyah, scooped up the box, and followed her daughters out of the basement.

Chapter 11

◀◆▶

One of Dorothy Ann's favorite songs played from Simone's phone through their wireless speaker. Simone was an adult before she understood how fruit could be strange. In a random conversation that had taken a turn from contemporary R&B to hit American jazz classics, her college roommate had explained the meaning. After that, Simone had listened to the song intently at least ten times, wondering how she could have missed the obvious. With Jada at her feet, reading one of her favorite books, Simone silently took in each word of the song again as she sipped a cup of decaf coffee and wondered what the world would be like for her son as he grew into a young man. Sure, it was no longer 1939, but little more than method and display had changed—nooses evolved to bullets, and salivating mobs now peered into the entrancing images of their computers and phones.

From the day they had begun living together, the sound of Mack's key in the front door lock—just as it was that evening—was a relief.

As Mack entered the foyer, leaning painfully to one side to stretch out a long-held cramp in his left flank, his coveralls smeared with grease, his nails—nails she had manicured herself—caked with grime, and a smudge of dirt above his left brow, Simone's faced softened as she realized the foolish nature of her vexation at his long absences.

"How was opening day?" Simone asked as she struggled to her feet.

"Daddy!" Jada crowed in delight as she jumped to greet her father.

"Don't get up," Mack said to his wife with a warm smile. "I'll come to you." Mack lifted Jada for a kiss before plopping down next to his wife, his large frame bouncing her. "Tired, but everything went good. I hired another guy—young kid, Nicco. Nowhere near as experienced as Sam, but he loves cars, so we can teach him a lot. It was nonstop from the moment we opened."

"I bet," Simone said, delighted, "Watson's is the only place in town."

"Parker Auto Repair," Mack corrected. "The sign came today too."

Simone's face lit in awe. "Wow, look at you."

"Look as us," Mack said before scanning the room. "I see you did well around here too."

"Yeah, me and the girls got a few things done." Simone rubbed her stomach. "But I have to be honest. My energy is waning."

"Don't worry about it too much. We'll get it done. What is this music?"

"I found a box that belonged to my mother in the basement. It had some of her old clothes and records, so I downloaded some of her favorites on my phone. For hours, she would sit in that sunroom, painting and listening to her music. My mother loved jazz singers. Ella and I were named for them," Simone recalled, picturing her mother there in the sunroom once again.

"We found jewels too." Jada demonstrated, holding her hand behind her ears like the game show glamour girls of old to show off the oversized gold, knotted, clip-on earrings she had pulled from the found treasure box. "I'm going to give these to Aaliyah. She'll like them."

"Yes, *jewels.*" Simone playfully raised her eyebrows at her husband.

Mack frowned at his wife's mug. "More coffee?"

Simone scowled. "It's decaf."

"This was Mommy's. Grandma Dorothy gave it to her. His name is Bobo," Jada interjected, presenting a stuffed animal.

Mack held the once white, disheveled, one-eyed bunny, taking in his musty smell and studying his patchy fur with narrowed eyes. "He looks like he needs to make a doctor's appointment."

"Daddy!" Jada whined spiritedly.

"With a specialist," Mack added as Jada snatched the toy and tucked it safely behind her back with a burst of laughter.

"I'm gonna check on Aaliyah before I hop in the shower. Is she in her room?" Mack asked, jumping from the couch.

"Probably listening to her headphones and sketching. She's not much for hanging out with us lately." Simone took a deep sip from her coffee.

Before bed, Jada—her face concealed behind a kitten mask—played in the bubble bath, splashing and blowing bundles of the iridescent bubbles onto the tile wall. Movement in the hallway just outside the door caught her attention. "Mommy?" she called just as the bathroom lights flickered, revealing the sudden presence of her new stuffed animal in the hallway.

"Bobo? What are you doing out there?" She lifted her mask to get a better view of the new toy she was sure she had left on her bed.

The pirate-eyed bunny stared back at her without a word.

Jada returned to her bubbles, then swiftly eyed Bobo, ensuring he was still in the same place before fully resuming her bathtub play. Shifting the bubbles around the water, Jada giggled to herself, then placed a dollop of them on her head.

An unwitting glance exposed Bobo's impossible mobility; he was closer now, just inside the bathroom door.

"Stop it," Jada whispered with the flat authority all children held over their metaphysically inferior friends.

Overhead, the lights shimmered again, and it moved near Jada. Something with spiritual dimensions that a stuffed animal lacked invaded the bathroom. A figure towered over her just outside the tub. Jada found herself staring at two thin legs with red rivers trickling from the knees that were now disfigured masses of bleeding flesh.

Jada's gaze floated up to the face of a girl she didn't know, Bobo extended from the strange girl's hand. Only a shallow wheezing escaped Jada's throat as she tried to scream. All the space in the bathroom went black, and the ripple of displaced bath water as something waned into the tub froze Jada in horror.

Chapter 12

A second later, the room was flush with warm light again. Aaliyah eyed her little sister strangely. "Why do you have the lights out?"

Wide-eyed, Jada frantically searched the tub. "There was a girl."

Aaliyah fished the soaking wet bunny from the bathwater, hardly hearing her sister's fantastic claims. "And why do you have a stuffed animal in the bathtub?" After removing the drain plug, Aaliyah pulled down a fluffy turquoise towel from the hanging rack and tightly wrapped Jada.

Following her sister from the bathroom, Jada glanced back one last time for any sign of the girl with the bloodied knees

That night, sleepless resentment twisted Simone's face as she studied her slumbering husband. They had only just crawled into bed, and there he was, snoring. His arm and back muscles curved and sloped under earth-colored skin, and Simone was reminded of one of those roughly drawn maps at the beginning of fantasy stories. For her, Mack was almost a fantastic place more so than a person, physically and otherwise, where she often lost herself in the delight of his weight and protection, a mecca to which she was desperately trying to find her way back. Mack loved her, she knew, but every passing year seemed to steal a little more passion from the marriage as if the longer the physical proximity, the more expansive the emotional gap. Marriage was a conundrum for intimacy. Each child added a unique and necessary layer to the family tapestry but was also a ravenous calf sucking furiously at the teats of marital attachment. Their once powerful brand of libidinous *in love* had downgraded into the doomed, generic blob of familial *love*.

Simone shoved her husband. "Mack."

"Yeah?" Her husband lifted from his sleep in the bleary yet panicked manner all expecting fathers trying to sleep knew all too well.

"I thought we could have some time together tonight. We haven't done anything together lately, just the two of us."

Mack opened one eye. "You're kidding me, right?"

Simone's face slacked in the indifferent mask of every wife who knew she was headed down a fallacious path of argument that would only end in mutual agitation but a path to which they committed regardless.

Mack continued with caution. "We just moved. We're still unpacking, trying to get the kids ready to start school, and getting ready for a new baby. You're working. I'm working. What did you expect?"

Good question. Simone realized she had no clue what she expected for her marriage. As with everything else up until now, she had only thought of their move in terms of family benefit. It was difficult to admit her relationship with her husband was an afterthought because that meant she was just as culpable in its current state as Mack. Its *current state* wasn't even bad, which is what made it worse. Simply put, their marriage was *just fine*, as Mack often stated. At least in a bad marriage, points of conflict occurred which was still a form of passion. *Fine*, Simone was fine with fine, but her fear was that, despite all his assurances, one day Mack would wake up, and *fine* would no longer be enough.

Let it go, Simone warned herself before her mouth somehow opened despite her reason. "Well, I certainly didn't think we would have no time."

"Simone, whether or not you can see it, I am stressed as hell. I haven't had a job in months, and I finally have a chance to have my own business, to build something for my wife and kids. I have worked my whole life and never owned a business—never owned anything—and now we have a home and a business. I can't fail right now. Everything is riding on this. Stop complaining." He was almost yelling, his tongue slipping to that accent she secretly adored to the point that she thought, perhaps, sometimes she purposely upset him to hear it.

"I'll stop complaining when you fix the sink or the refrigerator door or the lights that are still flickering." Simone's mind raced in a hysterical attempt to shut her mouth. "And, in the past when I was the breadwinner for this family, I still made time for you."

"Oh, okay. This isn't about me; it's about you! The big attorney making all the money, taking care of her broke husband. God forbid *I* have a chance to be the provider for my family." Mack turned to directly face her. "You just have to be in control of everything all the time! Well, it's no longer working for you or me. You want me to depend on you? Fine. Take my dream. You go back to work full time, and I'll stay home so I can fix a leaky faucet."

"*Your* dream? It was my idea. This was all my idea! You let me know when you have an original idea!" she snapped.

As if he were waiting for those precise words, Mack threw back the cover and jumped from bed. "Goodnight," he said with a snort as he grabbed a blanket from the chaise and slipped out the door.

At least now I'm sleepy. Simone thought. Despite the exhaustion from her undeniably selfish performance with her husband, her increasingly weak bladder forced her to the toilet where she sobbed into open palms.

A knock on the bathroom door at this hour should have startled her, but with a full house, nothing ever came as a surprise.

"Jada?" Simone called out for her daughter whose sleep cycle had recently regressed to an infantile state which drew her to her parents' bed nightly. There was a low scramble near the bottom of the door as Simone wiped and shuffled to the sink.

Little fingers wriggled through the thin space between the bottom of the door and the floor.

Simone sighed as she turned on the water to wash her hands. "Give me a minute, Jada. I'm coming."

Still, no one on the other side of the door replied.

"Jada …?" Simone called again just before the tiny childlike fingers mutated into skeletal, vine-like claws that elongated with the swift power of a lapping whip around her neck in a chokehold. The moment she grabbed her throat, she felt nothing but the pounding of her heart against her forearm. Her gaze went to the gap under the door where she saw only a strip of light. Simone yanked the door open to find her bedroom empty.

No Jada or Mack burrowed deeply in the covers, purring lightly, just her shadow floating through the ocean of moonlight.

Chapter 13

◆━◆━◆

A s the sun came up, coffee went down, and Simone filled the Parker home with the enticing aromas of waffles, eggs, and bacon, hoping to hedge herself from the fallout of the previous night's harsh exchange by filling her husband's belly. Bacon was Mack's sweet and savory kryptonite and always weakened her husband's defenses in her favor. She brewed an extra-large cup of coffee in the biggest mug they had which read, WORLD'S ~~BEST~~ OKAYEST MOM—the gag part of her Mother's Day gift from the previous year when she was working such long hours that her presence became foreign to her family. Simone grabbed the mug's handle, pulled her smoothie from the refrigerator, and shuffled to the living room on swollen ankles. The thing Simone loved most about this room was how much light streamed in through the front windows and the adjoining sunroom. At sunrise and sunset, the room dazzled, and as a girl, Simone would sprawl herself on the couch and watch her mother paint in the sunroom, natural light draping at Dorothy Ann's back in such a way that she resembled those holy figures in the colorful stained-glass windows of churches.

Simone suppressed a laugh at the contortioned lump that was her husband. He was already starting to stir when she placed the steaming cup near his nose and watched as he took in its earthy fragrance.

Mack sat upright with a wince, probably some miscellaneous soreness he had developed from his painful, overnight dance with the couch.

"You forgive me?" Simone asked.

"For what?" Mack took the cup into one hand without hesitation.

Simone drew back. Usually, it took at least three good meals and a backrub before her husband was ready to concede. "For being an oversensitive, hormonal witch."

Mack smiled. "You forgive me?"

"For what?" Simone asked.

"You're about to have my third baby, my little boy. I *should* be more sensitive. I've been too caught up in work. That's important, but so is my family." Mack leaned in to kiss his wife.

Simone paused. Yes, she wanted him to be more thoughtful, but not simply because she was the mother of his children. She needed him to do it because she was his wife—but before she started another fight, she submitted to his soft lips.

"Mmm." Simone touched her belly and tilted her head back with a groan.

"Another one?" Mack placed his hand over hers.

She nodded.

"What did the doctor say?"

"She said I'm fine,"

"What are you having today?" he asked, eyeing the green mush in her cup.

"I already had my coffee, so now it's spinach and green apples—tastes a little bitter though, maybe because I made it last night before bed.

It probably needs to be fresh. I'm gonna finish this, then get in some squats. I need to start opening up my hips so that this little boy slides right on out with no issues."

"I can help you open your hips." Mack nuzzled his face in his wife's neck.

"I just want to open my hips, I don't want to go into labor, Mack!" Simone screeched with a laugh. "Tonight," she whispered.

Mack pulled back. "You've already given birth to two children. You really think you would need a c-section?"

"No, of course I don't think so, but every birth is different, and I always start doing my squats about this time."

"What's so bad about it anyway?" Mack took another gulp of his coffee.

"Nothing is *so bad* about it when you need it, but it's still surgery. I'm not a doctor, but I have always been under the impression that you try to avoid surgery if you can."

Mack seemed satisfied. "How about you do what you need to do today, and I'll get the girls ready for their first day of school tomorrow?"

"*How about* ... that's great idea from an incredibly sensitive husband! I have a deadline for my brief tomorrow. Very smart move to have the shop closed on Sundays." Her cellphone rang from her robe pocket. "That's probably Katherine from the firm now. I'll take it in my office."

"What about your squats?" Mack called to Simone who was already sauntering down the hallway.

"I'll do them while I talk," Simone assured him as she swept into her office and closed the door.

The day seemed to pass Simone in a high-speed time lapse as she plowed through her work undisturbed. Mack shuffled the girls to the outdoor mall to do some last-minute school shopping, picked up school supplies, brought home dinner, and helped his daughters prepare their backpacks. After tucking the girls into bed early—and with the full day and lack of sleep from the night before—Simone was unconscious the moment her head touched the pillow.

Once Jada woke in the middle of the night—as it seemed she did often now—it was impossible for her to fall back asleep alone. She sat upright in bed with Bobo clutched to her chest as her gaze flitted around each corner of the room, checking for unusual shadows through the eye holes of her bunny mask. When she was sure she was alone, she fled the bed and scampered down the hallway toward her parents' room. The engaged lock restricted movement of the door handle. She was still pawing at it when the door of the hallway linen closet opened.

"Can you see me?" a raspy voice called from inside.

Jada wasn't sure if she were asleep or awake, likely the fuel for the bravery needed to creep toward the open closet door. Drawing closer, the stink that emanated from the dark space inclined her to believe in her consciousness as smell wasn't a sense her level of dreaming had often allowed her to grasp. "Mom?" she called as she opened the closet door farther with one hand, clutching Bobo deeper into her side with the other.

The basement light sputtered, casting a sour, lemon colored light through the chute before leaving the room dark again. Jada could only liken the stench to cooking aromatically brazen raw vegetables, like broccoli or cabbage. The scent worsened as she bent over the chute and pressed her face farther into the endless darkness as not even the unrelenting glimmers of moonlight that danced this house in nightly waltzes dared come this deep inside.

"I'm here. Stay with me," the voice called again.

Pressing her nostrils together, again Jada called out, her voice insulated in a nasal cloud, "Mom ...?"

Another sparkle of light allowed Jada to glimpse a figure draped in black float swiftly beneath the chute just as something grasped her arm.

"Seriously?" Aaliyah yawned.

Looking up, Jada discerned the familiar silhouette of her big sister. "I thought I saw Mom."

"Yeah, right. Mom hangs out in closets in the middle of the night." Aaliyah moved backward to clear a path for her sister to step out.

"Not in here. In the basement."

"Whatever," Aaliyah groaned.

"I was trying to sleep with Mom and Dad, but their door is locked."

Aaliyah crossed the hallway and tried her parents' room door handle which indeed stopped severely short of a full range of motion. "Weird." She started back down the hallway toward her room. "You can sleep with me tonight, but you have to take off that stupid mask," she insisted with an impatient flip of her hand that instructed Jada to follow. "What are you scared of anyway?" Aaliyah asked as they crawled into bed.

Jada's eyes made an obvious drift to the nightlight before returning to her sister. "What are *you* scared of?"

A question for which Aaliyah had hundreds of and zero answers simultaneously.

Fresh out of ideas for entertaining activity, Simone and Ella spread themselves across the wood floor of Ella's room, studying the shapes the glare of the setting sun made on her ceiling through the sheer, white drapes.

"What do you want to do?" Ella asked her little sister.

"It has to be something quiet," Simone reminded her. "Mom is sleeping, and Dad's working."

"Yeah," Ella agreed lethargically. "Hide and seek? Twenty seconds."

Five, six, seven, eight, Simone counted silently as she tiptoed through the hallway and down the stairs. Once at the foyer closet, a perfunctory glance highlighted the green ribbon tied around her father's doorknob. Careful to be quiet, Simone opened the door and had just scoped out a perfectly discreet space among the boxes within which to wrench herself when she heard the fierce growling of an animal from the other side of the door. Her legs were already trembling as she peeked around the door's edge. At first, all she could do was take in the multiple rows of serrated teeth, the pointed ears that resembled horns, and how its heavy breathing accentuated the animal's massively hunched back. Eventually, her brain allowed her to stack the images and process the monster as a single hideous thing.

It studied her, its snout sniffing her out, its body poised for attack. Oddly enough, it was the human features that made the creature terrifyingly strange as it arched its body on two hands and two feet.

From the waist down, Simone's body threatened to buckle as the beast began to leap.

"*Marcus!*" Simone heard her father's commanding voice as he entered the hallway from the bathroom.

The animal sneered in Simone's direction.

"I want you to get up. Answer me, Marcus." Simone's father spoke in firm but calm waves of commands like guiding a blind person through a minefield. Daniel stepped closer to the beast. "Marcus, you are a man. Not a wolf."

The beast tensed, ready to pounce.

With lightning precision, her father lunged forward and ripped up the mask.

A pathetic-looking man with a bald head and sunken eyes dropped to the floor with a gut-wrenching sob.

"It's okay, Mommy's here," Dorothy Ann said as she tightly swept her daughter into her chest.

Through her fear, Simone had not even noticed her mother and sister descend the stairs, but the moment her mother held her, every ounce of tension that had kept her body from disintegrating into a jellied mess fled her limbs, and the tension, anxiety, and fear collapsed neatly into her mother's chest. Temporarily unable to speak or move, Simone simply studied the reflection in the hallway mirror of herself tucked tightly into Dorothy Ann.

Ella and Simone laid in bed, listening to the harsh exchanges, and in the wee hours, Dorothy Ann finally won. Daniel would no longer see patients in the house. Marcus Sanden was gone, but the Sandman was inside now.

He never left ... a final crossover thought as the tightening of Simone's belly called her to consciousness.

Chapter 14

<hr>

O nce the false contraction passed, Simone crept to the kitchen for water. She pulled hard on the refrigerator door, once, twice, and on the third try, it popped open. As she gulped down the last of her drink, she noticed the drip of the faucet, the only affront to the comfortable silence. Placing her empty plastic cup under the drip, she seemed happy with her temporary solution for quieting the constant pinging.

At first, the sound from the back yard was a whimpering, but as Simone approached the door, the crying became louder. Through the glass, Simone scanned the yard. Everything seemed normal—the old clothesline, the rusted shed, the oversized garbage cans, the tree line of the forest just a few yards away. *A baby,* Simone thought as she flipped the lock on the back door and descended the porch steps, her bare feet now planted firmly in the moist dirt. Silence. Stepping forward, she listened intently for the cry, but there was nothing now but the incessant buzz of the crickets. Before turning back, she reviewed the yard one last time, her eyes catching on movement just inside the trees. The deep wailing of some forest animal rang, and Simone took the steps two at a time until she was safe again in her kitchen behind a locked door.

Before returning to bed, Simone went to Jada's room and found only an empty bed. Farther down the hallway, she pressed open Aaliyah's door and found both her girls; Aaliyah was pressed tightly against the wall, her face buried in the pillow, and Jada was sprawled diagonally, taking up more than her share of space. Her oldest looked most uncomfortable but better Aaliyah than herself fighting the bed war with the baby for one night, Simone thought as she pulled the mangled covers from between both girls and resettled them neatly on top in a tucking manner.

On the floor, Bobo peeked out from under the bed, his beady gray eye staring up listlessly. With a little effort, Simone crouched and rescued him from a doomed fate of being forever lost in the Bermuda Triangle-like underworld of children's beds.

"Come on, Bobo," Simone whispered as she went to place him next to Jada who was now sitting upright alongside her sister, their black, empty eye sockets staring down at her. She pushed herself back with a gasp.

"Mom?" Aaliyah croaked. "Are you okay?"

Simone blinked to find Aaliyah straining to see her in the dark, her beautiful, brown eyes intact.

Still sleeping, Jada stirred only slightly, somehow elongating herself even farther across the bed.

"Yeah, I'm fine. I was just grabbing Bobo from under the bed." Simone exhaled as she tucked the stuffed animal into Jada's side.

Aaliyah laid back once again as her mother re-tucked the blankets around her shoulders. "You heard it too?"

Simone's eyes caught her daughter's in the dark, "The crying?" Only now was Simone sure she had heard it. "Yeah. It's probably just a stray cat."

"It sounded like a baby," Aaliyah countered.

"Sometimes they sound like babies when they cry. Now back to sleep."

Unpacking boxes of the girls' old fairy tale books unto Trace's bookshelf brought the nursery one step closer to finished. Pleased with Mack's work, she admired the room's perfect soft-gray paint and the wood-paneled accent wall. Aaliyah and Jada had chosen the powder-colored crib and recliner which was draped with a ratty, blue quilt that Mack's mother had made for him when he was a baby. A dresser, charcoal-colored area rug, and a framed photo of Simone, Mack, and the girls decorated the open spaces, and now Simone just needed to place the wall hanging her husband bought. *Trace will be happy here,* Simone thought as she admired the neat rows of books organized by height.

"You're up early. Couldn't sleep again?" Mack asked, entering the room.

"I wanted to get a jump on the morning. Are the girls up?"

"I just woke 'em. They're washing up."

"I'll get breakfast started. You want coffee?"

"I always want coffee."

Simone lifted her chin for the customary morning kiss after which her husband stopped her, held her belly, then kissed her again.

"Are you working too hard?" Mack asked.

Ever sensitive to her enceinte self, Mack worked overtime with each pregnancy to ensure every expecting expectation was met. That was his way and why she loved him, but this morning, it felt … *demeaning.* It could have been the sacred setting; a nursery was a most dreamy shrine dedicated to the foolishly roseate hopes of motherhood—crisp new crib sheets to be vomited upon, freshly steamed carpet soon to be laden with a rainbow of juice stains, and painstakingly painted walls that would one day serve as little more than the canvas for crayoned squiggles and stick figures over which frazzled mothers feigned excellence before stomping out to locate a sponge and mop bucket for the one hundredth time. It wasn't Simone's first round on this ride. Twice before, she had built nurseries that went unused for at least the first year while she selected the pendulously positive or negative—depending on which blog she had read—co-sleeping option. In her mind, sleeping with her baby tucked in her side was more natural—it built the bond and gave her a sense of security—but yes, the prolonged pristineness of that room also reinforced the romantic fantasies of what was often a messy affair.

"What?"

"Maybe you should quit your job," Mack suggested.

Simone blinked hard and ticked her head to a tilt. "Quit my job? I am not quitting my job."

"I know we still have some time, but the shop is already doing great. I think we would be okay."

"What about our insurance? With us working independently, that's a big bill right now, and with the girls starting school, they'll need things."

"Simone …"

"I'm fine. I have to stop soon enough, so let me just get all I can out of this job before the baby comes."

Jada shuffled in between her parents, draping herself upon them. "I don't want to go to school. It isn't fair."

"Life isn't fair." Simone caressed her daughter's forehead before descending the stairs to start breakfast.

Mack lifted the girl and kissed her one-dimpled cheek. "Sorry, baby, but you have to go to school. C'mon, let's get ready."

Tripping into her favorite seat at the breakfast table under the veil of her bunny mask, Jada was first to join her mother in the kitchen. She playfully snatched a thick piece of bacon from the center plate as if a food shortage existed between her and invisible friends.

"Did Daddy get that outfit for you yesterday? It's pretty," Simone gushed over the long-sleeved shirt that featured a glitter-covered unicorn as she scrapped a fluffy bushel of scrambled eggs onto a plate.

"Yes, but you promised you would braid my hair for the first day of school, and I'm all fuzzy," Jada chirped.

"It is not fuzzy. It looks fine from last week, but I'll braid it fresh tonight, I promise. Yesterday was a long day."

Aaliyah slinked into the room. "Mom, seriously, does she have to wear that thing at the table?" Aaliyah moaned as she neatly put eggs, bacon, and toast on her plate. "It creeps me out."

"Good morning to you too, lovebug." Simone eyed her oldest as she yanked on the fridge door in search of milk.

"Why are you such a scaredy cat?" Jada hypnotically waved her fork at her sister.

"Says the girl who slept in my bed last night," Aaliyah quipped.

Mack joined them last, fumbling the buttons on his coveralls, a task his wife usurped effortlessly as he joined the sunrise symposium. "Who slept in your bed last night?"

"Jada slept with me. Your door was locked," Aaliyah said between gulps of milk.

"You're not taking those masks to school," Simone said, refusing to meet her husband's gaze.

Jada shrugged in response as she chomped another piece of bacon, her father's meat-loving twin.

Sunlight kissed so many surfaces in the kitchen that despite some inevitable first day jitters, it was impossible not to feel optimistic. Simone beheld the wholesome visual of her family's formation of a morning methodology like watching a film on mute. They traded plates, their mouths taking on a variety of dramatic shapes in conversation and laughter, and as Simone put the finishing touches on everyone's lunch, her spectral spectatorship of this new family narrative left her lost in the haunting fog that abstracted all seemingly perfect things.

"Girls, you ready?" Mack dumped his plate in the sink and gathered his things. "The bus should be coming in the next few minutes."

"Can you take out the trash?" Simone asked as she pulled her smoothie from the fridge and winced at the first sip.

"Yeah." Mack hoisted the trash bag from the can, tied it in one routine motion, and jogged out the back door only to return within seconds. "Can you replace the bag for me, bae?"

"I will once I get you three off." Simone followed her family out the front door.

A screech from the far side of the porch startled them. A small cat leapt from the railing and dashed around the side of the house in a tawny flash.

"Daddy, can we keep him?" Aaliyah sang, the girls' preliminary anxiety blooming into exponential excitement, the same amusing sensation that came after the opening dip of a roller coaster.

Before he spoke, Mack eyed Simone and recognized the mechanical downturn of her features. "I don't think so, but maybe Mom can give him some milk." He winked at his wife.

"Will you, Mom? Will you, *pleeeeeeease?*" Jada screeched. "Can we call him Whiskers?"

"Jada, enough whining this morning. Yes, I will give him milk. No, we cannot call him Whiskers. Naming him implies he'll be around more for us to call him. Now let's get a move on."

After waving to Mack, who was already backing his truck down the gravel drive, the girls crossed the lawn toward the path that led to the street. As if answering a subliminal call, Aaliyah looked back to spy her bedroom window.

"What is it?" Simone asked.

But before Aaliyah could say a word, the bright-eyed Jada declared, "There are monsters in the house," with the flat indifference of a scientist who had resolved themselves to the unavoidable fact that a catastrophic meteor was on track to decimate Earth.

Aaliyah shot her sister a menacing glance, a warning to keep her mouth shut.

Chapter 15

————— ◆–◆–◆ —————

N ear the road at the end of the curving, dirt pathway that led to their home, Simone waited for the bus with her daughters, shifting her weight side to side, a motion that pushed her deeper into the spellbinding state of reminisce this youthful practice triggered. Following the path home after school daily with her sister was a capricious ritual of sorts, the actions and orations of which varied depending on the day. Bright days were charged with laughter that resulted from the animated retelling of the day's events as they kicked rocks toward the house. On warm days, they playfully chased each other, tagging back and forth until they reached the porch, heaving for breath. Arguments along the trail were few, but as with all sisters, they had their time and place—especially on cold days when patience was thin. Toward the end on overcast, rainy days, dread took hold as they raced through raindrops, casting hasty glances across the pine-colored pasture to the tree line of the Langford Woods from where they felt something watching them.

That's where he lands. Simone's mind could not act quickly enough to block the thought. *"You know how your mother feels about the woods now."* Her father's voice played in her head.

"There is no such thing as monsters. They're like the made-up fairy tales we read," Simone blurted just as the long, yellow school bus bent the bucolic curve, lending to the illusion that it had materialized from the trees.

The Parker girls locked their synchronized gazes onto their mother.

Just then, the mechanical bus doors craned open.

"Good morning," Mr. Jeffrey's voice pounded, his personalized coffee tumbler faced outward, highlighting his name for everyone who entered the bus to see.

"Good morning," Jada chimed.

The riotous clamor of the morning bus ride simmered to a murmurous buzz as the girls staggered down the aisle to an empty seat near the back. Some kids stared at them, while others tried to discern the full form of the legendary house from the straight, clean lines the distant trees partially hid.

"They live in the Sandman's house," Russie Cunningham choked in a hoarse whisper, lifting his chubby body from the seat to get a better view of the aging farmhouse.

The chorus of mumbles erupted with new vigor, one name resurfacing repeatedly, a name of urban legend the children of Black Water had been taught never to speak—the Sandman.

As the bus jerked forward, Simone waved before starting back on the trail. Once she approached the curve that put the house in full sight, her eyes were drawn to the edge of the Langford Woods at its right side. There was a point, a natural opening of sorts where her family had most often entered and exited the forest. A breeze blew over Simone, conjuring the memory of her and Myeisha emerging from the portal in the trees, screaming for help as they carried an injured Ella. The old screen door wheezed open, and Dorothy Ann carefully scrambled out, still healing from giving birth only a week before, the stress of hearing her daughters' screams etched plainly across her weary face. Racing behind his wife, Daniel Mills crossed the lawn to assess his daughter's injury—a broken ankle.

The thud of Ella hitting the soft ground pounded in Simone's head once again as she rewound the memory. Ella writhed on the ground, crying and clutching at the ankle already swelling to absurd proportions as the last of the butterflies disappeared into the canopy of treetops.

Myeisha pushed Simone, jolting her from her trance. "I'll get under her arms, and you grab her legs."

By now, the dam of dry shock from the fall had dissipated, and tears that signaled not only the painful throb but the raw emotion of embarrassment and disappointment that came with such an accident flooded Ella's face.

"Gently!" Myeisha chided as Ella screeched in response to her sister's grasp.

A young Simone loosened her grip and better positioned her hands under her sister's knees to support Myeisha in lifting Ella's upper body from the ground. "We have to hurry. It's starting to get dark."

Simone noticed that under the influence of dusk, the landscape was undergoing the evening transformation that mutated playful silhouettes and ditches into sinister shadows and dungeons.

Descending a slight hill, Simone's foot slipped in a wet patch of dirt, momentarily distracting her from her task. When she looked up, she saw him at the top of the knoll—not through narrowed eyes that she would cover with her blanket as the heaving beast stood over the bed in her darkened room as she had several times before. For the first time, the sighting was clear. The Sandman's milky orbs were dotted with single circles of black in the middle and glued to the fumbling girls. His snout pulsed with rotted breath, and his spire-inspired ears sat straight up on top of his head just outside the hood of the black cloak that swept around his veiled body. The sisters' eyes connected, and Simone knew Ella saw him too. Through some shared sibling intimacy, both intuited the fact it wasn't the first time for either of them, and for a brief moment, Simone allowed herself to wonder why people—especially sisters—kept their own confidences on things clearly less burdensome when shared. Perhaps clarity came only after calamity, particularly when sibling rivalry rose to the mundane heights of the appearance of normalcy.

"Come on!" Myeisha yelled, dashing Simone's belated reveries.

Simone wiped her sweat-laden hands before regripping the backs of Ella's knees, scuttling farther down the hill. Before he was completely out of sight, Simone looked up for one last glimpse.

His billowing cloak opened to a gruesome reveal. There, in the belly of the cape, was Ella, her face the ashen shade of death, bloodied with rich maroon smudges and one tantalizingly brown eye peering out wildly, the claw that covered her mouth silencing her screams. On the other side of her face sat a gaping black hole that once housed a now missing eye.

Simone's eyes darted to the sister she carried who had her eyelids pressed tightly closed. Simone's body went numb. She could hardly feel her hands or her feet which found another patch of damp dirt, causing her to slide.

All three girls toppled down what was left of the mound. Once on flat ground again, they untangled themselves, lifted Ella, and ran the short distance to the opening of the trees which led into the Mills' side yard.

Covered in wet leaves and mud, they yelled for help, their voices mimicking the screech of scared animals.

An adult Simone stood on the path, watching the silent scene, her former self, sister, and friend lumbering from the trees, their mouths wide in screams of panic. The broken ankle was nothing against the terror of the Sandman sighting, and while Myeisha had seen nothing more than trees and dirt, the sisters' shared terror had infected their friend, filling her with the overwhelming sense of dread.

Simone's eyes peered passed the girls whose shapes soon disappeared into the landscape. In the shadows just beyond the lip of the trees, Simone spotted movement.

A murky figure stood, watching and bellowing her name in its animalistic call. It never moved, but the calling got closer and became lighter until it was no longer the howl of an animal but the voice of a woman. "Simone?" the voice called.

Simone turned to find a slight, dark-haired woman jogging up the path from the road. Facing the woods once again, Simone confirmed that the gloomy silhouette had only been a byproduct of her momentary childhood recollections.

"Simone," the woman called again.

Spotting the light pattern of freckles that dotted the woman's face in a wave—under one eye, over the bridge of her nose, and down again under the other eye—Simone recognized her friend. "Myeisha."

"Yes!" The woman embraced Simone in a deep hug and laughed which activated the sparkle in her honey-colored eyes. "It's so good to see you!" Myeisha finally released Simone. "I'm sorry. I probably smell awful, but I had to hug you."

"Don't worry about it. It's good to see you too. I had no idea you were back here. Last I heard, you were in Seattle or something."

"Yeah, well, Mom hasn't been well, so when a spot opened at the newspaper, I couldn't say no to the opportunity to move home to care for her and at least have a job in my field. Number one reporter." Myeisha grinned sarcastically. "But it works, I guess. A guy named Gus Farley—you know, Rita Farley's grandfather—is still the editor, but he's ready to give out any day now, so there may be some opportunity there."

"How *is* you mother? I've been meaning to go by and see her."

"All that drinking has finally caught up to her, and it isn't being so nice."

"She drinks?"

"Of course, always has, even when you lived with us after …" Myeisha's voice faltered. "She was much better at hiding it back then. What about you? When did you get here?"

"A couple of weeks ago. We're here permanently now. My husband and my two girls. We bought Mr. Watson's old auto shop."

"And you're staying *here?*" As much as Myeisha tried for the opposite, the words still sounded strangled and awkward.

"We are." Simone responded firmly. "It's time."

Myeisha nodded eagerly in a show of support. "Well then, that is … amazing. And look at you, another on the way, huh? You're absolutely glowing." Myeisha playfully touched her friend's belly.

Simone chuckled. "Yep, another one. I really want to catch up, but I must get back to the house. I work from home, and I'm on a deadline, but let's get coffee. Call me." Simone waited as Myeisha retrieved her phone to enter the house number before starting back.

"I will!" Myeisha said, heading toward the road. After a few strides, she turned and took another long look at the home barely visible through the trees before replacing her headphones and sprinting from the property.

Chapter 16

N o sooner than Simone walked through the door, her phone rang. "Hello? ... Hi, Katherine. ... Yes, I sent you an updated version last night. ... Sure, I can make those changes. ... I know, I'm sorry the work has been a bit slow. I've just been a little busy—but no worries, I will research that issue and get back with you ASAP. Can I give you my landline number? My cell doesn't always get the best reception in the house." Simone rattled off her home number as a fierce tightening tensed her stomach. She groaned and rested her weight against the wall. "No, I'm fine. Thank you. I'll get to work on this right away," she assured Katherine before ending the call and wobbling down the hallway toward her office.

The muffled buzz of the washer filtered through the house, and happy with the work that she completed over the morning, she rose from her desk with a satisfied stretch. As she passed through the foyer, she studied her mother's painting recently brought from the basement and wondered where to place it. Once in the cellar, Simone cautiously eyed the cement shower before moving the wet clothes from the washer to the dryer, then loading the washer again with the fresh pile of clothes under the chute. As she sorted and tossed the shirts and jeans into the machine, one flew too high and dropped behind the washer into the dusty depths that all large household appliances seemed to hide. "Crap," she whispered.

Positioning herself on the floor against the wall, she pressed her arm through the thin opening between the machine and the wall but still couldn't grip the t-shirt. Scooting closer, she plunged her arm as far into the narrow opening as it would go, turning her face so she could cram herself further. There it was; she felt the damp cotton, then something else, something cold and metal, tucked into a small crater of wear and tear that had opened at some point in the cement floor. Simone grasped the shirt and the metal together and carefully pulled them out.

Tears welled in her eyes when she saw what she was now holding. *It couldn't be.* She glanced into the darkened crevice behind the washer and dryer and pondered what other familial curiosities this house was concealing, ready to offer up only at precisely premeditated moments. Besides the broken clasp and slight tarnish, the silver chain and its charm—a small circle attached to a crescent at the top and bottom, allowing it to spin, two moons that made a larger one when pressed together—was still in excellent condition. It had been a gift Simone envied, one from Dorothy Ann to her eldest daughter, Ella.

Simone ran her thumb over the inscription etched in the circle before bursting into powerful sobs, each accompanied by a fresh barrel of tears and an army of uncategorical feelings. Eventually, her powerful grief dwindled to an ongoing tearful moan, and her elusive emotions gave way to more clear-cut thoughts. This inconsolable mourning session was inevitable with the move back, Simone knew, and she was just grateful it had taken her when she was alone. It was the crux of this prodigal return. Out in the world, she had dulled her emotions to travel through life, but she had come to a point, as many do, where it was time for the undesirable task of unpacking. She missed her family, she missed her sister, she wanted her mother, and she was ashamed she couldn't even recall the last time she cried for them. She could not continue to compartmentalize them in that tragic box of her memory, like dolls tucked lifelessly away in the dollhouse at night. It was time for all of them to come home, no matter how many ghosts Simone had to uncloak to make way.

Simone's tear-stained face jerked upward to the main floor as it came to life with music. "Hello?" Simone called as she climbed the basement stairs.

No one answered. It was no wonder, as she could hardly even hear herself over the moderate horns and distinct drawl of one of her mother's favorites about the Bible and blessings for the child who frees themselves of their mama and papa.

As Simone stepped into the light of the kitchen, she called again, "Mack?" The melody grew louder as she crept to the front of the house. "Mmm." Simone stopped to let a contraction pass before she peeked around the corner into the living room and saw the beaming red light on her wireless speaker. She spun on slippered feet and trotted down the hallway to her office where she spotted her cellphone on the desk.

She pressed the pause button on her music streaming app and brought the house to an abrupt silence. A crashing noise she immediately recognized as the slamming of the back screen-door tensed her chest. Simone raced out the office, down the hallway, through the foyer and dining room, and into the kitchen to find the back door wide open. She pressed through the wiry screen-door but found only Whiskers the cat purring on the grass. *Mack must have left the door open this morning when he took out the trash.*

She noticed thin, dirty footprints leading up the stairs into the house. The slight outline of dirt stopped only a few steps into the kitchen and were much too small to be from her husband. Pulling off her slippers, Simone studied the shadow of dirt that remained on her feet from stepping outside the previous night.

"Good job, Simone," she whispered to herself. "Make even more of a mess for you to clean up." As the tension in her body abated, it revealed pain in her fingers, and she realized her fist was still clenched. Lifting her balled hand, she allowed the moon-shaped charm to drop and dangle in front of her face by its chain. "*I love you to the moon and back,*" Simone read the inscription aloud as it spun, reflecting the stale afternoon sunlight.

When the girls trampled through the front door, finally home from school, Simone stood in the kitchen, preparing their snack and finishing her last conference call of the day. "I understand that, Kathrine, but I really don't think they have any room for more damages than what they originally petitioned for." Simone stretched the phone cord to plop the paper plates of peanut butter and jelly sandwiches and grapes on the dining room table.

Aaliyah had dropped her purple zebra-striped backpack and headed straight to the living room to watch television.

Jada marched defiantly toward her mother, and despite how she had been taught to behave when her mother was on a work call, started shouting, "You lied to me!" The child's voice was laden with the subtle cracks that revealed her proximity to the edge.

"What?" Simone responded with a retraction of her neck. "Katherine, can you hold for a moment?" She tightly pressed the face of the phone to her chest without waiting for an answer. "Calm down. What is *wrong* with you?" Simone reached to touch her disheveled daughter before the girl stepped swiftly out of reach.

"You lied to me! You told me the Sandman was good, a magical creature who came to sprinkle glittery sand in kids' eyes to help them sleep, but you *lied*. He's not good; he's a monster with glowing eyes and the face of a wolf!"

Simone stepped backward from her daughter's thundering words.

"He goes to bad, little kids who won't sleep. He uses razor-sharp sand to loosen their eyes until they bleed. Then he rips them out so he can feed them to his children on the moon!" Jada recited the legend as she must have heard it that day, not missing any key details.

"No," Simone whispered to her baby whose anger made her innocent face almost unrecognizable. Another one. Simone had been sure there would be plenty of tests that came with moving back to Black Water, but she hadn't expected them in such rapid succession.

"That's what the kids at school said!" Jada snapped with the confidence of all kids her age who believed anything held as truth by the collective of the *kids at school* was automatic fact.

"That's not true, and I don't care what those little heathens at school said," Simone insisted firmly, gathering enough maternal ballast to misname the kids at school in discredit—a cheap but effective tactic her own mother often used in disagreements with her and Ella. "And you will not be disrespectful to me like this, young lady!"

Lips quivering, Jada fought the moisture swelling in her eyes.

"Now get your butt up to your room right now!" Simone added, despite the tugging of her baby's budding tears at her heart.

Jada ran up the stairs only slowing to scream back, "I hate it here!"

Simone sighed before bringing the phone to her ear. "Hello, Katherine? Katherine? Hello? Dammit!" Simone placed the phone on the hook and headed for the stairs. In the living room, she noticed Aaliyah slouched against the back of the recliner, staring at the television. "Aaliyah, go wash up and get ready for a snack. No television right now."

Aaliyah didn't move.

"Aaliyah," Simone snapped as she filed through the foyer, not in the mood for a second outburst. "Aaliyah, are you ignoring me?" She grabbed her daughter's shoulder.

As the girl turned, her glazed eyes peered in her mother's direction.

"Aaliyah?" Simone called, casually shaking her daughter.

"Yes, Mom?" Aaliyah finally responded with a firm blink.

"I said no television—" Simone noticed only their distorted reflections in the blankness of the television screen. "N-nothing. Do you have homework?"

"I have to make a solar system," Aaliyah grumbled, instantly dulling the potential wonders of the universe. "Can you help me?"

"I guess they don't waste any time, huh?" Simone snickered. "Go upstairs, wash up, and get ready for snack, and yes, I'll help you."

That evening, Simone sat on the edge of Jada's bed, grabbing portions of her baby's freshly washed and dried hair, then layering them in an intricate pattern that crowned the side of Jada's head with a thick braid. With her back against the pillow placed between her mother's legs, Jada slouched in stubborn silence, clutching Bobo to her protective chest.

As Jada's hairstyle came to completion, Simone dropped her shoulders. "Jada, I want you to know what you heard about the Sandman at school today is not true. Those stories just come from bored, small-town kids who have nothing better to do than make up things to scare other kids."

"But they swore he was real," Jada squealed, jumping around to her knees to face her mother.

In Jada's face, Simone could not help but notice the delicate physical evolutions that were aging her baby into a young girl. Her eyes had grown wider, like flowers in bronze bloom, and they sparkled with wild curiosity. Accounts from her mouth became laced with the confidence of firsthand experience, and answers to her questions demanded more accountability. The once infantile roundness of Jada's face was thinning to a preadolescent eloquence that changed her interpretation of her own reflection. It was a critical point where many began the shed of their innocence-laden baby fat, and Simone was not ready.

"Shh. I mean it, Jada. The Sandman is a make-believe story like the fairy tales we read. Falling into rabbit holes and becoming king in a land of monsters are just—"

"Cannibal witches, wolves that eat grandmothers, creatures who spin straw into—"

"Aaliyah!" Simone said as her oldest child wandered into the room. "Why did we ever give you the internet?"

"What's a cannibal?" Jada chirped.

"After all the stuff the kids told us today, I just got on the internet, and there it was. All those fairy tales are really creepy. You know, what they really mean."

"No, just no. We are not doing this tonight. Like I was saying, regardless of variations on these stories, they are just that—stories—and people tell them and retell them so many times that other people think they're true. They themselves even sometimes think they're true, but they're not. You can't live your lives in fear, especially of imaginary monsters. The Sandman is not real. Do you understand me?"

"Yes," Jada responded. "What's a cannibal?"

"Not today, girls, okay? We can talk about it another day." Simone's hands rose in a motion that wiped away the conversation.

"Okay, but promise me he's not real." Jada searched her mother's face for the slightest sign of deceit.

Aaliyah, also having a dog in the race, carefully eyed her mother from the corner.

Simone hesitated. "I promise. Are we good?"

After a long silence, the girls spoke in unison, "Yes, ma'am."

"C'mon, let me wrap your hair." Simone used the silk scarf in her hand to motion Jada to the vanity. "Can you do me a favor and stay in bed tonight so we can all get some sleep?"

"I'll try," Jada said in a groan as her mother finished tying up her hair.

"Perfect. You look gorgeous," Simone said as she and her daughters admired their reflections in the mirror. "Both of you are gorgeous, and you look just like your mother." Simone giggled as she rubbed noses with her oldest.

"Who do you look like?" Jada asked.

Simone stared at herself in the mirror for a moment. "I look just like Mommy." She paused. "My mother, I look just like my mother."

"Does that mean that we look like Grandma too?" Aaliyah asked.

"Yes, you do." Simone tried hard to suppress the tears. "I know you didn't know Grandma Dorothy, but there's a thing called DNA, and it's basically a piece of you. Babies leave a bit of it behind in their mothers. I did it with my mother, and you both did it with me, and in a way, that makes us all connected. You both would have loved Grandma and Grandpa and Aunt Ella and Charlie, and they would have loved you."

"Where did you get that ring?" Aaliyah asked of the onyx stone set atop a gold ring Simone wore on her finger.

"It was Grandma Dorothy's." Simone caressed the ring. "It was in that box we found in the basement. Time for bed, girls."

Jada flopped into bed, and Aaliyah shambled toward the door as Simone drew the curtains. Movement in the yard below froze her, a stealthy figure navigating the dark with ease highlighted by only the porch light's delicate white blaze. Leaning closer to the window, Simone lost view of anything suspicious as the night grew still once again. The porch light sputtered, casting the entire front of the house in brief blackness before relighting and revealing the wiry shape of a person. Simone gasped at the sight of the stranger swathed in black, his face an oversized mass of hard features indecipherable in the shadows.

A second after he disappeared beneath the overhang of the front porch, three loud knocks rumbled through the house.

Chapter 17

———◆—◆—◆———

With their bedtime ritual already interrupted, Simone cut short the maternal pleasures of multiple goodnight kisses and sweet farewells. She instructed Jada to stay in bed, then pushed Aaliyah into her room before ducking into her own to open the bathroom door and find Mack in the shower. "Someone's at the door."

He was covered with suds, including those oozing down his face like a sagging mask. He wiped his eyes clean with wet hands. "What?"

"Someone's at the door. Some guy."

"A guy?" Mack mumbled, turning off the shower, then taking the towel Simone held for him.

Three more intrusive knocks sounded through the home as Simone crept down the stairs close behind her husband.

"Are you sure you saw someone?" Mack asked as he reached the bottom of the steps.

Peeking from one of the two long rectangular windows that bookended the front door, he spoke in a faux firmness his family rarely heard, and even then, it was never directed at them. "Who is it?"

No answer.

"I don't see anyone, Simone." Mack grabbed a baseball bat from the hallway closet and unlocked the top lock. "Anybody out there?"

"Mack, don't go out there," Simone begged, but her husband opened the door, the night chill activating a pronounced layer of goosebumps across his broad back. Simone disappeared into the kitchen and returned moments later with a cleaver knife from the butcher block. As uncertain as she felt, Simone followed Mack's lead, the tail of her husband's tactical team. Had someone been watching, she was sure this scene of their partnership would have looked comical—a baseball bat-gripping, bare-chested Mack, his lower half covered only in a peach-colored towel, and his large-knife-wielding sidekick in full gestation.

Mack descended the front stairway, his wet feet marking his path on the wood. Tightening his grip on the bat, he scanned the premises multiple times before facing his wife with a shrug. "Nothing."

Exhaling a long-held breath, Simone dropped her shoulders. "Then who was knocking?"

"I don't know, but whoever it is, they're gone now. Probably just kids or someone who realized they had the wrong—whoa, where did the knife come from?"

Simone dropped her hand with a smile before speaking softly, "Shut up."

"You weren't playing, were you?" her husband teased as he pressed his free hand against her protruding belly and herded her back through the door.

When Aaliyah woke, the house was bursting with the silvery wisps of moonlight that only midnight can create. She sat upright in bed just as the creaking of her closet door came to a stop, and she stared into the blackness of it. "Hello?"

"*Hello,*" a weak voice echoed back.

Her trembling hand flailed to find the knob of her bedside lamp. When the ridges of the dial were under her fingertips, she turned it over, washing her room in pale, welcoming light. "Hello …"

"Hello," the voice sang back so immediately it almost overlapped hers.

As she put her weight upon the feet she had planted on the floor, they shook to the point that she never imagined they would carry her across the room as they did. In one swift motion, Aaliyah flipped on the light and flung open the door to find her clothes hanging lifelessly. After moving things around and finding no culprit, Aaliyah settled on the unsatisfying but necessary truth that, after waking, she hung in that thin purgatorial realm where elements of a dream momentarily gain the power to cross into the waking world.

Aaliyah yelped as she turned toward the bed to see an impish, little creature with the face of a deranged bunny. "If you wear those masks in my room ever again," Aaliyah started as her racing heart slowed, "I will take you into the woods and leave you." She advanced on the retreating little creature. "Then a wolf will stalk you and rip ya to shreds!"

"Jeez," Jada griped as she ripped off the mask and placed in on the nightstand.

"Just get to bed and be quiet," Aaliyah finished. Turning out the lights, she climbed into bed next to her sister.

Over the coming nights, sleep eluded Simone more and more. Breathing through occasional Braxton Hicks, she stared at the white ceiling as the changing shadows signaled the morning. Turning onto her side, she watched her husband's body rise and fall in a light snore.

As per usual, he was unbothered while his wife obsessed over the shadowy figure that had recently knocked upon their door.

No sooner than her husband opened his eyes, she was talking. "Mack, I want to get an alarm for the house."

He pressed his hands into his eyes with a hard sigh. "Simone, we don't need an alarm. We live in a sleepy town where kids sometimes knicker-knock."

"Mack …"

"Simone. I'll put another lock on each of the doors if it'll make you feel better—a heavy deadbolt."

"Right … is that *after* you fix the leaky faucet and the sticking fridge door?"

Mack lumbered out of bed toward the bedroom door. "Don't start."

"Am I lying?" Simone followed him down the stairs.

"Can we not do this?" he begged as they entered the kitchen where Aaliyah quickly closed the fridge door and fled up the stairs without a word.

"Good morning," Simone said to her daughter in a heavy tone carried over from her marital quarrel before refocusing on her husband. "Do what?"

"I painted the house, didn't I?" he rumbled as he added water to the coffee machine. "You want a cup?"

"That was weeks ago, Mack." Simone pulled her smoothie from the refrigerator and shook it. "And yes, I do."

"I don't want to argue with you." Mack answered the call of the blinking blue light by slamming the handle on the fancy coffee maker. Facing his wife, he swiped his hand over his stress-lined expression. Next, he drew her close. "If an alarm will make you feel safe, we'll get an alarm. It's that simple."

Simone smiled before hugging her husband tightly around his neck.

"Nicco, the guy I hired, invited us to his church this weekend. You want to go?"

"Since when are we church people?" Simone craned backward from the sweet musk her husband's skin emitted naturally.

Mack shrugged. "We're not ... *church* people. I just thought, since he offered, I would bring it up."

Simone sat, sipping her black coffee and unpleasant tasting smoothie in silence.

"What's wrong?" Mack sat across the table, stirring what his wife often complained was too much cream and sugar into his coffee.

Before she knew it, her mouth was moving. Her parents had always been holiday Christians—Christmas and Easter mostly with a couple of Mother's Days and random Sundays. As a family, they attended church out of tradition and social habit, but religion never played a substantial role in their daily lives. Simone could count on her hands the number of times she recalled attending church, but they attended even less after their encounters with The Church of All Saints—a fringe religious organization that viewed the words of the Bible in such a literal sense that only the most rigid disciples could maintain their standing. Such wild beliefs kept them from making a permanent home in any of the more established towns, but they purchased some acres of land a few hours south of Black Water in a tiny place called Beckstown where they built a church and several simple homes for their followers. Over the years they grew, developing into a dispassionate and colorless sub-town of their own. Perhaps they became bored with one another or needed more direct and effective ways to project their misery, Simone never knew why, but the group eventually took their beliefs on the road—a bizarre circus indeed. A curious band of hate-breeding, sin-juggling, scripture-contorting carnies, they took to harassing people in nearby towns. Their targets were mostly unmarried, pregnant women, and pharmacies that distributed birth control. Sometimes they gathered to disrupt military funerals with signs that stated how most—everyone but them presumably—were going to hell, ironically enough, a place with which they seemed so familiar. All the scurrilous performances led by their underwhelming ringmaster, Jonathan Cramer.

Somehow, they had learned Daniel Mills was a psychiatrist practicing in Black Water and, from that point on, made him and his evil science the mark of one of their odious campaigns. Day after day, the group gathered just off the Mills' property, close to the tree line with their signs, chanting the ills of psychiatry. A young Dorothy Mills would sit in her sunroom for hours; at first, she had tried to maintain her hobby of painting, but over time, relinquished to watching the protestors as much as they watched her, chewing the nails on one hand and rubbing her swollen belly with the other. Dorothy would study Jonathan Cramer especially closely. While the others around him would chant fiercely, saliva sometimes slinging from their jowls and thrust their homemade signs into the air for hours on end, he would barely even open his mouth, his uniform of a crisp white collar shirt and khaki pants as pristine at the end of the day as it was at the group's morning arrival. Simone could remember her father's exasperated calls to the sheriff who had already dispatched his deputy a couple times to ask the angry mob to disperse, but since they weren't on the Mills' property, could do little more.

"Why won't they leave us alone?" Dorothy would ask her husband's mentee, Dr. Duran, who had also become her friend.

It would be weeks before they moved on to the opening of a strip club in Salem, and by that time, young Deputy Handow had threatened Jonathan Cramer and his followers with arrest for the slightest infraction enough that the move from Black Water was long overdue.

Dorothy Ann had especially been glad they were gone as her due date approached, and she rued the thought of bringing her son home to the raging mob who, despite all their claims to heaven and God, were devils. Despite the endless litanies at his property line, Daniel's practice had grown which led to him taking on Dr. Duran—a beautiful, young woman with a sweet smile, a plump figure, and a sultry beauty mark just beneath her left eye. She had always been nice to the girls and would give Simone's mother someone to talk to in quite whispers behind the glass sunroom doors during the last weeks of her pregnancy.

"I'm sorry I never told you any of this stuff before," Simone said, blinking back to the present.

Mack kissed her hand. "I get there's a lot of history for you in this house, in this town, but you have to communicate with me. No secrets."

"It wasn't a secret, just something that never came up. We've never even considered church before."

"I'll tell Nicco no thanks, and we can have family movie night on Sunday, popcorn and candy. It's been a while since we've done that."

"Thank you," Simone croaked before changing the subject. "I saw Dr. Duran at the grocery store."

"How is she?"

"She looks good. She suggested we go to lunch or something."

"Do you want to?"

"I don't know. I mean, she was very close to the family. She was one of the first people on the scene after what happened. She treated me for years afterward. I suppose that I should, but I'm going to lunch with Myeisha today after we get the kids off."

"Oh, ya'll finally hooked up?" Mack gulped the last of his coffee.

Simone rose to start him another cup. "She was out for a run when I was at the bus stop with the girls the other day. By the way— " Simone gestured toward a piece of paper on the fridge— "as we get closer to baby time, I printed a list with the phone numbers of important local people, including both of them."

"Got it. I'm glad you're getting out. I'll probably have another long day. We're packed with cars and still trying to get organized and get all our systems in place." He kissed her and headed upstairs with his fresh cup of coffee in hand.

As her lunch date approached, Simone didn't know if the fluttering in her stomach was nerves or just Baby Trace taking to his daily acrobatics. Simone finished a light makeup application, inspected the job, then added more concealer to cover the fatigue that had manifested as pools of dark space under her eyes. As she was about to leave her room, she went to her bedside table, opened the drawer, and retrieved Ella's silver necklace. Next, she fetched her mother's gold watch—another forgotten trinket from the abandoned basement box—and slipped it on her wrist, admiring it for a moment alongside the onyx ring.

About a block from the diner was Black Water's only jewelry store, Illumination Jewels. Simone parked on the side of the street and went inside. Grady Thompson had always owned the store; his son, Toby, had committed suicide when they were in high school. Simone was in ninth grade and Toby in tenth. He had hung himself on Halloween night from a tree in their front yard.

Chapter 18

N either Grady nor his wife were home that evening. Everyone in the neighborhood, from the demanding little monsters that crisscrossed the streets to the officers who had long ago lost their enthusiasm for this night in their patrol cars that paraded up and down each avenue, passed the swaying corpse with nothing more than a word of admiration on its authenticity. In Black Water, Halloween was a revered holiday, one in which the community appreciated a gruesome and realistic trick, like the one the Thompson family had prepared. With that prank, they easily topped all their elaborate yard-decorating schemes of years passed. The previous year, their yard donned a classic but extravagant witch theme. Countless figures of shaped chicken wire were draped in black chiffon and topped with pointed hats strategically placed in a sea of carved, orange pumpkins—their wicked expressions aflame with the delicate tealights placed in their gutted hollows. It was a zombie theme the year of Toby's death. The lawn was a graveyard tableau, a hopeless landscape of dilapidated tombstones and corpses awakened from all stages of death pawing up from the ground or frozen mid-stumble across the grass. Green and violet holiday bulbs in their light landscaping cast ghastly hues in every direction, all leading to the front of the elaborate Victorian swathed in lemon-colored Do Not Enter crime scene tape and a ragged wooden door sign that warned, *Dead Inside*, in crimson-splattered strokes.

Upon their return home, Grady instantly recognized the new and unfamiliar insert in the meticulous design of his yard décor. Though a black sack covered the hanging body's head, in that same intimate way that blindfolded children recognize their mothers based only on the feel of their faces, Grady discerned his son's faceless form.

A mix of superheroes, seraphs, devils, and flashy 80's R&B/soul legends gathered in awkward observation as Grady Thompson clumsily pulled down his best decoration in sobs. The only bare yard on Black Oak drive every Halloween thereafter sat as a monument to the Thompson family's impenetrable and irreversible burn out on all things that symbolized the last day in October.

"Hi, Mr. Grady," Simone greeted lightly, as if any sudden volume would be too much for the man, the endlessness of his grief apparent in the hunch of his shoulders and the glaze of his eyes that always made him seem as if he was never wholly present.

"Hello there, young lady," Mr. Grady said, his voice laced with a bit of the shakes. Presumably, she looked familiar to him but not so much that he recalled her name.

Simone pulled the silver necklace from the side pocket of her purse. "Can you fix the clasp on this?"

Mr. Thompson pulled the broken necklace close to his eyeglass. "Yes, sure. To the moon and back ..." he recited the engraved words. "What does that mean?"

In the cavernous pools of sorrow where only people who had suffered the loss of someone close to them could swim, Simone's eyes met Grady's, and she cleared the pinch in her throat. "Uh, well. Honestly, I've never really thought about its meaning so much as just accepted the words. It's something my mother used to say to us kids when we were little. *I love you to the moon and back.* A simple way to express the far reach of a mother's love and care. Otherworldly, I suppose."

For a moment, the glaze in his eyes cleared; he knew who she was now. "The Mills girl," he confided in himself with a slow nod. "To the moon and back. I can understand what she meant. I'll have this ready for you in about an hour, maybe less."

"Fantastic. Thank you," Simone said. After paying, she took the short walk down the block to the Old Country Diner—the OC for short.

No sooner than Simone passed through the heavy glass door, Myeisha waved from a booth at the far end of the diner. A smiling Simone hurried over, unbuttoning her jacket along the way. They hugged, then sat, Simone contorting to fit her belly into the narrow space between the table and seatback. Almost thirty minutes of mindless chatter before they ordered reminded Simone how good it felt to have a friend. With work, two kids, and a husband, she hardly had any before the move.

Myeisha opted for a garden salad with chicken, and Simone requested the steak and eggs. Baby Trace was shaping up to be a meat and potatoes kind of boy, and after ordering, the pair dove back into the non-stop, separation-fueled babble that belonged only to old friends.

"Remember how Handow wanted to, quote, *clean up* the youth of Black Water, so once he got wind that kids would skip class and loiter in the grocery store parking lot, he started sitting out there every day, doing his crosswords and trying to catch us?" Myeisha screeched with laughter.

"Yes, so we had to start moving the skip location each day so he couldn't find us." Simone laughed.

"He still does that, you know."

"Really?"

"Yep." Myeisha choked her tea down through a cackle. "The kids don't go there anymore, but he sits in the grocery store parking lot every afternoon for lunch and does his crossword. Habit, I guess. Isn't it sad I'm still in this town to even know that?"

Both women snickered.

"Well, I'm here too." Simone cut into her medium-well steak. Medium-rare steaks were one of the many food items she missed.

"Sure, but you left."

Simone shook her head lightly. "So did you. We came back because it was best for our families."

"Yeah, not so much best for our careers. I'm still waiting on that big story. Black Water for all its mysterious happenings has been rather quiet lately—occasional runaways, domestic disputes, and accidents, but there *have* been some minor burglaries lately."

"Burglaries?" Simone's mind returned to the dark man on her porch.

"Not exactly burglaries, but a hose was stolen from the side of a house and a bike from another, the small town usual. So, tell me more about your family, your husband, that baby! Are your girls anything like us when we were kids?"

"We were outdoorswomen. My girls are not big on outside. They'll have to get used to this country life. My little one, Jada, loves to read and play with her stuffed animals. Aaliyah, my whippersnapper, loves to sketch and listen to her music."

"Whippersnapper, eh? That sounds like El—"

"It's okay … Ella." Simone finished her friend's sentence. "Yes, they're alike in many ways."

"What about the baby?" Myeisha asked before shoving the last of her salad into her mouth and chewing through her follow up. "Boy or girl?"

"A boy." Simone exhaled. "Black Water's only two midwives were booked, so I'm stuck with a doctor I don't love and just trying to prepare for lack of sleep, breastfeeding, the—"

"Breastfeeding? We don't do that!"

Simone smiled. "Actually, we do. It just shrunk in desirability after slavery. We were so often forced to wet nurse children that weren't our own that, over the years, it became reviled as a slave task we wanted to separate ourselves from."

"Nu-uh." Myeisha scrunched her face in spirited disbelief. "I should know that, right?"

"Not necessarily. There are so many facets to pregnancy and birth. I didn't know most of this stuff until I started reading about it when I became pregnant with Aaliyah. Once I learned that about breastfeeding, I became determined to reclaim it. What about you? You want kids?"

Myeisha hesitated before slurping from her glass. "I don't know. I just don't know what kind of mother I would be. I mean, I love my mom, but I don't want to be anything like her as a mother, and I don't want to pass on some drinking gene to my child. You know with things like that they say doctors don't really know if its nature or nurture."

"Really?" Simone cut the last few pieces of her steak.

"I don't know a lot about having kids, but I have done a lot of research on alcoholism. If a child is subjected to an addicted mother or something similar, their chances of becoming addicted or having similar behaviors is even higher, but they don't know if it's because they carry a genetic marker for addiction or because the parents have exposed the child to that behavior."

"Children are hard, no matter what, but I'm sure you'd be a fantastic mother." Simone's words seemed to touch an intimate place in her friend. She continued so as not to draw further attention to Myeisha's discomfort. "As a mother, you want to be everything for your children—loving yet strong—and anything short of surpassing those expectations feels like failure. That's one of the reasons I wanted to go to law school. I wanted to be a provider. In control. Aaliyah was always resentful that I was never home, so I moved to contract work so I can stay home, and even though we moved here, she still doesn't seem quite impressed with me. At least my baby, Jada, was on my side, but since we've moved into the house, it seems Aaliyah has grown more docile, and Jada is all out of whack. No matter how much we try to be everything to our children, it will never be perfect. You know, I saw a talk show one time about a troubled kid, and do you know what he said? He said his parents loved him too much. Have you ever heard such a ridiculous thing? So, literally, you can *not* love your child enough, love them too much, never be there, be there too much, etc. Motherhood is nothing if not a constant lesson in your own imperfections."

"Unbelievable."

"You still don't drink?"

"Just a little. I don't have a problem. I never get drunk. I don't even like it. I just drink a little because not drinking at all scares me shitless. Not drinking at all means I can't control it."

"Whatever works. Same with parenting. Whatever works," Simone said before segueing to safer, less abstract topics. "I saw Dr. Duran."

"Oh, good. I see her every now and then, but she's always working, dedicated to the hospital. They have a full-on psychiatric ward now. All small towns probably need one. These places drive you nuts."

"She wants to get together for lunch or something."

"She doesn't want to talk about that night, does she?" Myeisha cringed. "Seems like that would be too much."

"I don't know, and honestly, I don't know that I would be so against it. Being back has brought a lot of things to the surface I need to clear away. It's part of the reason I moved back. I'm moving to a different stage in my life. This is my last child. I want to confront the residual shit and be done with it."

Rolling her jaw as if she had a sweet piece of hard candy in her mouth, a signature move that indicated her tumbling thoughts, Myeisha focused on her friend. "I'm not judging you, and I am so happy you are here, but did you really need to come back here to do that? To move into that house?"

Myeisha *was* judging her. Maybe she needed to be judged; isn't that what friends were for occasionally? To abruptly ask errant but calculated questions that forced us to revisit questionable decisions? No one, not even Mack, had asked the question just so, and within the fresh context of being back now, Simone was forced to reconsider her purpose. "I think so. I need to hear those old squeaks in the doors, face the familiar shadows in the hallway, and study the stains in the wood where the blood never came all the way up. If I'm scared in my home, I'm scared everywhere. Look at you. You don't have to be here, but you are. Facing your past and focusing your future all in the same tough act that is caring for your mother. It must be hard, but you're here. I'm here."

Myeisha nodded slowly, then smiled. "This was supposed to be a light lunch."

Simone laughed. "But seriously, do you think talking to Dr. Duran would help?"

"Can't hurt. The greatest secrets are always hidden in the most unlikely places." Myeisha motioned for the check. "Talking to her may uncover just what you're looking for."

On her way home, Simone retrieved Ella's necklace. Mr. Thompson had replaced the silver clasp with the expert precision of a man who focused every ounce of his remains, including the angular sharpness of lasting but functional sorrow, into his craftsmanship.

As Simone's minivan bounced up the gravel drive to her home, she braked hard when she spotted a hulking, squarely built man under the cover of black clothing and a baseball cap, shuffling from behind her house, across the side yard and into the trees.

Chapter 19

———————◆━◆━◆◇»———————

Without ever taking her eyes from the point at which the man stumbled into the woods, Simone muttered to herself as she fumbled through her overstuffed purse filled with everything from mints to a mini first-aid kit, "Where is it? Where is it?"

When she felt the textured glittering gold of her phone case, she wrenched it up but had to stop and take a calming breath in order to persuade her shaking hands to enter the passcode and dial her husband.

Not even eight minutes later and Simone spotted Mack's truck in her rearview, barreling up the drive. Simone's heartrate was restored to normalcy, and she shifted her car from reverse—prepared to peel out if necessary—into park and removed her foot from the brake.

Like a veteran first responder, he jumped from his truck with the textbook amalgam of urgency and confidence. The defined lines of his chest and torso pressed through his sweat-soaked t-shirt.

"I thought you were at work," Simone said, noticing the black basketball shorts he always wore for occasional pickup games in the city. At once, she forgot about the loitering stranger and focused on the husband whose midday costume change struck Simone as perfidious at best.

"I was, but I met some guys yesterday who play, and we set up a quick lunch game." He crossed the lawn, inspecting the property with the parodic investigative eye all men mimic when called upon to flesh out perilously odd noises in slasher films. "You saw someone over here?" He pointed to the tree line left of the house.

"Yes. He came from the back of the house." Simone's squinted stare lingered on her husband's athletic attire. "You didn't tell me you were playing basketball today."

Mack sighed, then headed to the front porch where Whiskers padded around anxiously. "I didn't think it was a big deal. Did you recognize the man? Maybe he was just going for a jog and cut across our yard."

"He didn't look like he was jogging, Mack. I saw his face, but I didn't get a good look. His face was kind of ... distorted. His features were hard to decipher. They seemed uneven."

In the foyer, Simone waited, rubbing her belly with both hands as Mack searched the entire house, looking behind doors and under beds with the bat that now had a secondary purpose by the front door as home security. Usually, she would be at her husband's side for any dangerous domestic missions, but she wasn't overly concerned with ideas of people under the stairs or crouching in the attic, seeing as how the man had been running away from the house and not into it.

"Nothing," Mack declared, appearing at the top of the steps.

Simone went to the kitchen, dropped her purse, and pulled a glass from the cabinet. "Mack?"

"Yeah?" he called as he entered the room.

"Did you leave the shed open?" she asked, peering out the back window.

"No." Mack looked over his wife's shoulder at the shed door flapping lightly in the breeze. He unlocked the back door and darted across the yard. Once inside the shed, he scanned the small storage space before shutting the door securely, then jogging back to the house. "I don't think anything is missing, but I'll get a lock just in case."

"We should report this. Myeisha said there have been some minor burglaries recently."

"Bae, nothing was taken."

"You don't *think* anything was taken, and he could have still been a prowler or, even worse, a peeper of some sort."

It took Sheriff Handow about twenty minutes to arrive. Simone greeted him at his patrol car.

"Simone Mills, it sure is good to have you back."

"It's good to see you as well. Parker—my last name is Parker now. This is my husband, Mack Parker." Simone motioned to Mack who was approaching briskly.

The men engaged in a firm handshake before Mack launched into a straightforward debriefing of the events preceding their call as he guided Handow to the back of the house.

"You notice anything missing?" Handow asked after Simone couldn't give a detailed description of the bulky man she only saw for a few seconds from the side.

"No, but we thought we should still report it."

"Course, you should," Handow confirmed, his smile authentic as always. "Well, we've had a couple of small things stolen from homes lately, bikes and such, but nothing too critical. I'll make a report, and if you notice anything missing, you give me a call."

"Will do," Mack said before excusing himself for a shower.

"You all coming to the Summer Closing?" Handow asked as Simone walked him to his car.

"Probably. I'll have to see how I feel."

"It'll be a good time." His voice was low, and his gaze swept the ground as he dipped into his driver's seat. "How you doing in this old house?"

Simone wanted to roll her eyes but didn't. He probably thought she was crazy to move back, and now she thinks strange men are digging around in her shed. "I'm fine. Old ghosts, you know, but we're cleaning them out."

"Good, good, good." His voice was smooth like well-creamed coffee, and the skin around his dark eyes crinkled about the corners as he analyzed her words for authenticity. "Well, you call me if you need anything. Anything at all, you call. I'm keeping a special eye on you."

Simone watched his car disappear around the gravel path and through the trees before she went inside.

Dressed in a fresh set of work clothes, Mack trotted down the steps. "Will you be okay if I go back to the shop?"

"Do you have to go?" Simone detested the whine that slipped into her voice.

"We have a couple more cars. I wanted to get ahead so I can leave the shop to Nicco on Saturday and take a day off. Do you need me to stay?"

"I don't understand how you had time for basketball but now have to go back to work."

"Bae, I need a break sometimes too. You went to lunch with a friend, I used my lunch to hoop. Give me a break." Mack's words became short and sharp with annoyance.

"Well ..." Simone rolled her eyes at her own ridiculous paranoia. "I'm fine. Besides, the girls will be home soon."

"I'm sure they can protect you," Mack joked.

Simone didn't smile.

"Tell you what. I'll go back to the shop, get as much done as possible, and be back no later than five. Oh, and I'll bring dinner."

"Okay. What about the alarm?"

"We'll look into some systems this weekend," he assured her as he shuffled down the porch stairs and into his truck.

"You promise?"

"Yes," he said and kissed her through the driver's side window. "Now you and Trace get back in the house and lock the door, but I don't think there is anything to be afraid of. If I did, I wouldn't leave."

Simone sunk into the security his chestnut-colored eyes always provided for her, and she believed him—she always believed him. As soon as she was inside, she locked the front door and peered out the side window.

Mack was far down the drive but kept his eye on her until she was safely behind the door, at which point he turned his truck to head toward the main road.

He was on his phone, Simone noticed. *But with who so soon after leaving her? Must be the shop. Just letting this Nicco person know he was on his way back.*

All through the house, Simone took her time ensuring all the doors and windows were locked securely. She insisted to herself she was overreacting but could not scrap the prickly sensation of someone watching her. At last, she finished her round through the house at one of the sunroom windows where she studied the deceptively still tree line that had, just an hour ago, swallowed up her stranger. First, the man at the door, and now the one in the yard. *Had they been the same? No. Today, the man was big but clumsy. The man waiting at the door was smaller, sturdy, and menacing beyond description.* A chill coursed through Simone's shared body. *One was running away while the other was demanding to come inside.*

Chapter 20

Storm clouds moved in, blocking the light and warmth. It had a leavening effect on Simone as she had grown to prefer weather that kept everyone safe inside. Before checking the house phone's voicemail, she streamed her mother's moody jazz music through the wireless speaker and put on the water for tea.

There were three voicemails. The first was from Dr. Penny's office reminding her of an upcoming appointment. Next, she heard Dr. Duran's voice. Had a foreigner landed on new shores and asked to be taken to the elder female leader of the land, her voice would be that of Dr. Duran's—melodious with an inherited confidence buried in its drawling depths. Dr. Duran was just checking and wondering if she were free for lunch this week. Last, Katherine informed her that she emailed some questions on the updated brief and needed a response ASAP.

The kettle whistled. Simone made her tea and threw herself into her work, blocking out everything but the words on her computer screen. By this time, the rainstorm was raging.

When Mack poked his head through her office door, she could hardly believe it was evening. Besides a short break to prepare an afternoon snack for the girls, Simone had devoted herself to her work without distraction.

"I come bearing gifts." He smiled.

"Just give me one moment to finish sending this email," she explained, all the lines in her face drawn tightly as she squinted at her computer screen. "You would not believe the amount of research and unnecessary changes these people expected today. They're impossible. I don't know how much more I can deal with them."

"Well don't. Soon the shop will be doing so well, you won't have to return to work after the baby is born. We won't be rich or anything, but I think I can keep us fed and clothed."

Simone smirked before pressing the send button. "I know."

Chinese—Simone immediately recognized the greasy-bottomed bag when Mack held it up. "Your favorite!" he said.

As Simone closed her laptop, Mack fully entered the room, and she saw him holding something else in his other hand. "What do you have there?" she asked as he turned it around to reveal a painting.

"Another surprise," he said, a soft grin lighting his face. It was a square, gray canvas with the silhouette of a strange little creature. Alongside it, the words, *I'll eat you up, I love you so,* were painted in white. Once again, she was eight years old, in bed, listening intently to her mother as she read Simone one of her favorite bedtime tales of wild rumpus and fantastic beasts. Dorothy Ann was draped in her favorite full-body painting smock. It was black but covered in spontaneous splatters and drops of paint. As her mother read, altering her voice to fit the characters, Simone focused on the streak of shamrock-colored paint across her mother's left cheek.

"I love this, Mack," Simone gushed over the quote. "It's perfect for the nursery. Thank you."

That night as Simone read the words in the story where the little girl looked into the oversized orbs of her suddenly strange grandmother, Jada stopped her. "Does this story have a happy ending?"

"No. The grandmother eats her." Aaliyah lifted from the opposite end of the twin bed.

"Aaliyah, please," Simone said as she pulled Jada's bear mask from her face and placed it on the nightstand. After motioning for Aaliyah to hop out of bed, Simone pulled Jada's covers around her chin with a song. *"Twinkle, twinkle, you are my little star. I'll rock you and put you to bed."* The words melted into a hum as that was all Simone could recall of her mother's lullaby thus far. "Stay in bed tonight. I love you." Simone walked to the door, goading her eldest alongside her.

"I love you more," Jada chirped.

"I love you four," Simone said before flipping off the light.

In the dark hallway, Simone pulled Aaliyah's face to hers and kissed her lower cheek. "I love you. Get to bed."

In her bathroom, Simone removed her mother's watch and ring. She lifted the crinkled corners of her eyes, reminded of a time when that delicate skin was smooth. She massaged a glop of moisturizer into her belly, the daily routine that had twice before prevented the fissures of expanding life that babies often left on their mothers, like a marking of their human territory.

Rubbing the remnants of lotion into her hands, she leaned against the doorframe, watching her husband as he counted his one hundredth pushup under his breath. "Hmm …" she moaned softly.

"What's that?" Mack called.

"Nothing," Simone replied for fear of launching another argument over her likely ridiculous suspicions of his sudden preoccupation with working out when he had allowed his gym membership to lapse at least two years ago without so much as a word.

"Whose necklace is that on the sink? That silver one." Mack lifted himself from the floor.

"It was Ella's. I found it lodged into a floor crack in the basement." Simone crawled into bed. "Pushups, huh?" Control of her mouth seemed in short supply lately, especially when it came to her husband.

"Huh?" Mack responded as he removed his watch and bounced into bed beside her.

"First basketball and now pushups—what's next? IronMan?" Inside, Simone was screaming at herself to shut up.

"It's good for me. I just feel good being in a new place, trees and fresh air."

"It would be nice if you could work on some of the things around the house you promised you'd work on—the sticking fridge door, the dripping faucet."

"Simone, I'll get all of those things done. I said I would." Mack leaned across the bed; lips pursed sardonically.

Reeling backward from his mocking kiss, Simone fired, "Why now? You stopped working out years ago."

An exhausted Mack pushed his finger into the inner corner of his eye to remove something that wasn't there, more a gesture of frustration than function. "If you recall, that was about the time I lost my job and couldn't find a steady new one. Have you ever thought I'm just happy and enjoying life a little? Have you even thought I have a little more energy and confidence with all of the great things happening for us now?"

Ever ready with a logical rebuttal, one would think that, over the years, Simone would have become wary of Mack's uncanny ability to say just the right thing with unquestionable timing. She hadn't, because the one thing she could never deny was his authenticity. A man's man for sure, especially in the sense that if he was anything, he wasn't calculating. He said what he thought with little measure of appearance.

Simone had been sure Mack would not call her again after their second date, which marked the first time they had made love. Not because Mack had indulged in any of the toxic masculinity that prescribed that a man—to be considered a man—must always be on the prowl for sexual gratification, but because, as he would later tell her, he had known immediately that she was *the one*.

Mack was right. It was possible that she was too busy working, planning, and trying to be in control, but lately, she had given little thought to his happiness in ways beyond how it affected her and the family.

"I'm sorry." Simone reached for her husband, cuddling him in her arms and kissing his forehead gently. "I'm glad things are better for us. I just want them to keep going that way, and I will do whatever it takes to make that happen."

"You really want to make things better?" Mack gently pushed from his wife's embrace.

Simone jerked her head backward before speaking slowly. "Sure …"

He hesitated still. "I need to talk to you about something, but I don't want to upset you."

"What?" Simone asked, resolving to stay calm.

"First ..."

Simone's eyebrows lifted. *"First?* So, this is a two-part conversation?"

Raising his hands in a deescalating gesture, Mack spoke calmly. "First, can we stop locking the door at night? I don't feel comfortable with Jada being locked out if she's scared."

"She's fine. She's been sleeping with Aaliyah." Simone rolled her eyes. "So now I'm a bad mother because I want to actually sleep every now and then?"

"Whoa, whoa. Never said that. In fact, you're an excellent mother, which brings me to what I'm about to say next."

Simone straightened her back, squaring herself defensively to the attack on her motherhood she was now sure was about to drop from her husband's lips into this marital minefield. "Go on," she commanded stoically.

Mack was far from foolish and knew the lump growing at the base of his throat was a trustworthy self-warning. The one thing a man did not do was question his wife's maternal motivations and actions. He chose his next words as cautiously as a tightrope walker chooses their footfalls on a tiny line between skyscrapers. "It's just that sometimes it seems like Jada is your ... favorite." He flinched, somewhat jokingly, as if she would hit him.

Surprisingly enough, at first, Simone wasn't angry at all. Her preliminary feeling was that of curiosity, as she had never considered such a thing. Sure, her relationship was different with each of her girls, but she had never intentionally favored one over the other. "Did Aaliyah say that?"

"She doesn't have to say it, Simone. I know her."

"And I don't?" Simone snapped.

"You said you wouldn't get upset."

"I never said that, Mack! I never once said that."

"I'm not criticizing you, Simone. All I'm saying is sometimes it seems your bond is stronger with Jada. Especially with the, *I love you more, I love you four,* thing. You have these little moments with Jada. Aaliyah notices."

"I can't believe you!" Simone jumped from the bed.

"Where are you going?" Mack's shoulders slumped.

"To make this right, I suppose," Simone retorted before dipping into the bathroom and then into the hallway.

Chapter 21

————— ◄═══●══►═══ —————

Clutching the cool metal in one hand, Simone knocked gently with the other. "Aaliyah?" When there was no answer after another knock, she pressed open the door and found her daughter sitting upright in bed, sketching, her earbuds pressed tightly into each side of her head. The lightest scent of bubblegum permeated the air. On the floor against the far wall, Simone spotted a model of a solar system that appeared to be in mid construction. At the bottom left corner of the black poster board was burnt-orange construction paper that represented the sun, curved white lines were painted out from the sun diagonally across the rest of the surface, and a ranging size of painted colorful balls were starting to be glued along the white lines—only Mercury, Venus, and Earth and its moon so far. At once, Simone decided Mack's implications were wrong, but he did have a point. In no way did Simone have a favorite child. Such a thought was something she willfully abhorred. Nevertheless, in some indiscernible familial evolution, Simone had allowed preoccupations with seemingly more urgent matters, along with the parental way given for independence that preteens need to blossom into teens, push her relationship with Aaliyah in a damaging direction.

Neglect. Even tumbling around in Simone's thoughts, the word was a perversion. Under her bare feet, something sharp dug into her heel. "Ow."

A startled Aaliyah removed her earbuds. "Mom, are you okay?"

Simone lifted her foot to study the light coating of gritty dirt that contained a few reflective specs. "I'm fine. Did you track sand in the house?"

"I don't think so." Aaliyah's face scrunched in confusion.

Dusting the heel of her foot on her opposite leg, Simone spoke, not yet looking up. "I see you started your solar system. I thought we were going to work on it together?"

Her daughter shrugged. "I know you're busy, so Dad was helping me."

Every inch of flesh under Simone's skin warmed with the light shame all mothers felt at the slightest expression of their children's disappointment in them for every innocuous misstep, from forgetting to pack a swimsuit for school splash day, to tardiness to the amateur dance recital due to a glitch in the digital calendar. It was *okay* for moms to be busy and okay for dads to do their parts, Simone reminded herself. But it wasn't. Mothers were different, a being from which omnipotence and omnipresence were standard expectations.

"I'm sorry, sweetie. I know I've been preoccupied lately, and you must be worried I will be even more so once Trace gets here. One of the reasons we moved to Black Water was to have our own business, and it's going really well. I may not even need to go back to work for a while after the baby is born. I'll have more time for all of us, okay?"

Aaliyah nodded.

Simone held up the necklace for her daughter to read the words adorned across the charm. "This necklace belonged to my sister when she was a little girl. Grandma gave it to her."

"*I love you to the moon and back.*" Aaliyah's eyes sparkled as she read. "Honestly, I kind of always envied it."

"Why?"

"Well, Ella was always closer to Grandma. As the oldest, she knew her in a way I never would. I was closer to Grandpa. I would sit with him, rocking in his recliner, very much like the one we have, watching television." Simone motioned for her daughter to turn so she could fasten the clasp around Aaliyah's neck. "Even though Ella was older than me, we played together endlessly. Hide and seek especially. She would hide underneath a bundle of covers, and when I got close, she would raise up, pull me in, and tickle me. Like her, you're a wonderful big sister, a wonderful daughter, and I love you more than anything."

"Thanks, Mom. I love it," Aaliyah gushed.

"Bedtime," Simone announced. She took Aaliyah's sketchpad, then straightened the covers.

"Can you close the closet door all the way?" the girl asked before her mother departed, leaving her to the oozing glow of the orange nightlight.

It was a beautiful day for Simone to take the girls for an exploratory walk in Langford Woods. The sun was high and offered some of the last of summer's warmth before fall fully took the reins. Fused from the aromas of dirt and a variety of green matter and wildflowers, the scent of the forest was mesmerizing. Ahead of her, Jada and Aaliyah chased one another along the trail, stopping occasionally to share secrets and bursts of laughter before shooting out in joyful sprints of play. Along with the sounds of twigs breaking underfoot, the scampering of smalls animals and sway of the branches brought the mass of trees to life. The girls were farther ahead now, almost too far, and over the course of a second, the sun had given way to the moon, the seduction of its silvery light infusing the night.

To gain on the girls, Simone quickened her pace, one hand pressed to the lower part of her bulbous belly. Shadows danced around her, threatening to close in, and what, in the light, had been the harmless hoots of friendly wildlife were now the depraved howls of carnivorous creatures. It was impossible now for Simone to keep up with the girls, and nothing more than a dusty croak clicked from her throat when she tried to call to them. Up ahead, Simone witnessed three startling bursts of light that transformed her jumping girls into butterflies, their vibrantly colored wings flapping elegantly against the night sky as they floated purposefully toward the round moon. Glimpsing a third butterfly that lagged in the skyward ascension, Simone's attention shot to her flattened belly.

Bolting upright in bed, Simone's instinct led her hand to her stomach which still held her son.

A scream ripped through the second floor, and within seconds, Mack was out the door, racing down the hallway.

Simone arrived in Aaliyah's room only a few steps behind her husband.

"What is it?" Mack asked in a raised voice.

"It's blood. I'm bleeding!" Aaliyah's eyes were trained on some unseen force beneath the blankets with her.

Still lost in a heightened state of confusion, Mack pulled back the covers. At the fresh blood pooled around his daughter, he gasped.

Shaking off the remnants of sleep, Simone moved to the bed and pulled the covers back up before turning to her husband. "I'll handle this."

"What is—"

Simone narrowed her eyes in a way that begged his common sense, suddenly making the situation clear.

"Oh, wow. This is new. Uh, honey," he said in a whisper, "If you need Daddy at all, I'm here for you, okay?"

Aaliyah's eyes darted wildly between her parents.

"It's okay. Mommy's here," Simone assured her, waving Mack away.

A knock sounded as the door swayed open to reveal Jada in her white pajamas with pink polka dots, Bobo in one hand, rubbing her eyes with the other.

After helping Aaliyah to the shower, Simone took her daughter's sheets, nightgown, and panties to the basement where she scrubbed them with stain remover before throwing them in the washer. Next, she used detergent to scrub the drying stain from the mattress before unfolding a towel over the now wet spot and making the bed with fresh sheets, the whole time barely fending off questions from the diligent, little assistant who shadowed her every move.

"Jada, you can sit in while I talk to your sister, but for now, let's just get this done. I'm exhausted."

Once Aaliyah was back in her room, she consented to allowing Jada to stick around a few moments for their mother's words.

In a calm tone, Simone showed her daughter how to apply the sanitary pad to her underwear. "See? Just like that."

The girls stared at Simone blankly as if she were hiding something, like she was a fraud—and she was in a way. She was trying to simplify the explosive emotional, biological, and psychological mechanics of the menstrual cycle to the application of a sticky pad.

Simone sighed, the narrow slits of her eyes begging to close. "We discussed this before, Aaliyah. Granted, I didn't think it would come so soon, but it's completely normal. It happens to all women."

"To you too?" Jada asked, more interested than her affected sister. "You bleed too?"

"Not right now, honey, because I'm pregnant. It happens to all girls and women once they reach a certain age, except when they're pregnant. In fact, that is really what it boils down to—the transition from maiden to mother. Our parents used to say it meant you were a woman, and that's false in so many ways, but it does mean you can carry a child."

Aaliyah's eyes bulged before all her features drew into the center of her face in disgust.

Rushing her words, Simone explained further, "Not that you or any girl your age would. It just means your body is starting to get in the process so one day, far from today, you can. Do you have any more questions?"

With only two words, Aaliyah responded, "Every month?"

"Every month," Simone confirmed as her daughter scooted under the covers. "We can talk about this more, of course, but let's talk about it tomorrow. How about everyone get some sleep, okay?"

"Okay," Aaliyah whimpered as her mother tucked the covers around her chest.

The expected curious chirp response was palpably missing from her youngest. Simone scanned the room and saw Jada had spotted her sister's science project. "Jada …"

Fixed on the mesmerizing glittered replica of the most perilous environment known to man, Jada herself seemed lost in a far-off space of her own. "The moon. That's where the Sandman lives. On the dark side."

"Not tonight," Simone started.

"It's true! That's where he takes the eyeballs to feed to his children."

"Enough!" Simone kneeled in front of her daughter. "Look at me. There is no Sandman, do you understand? I want you to stop it."

Jada looked at her mother. "He's trying to get in."

"Inside the house?" Aaliyah asked, sitting upright in bed.

Simone panned from Aaliyah to Jada who nodded. "Aaliyah, don't encourage her. No one is trying to get inside." Simone huffed.

Then they all heard it. Through the window, the distant screeches of the baby filled the room. All three of them strode to the glass and peered into the darkness, each of them placing a hand: Jada's to the window, Simone's to her belly, and Aaliyah's to the coolness of the silver charm around her neck.

"There's a baby outside," Jada declared.

A tiny, nimble creature shot through the yard and onto the back porch.

"Freaking cat," Simone mumbled.

"Can we let Whiskers in?" Aaliyah begged.

By now, Simone was in no state to argue. Aaliyah was having a particularly rough night; they had already named the damned thing, and Simone just wanted everyone content so they could all sleep. "Only for tonight," Simone relented, launching the girls into a race through the hallway and down the stairs.

By the time they got Whiskers inside, gave her milk, and headed up the stairs, Simone knew the darkness would soon be evaporating into light.

"Can I sleep with Aaliyah?" Jada asked, jogging ahead to her sister's room.

"It's okay, Mom," Aaliyah said.

The last thing Simone needed was her youngest swiveling her form into a horizonal bar between herself and Mack. All night, Simone would be adjusting the position of Jada's feet only to have them repeatedly planted into her side until morning, but Mack had already expressed his disdain with his wife locking their bedroom door, so she did as any mother should. "Jada, are you sure you don't want to sleep with Mommy and Daddy?"

"Not tonight. I'll stay with Aaliyah," she confirmed to Simone's secret relief.

After Simone left the girls tucked warmly in bed, Jada faced her sister. "It's not the Sandman that's trying to get in."

"I know." Aaliyah placed her arm around her sister's waist. "It's the baby. The Sandman is already inside."

Chapter 22

—◆—◆—◆—

R ain dropped from a cloud-marbled sky in unforgiving sheets, affording Simone the soothing luxury of waking to a house brimming with its white noise. Her dry mouth ached for the creamy warmth of coffee, but despite the collusive sleeping arrangement made the previous night with her daughters which left the master bed to Simone and her husband alone, she was still too exhausted to get up. Instead, she silently counted the seconds between rumbling bursts of thunder, a trick of her mother's conveyance. Reminiscent of the early mornings when her mother would sit in her sunroom as storm clouds descended on the house, Simone peered out her own rain-battered window, consumed with what she assumed was the same peaceful numbness her mother had felt in similar weather. With the sun came an exhaustive and endless exuberance, and with more extreme, destructive weather, a terrifying anxiety and scramble for safety, but the thunderstorm brought acceptance. The rain was coming, you made your peace with it, you sat and waited for it to pass.

Dorothy Ann would watch the rain come down for hours. Simone would climb into her mother's lap and nuzzle up to the pine-colored terrycloth robe that wrapped her mother's pregnant middle, and the two would watch together, rarely ruining the moments with words. It was some of the only times she had alone with her mother, as Ella preferred to sleep late, especially when it rained. Once, her mother broke their sacred silence and spoke just as a cacophony of thunder pinged the air. *"You know, if you count the seconds between the thunder, you can tell how far away the storm is."* Dorothy Ann counted, *"One ... Two ... Three ... Four ..."* Another raucous symphony of thunder rang out. *"It's close."* A steely clang of lightning followed, shuddering a young Simone, like a kitten stuck in a tree. *"It's okay. Mommy's here."* Dorothy Ann rubbed her hand up and down Simone's arm with a squeeze and a hum that grew into song. *"Twinkle, twinkle, you are my little star. I'll rock you and put you to bed, my house is made of gingerbread and candy..."*

At once, Simone was back in her bed with Mack lying next to her. The obnoxious buzzing of the alarm from his phone failed to stir him. Hoisting herself from the bed, Simone shut off the alarm and nudged her husband to an on-time start so he could drop the girls at school. Waiting at the bus stop in the pouring rain was not an option she felt much like pursuing.

The morning's mad scramble included cooking bacon, locating rainboots and missing homework, and concealing sanitary pads in a sequin backpack. Such frantic passing of the time made Simone realize, once the house was empty and she sat at her desk, that she had barely spoken two words to Mack.

After a while, Simone noticed the delicate tapping of her laptop keys was the only sound in the house. Stopping, she sat back, closed her eyes, and let the silence envelop her. Simone smiled at the thought of her baby boy. When she opened her eyes, she noticed the rain had finally subsided. She checked the time at the bottom of her computer screen to see it was almost noon. This baby was different; her appetite was waning. Even after skipping breakfast, she still wasn't hungry but knew it would be irresponsible not to force at least something small down. In the kitchen, she found Mack's oversized, metal lunchbox forgotten on the counter.

Wrangling even maternity jeans over her midsection was now officially a struggle. Simone plopped across the bed to complete the last pull that successfully anchored the elastic around her waist. There she rested for a moment to catch her breath before rolling unto her side and up to put on a thick, sea-green sweater. In the bathroom, she searched the little box on the counter for her gold hoops but came across her mother's pearl earrings first which she caressed before poking them into her earlobes.

Before heading out, Simone grabbed her smoothie from the fridge. Despite preparing it the day before with all fruit, as the dense concoction rolled across her taste buds, the flavor hinted at salt and spoliation. Gagging violently, Simone was grateful she had not eaten that morning else she would be looking at a gross rainbow of half-digested breakfast foods instead of the bit of bile that speckled the stainless steel of the sink.

Perhaps the baby was changing her tastes, Simone thought before pouring the remainder of the drink down the drain and grabbing Mack's lunchbox.

Once in town, two of the three Black Water patrol cars sped by her in the opposite direction, sirens blaring. Checking her rearview, Simone tried to get an idea of where they were headed, but they soon turned off and were out of sight.

Each of the three bays at the shop housed a car with plenty more lined up behind each of them. Mack wasn't exaggerating about the amount of business coming through. Inside, the shop felt bright and warm against the outside gloom. Simone admired the shine of new management on all the surfaces.

"Can I help you?" A young woman smiled brightly from behind the front desk. Her sharp, black hair was cut into a pixie, her brown eyes seemed to ripple with hypnotic affect, and her teeth were offensively white. Artfully created rips in her black jeans undoubtedly made them more expensive, and a bright canary-colored t-shirt read, CAMP CRYSTAL LAKE, with an imprint of a wood cabin pressed tightly against her pointed breasts.

"I'm Simone. Simone Parker."

"Mrs. Parker!" she erupted sweetly, hand extended. "I've heard so much about you. I'm Nita, the receptionist."

"Oh yes. Nita," Simone quipped sharply, pretending she had been made aware of the young woman's employment. Was Nita gorgeous? Simone couldn't be sure what passed for attractive with middle-aged men anymore, but she was young, and often the concepts seemed interchangeable.

Reminded of Mack recently arriving home all sweaty, Simone quickly dismissed her dubious mind. He *did* have a basketball, and it was likely he had simply discovered local friends to help him rekindle an old hobby, but then there were the pushups every night on their bedroom floor.

Not on purpose, Simone scrutinized Nita's Playboy-worthy breasts before lowering her gaze to her own, and while she had managed to avoid stretch marks with an expensive homemade mixture of oils and cocoa butter, after Jada, her breasts had never recovered.

"Is my husband around? I brought his lunch." Simone limply lifted the metal box.

The door that led to the garage strained as Mack pulled it open and shuffled inside, his large hands covered in grease. "Simone …" His eyes widened at the sight of his wife before he glanced at Nita who had moved on to helping another customer.

Simone flashed an elaborate grin. "You forgot your lunch."

A hint of delight flickered in Mack's eyes. He wiped his hands on the oil-marked towel slung over his shoulder before kissing Simone and leading her passed the receptionist desk into a tiny back office where he helped her sit.

"You told me you had hired another mechanic but failed to mention *Ni-ta.*"

"Here we go," he muttered before ripping into his sandwich.

"We're not *going* anywhere. I just wish you would keep me informed about things that are going on here."

"I just hired her yesterday. She came in with her boyfriend who was getting his car fixed. Between the front and the garage, we were swamped. She noticed and asked if we needed some help. I was going to tell you, but this is what I wanted to avoid," he explained between chews.

"What? What were you trying to avoid?"

"You trippin."

Simone rolled her eyes right before a contraction tensed her body.

Mack touched her belly. "You okay?"

"Yes. I'll probably keep having them until I deliver."

"When is your next doctor's appointment?" He shoved a whole chip into his mouth.

"Tomorrow, I believe."

"You want me to go?"

Simone thought for a moment. "Nah, it's routine."

"Where are you going anyway? You look nice, jewelry and all." Mack smiled.

"You think you're really cute, don't you? Actually, I was just coming to bring my husband lunch, but it looks like you've got your hands full. Guess I'll go home now and try to fix the leaky faucet, something you just can't seem to find time to do. Tools are in the shed, right?"

"Bae, go home and rest please. You look tired. Let's make a deal; if you go home and get in bed, no matter what time I get home and no matter how tired I am, I will fix the faucet ... tonight."

Simone launched herself from the chair before Mack could assist and sauntered to the door. "No, thank you. I've got lots of work to do, just like you and Nita."

"Let me introduce you to Sam and Nicco before you go so you won't have any silly thoughts about me and Nita sitting around here alone together."

After the short tour and introductions, Mack walked his wife to their minivan. "You're not really mad, are you? You know all of this is for you and the kids. For us."

"I know." Simone put her palm to Mack's cheek, his stubble tickling her. "I'm not mad." She giggled as her husband leaned through the window to graze her neck with his lips.

Black Water's sidewalks glistened from the morning rain, and as the air cooled, dense fog rolled through town. Simone carefully made the turn onto the private path that led to her house and pulled her van as close as possible to the front door. Though she could hardly see anything beyond a few feet in the maze of gray mist, she scanned the property for strangers and firmly gripped her house key in her hand before stepping onto the soft ground. As she climbed the porch steps, a flock of black birds erupted from a nearby tree, startling her with the wild flapping of their charcoal wings. Once inside, she snapped the locks, then peered through the curtain of the door-side window to ensure no one had followed.

Armed with a cup of tea, Simone stood in the doorway of her office, staring at the neat and organized stacks of paper on her desk that comprised her research. Mack was right; the time was coming for her to rest and nest. Staunchly focused for the next few hours, she shuffled through her papers, reading, cross-referencing, then clicking away at her computer keys until she was satisfied all the requested updates were made with masterful insight.

"Send," Simone whispered to herself, and she punched the mouse button, shooting the final document through email. By now, she noticed the discomfort of the elastic of her pants digging into her skin at the hips. Her body felt taut, and she was at a familiar point where any clothing at all felt uncomfortable. A shower before the girls got home and the loosest-fitting cotton ensemble she could locate may provide some relief.

As she passed Aaliyah's open bedroom door, Simone saw wrinkled clothes hanging from the chest of drawers, as if trying to escape. Her daughter's sketchbooks littered the floor, and the covers of her bed were crumpled in a pile. The mother in Simone could hardly continue without tidying the space. Squatting, Simone straightened the sketchbooks before placing them on the bookshelf. At the chest, she folded her daughter's clothes and tucked them into the drawers before closing them fully. Before turning to the bed, her gaze lingered on that photograph of herself, Ella, and Myeisha. Remembering the day Ella fell from the butterfly tree, she abruptly felt accompanied. A whiff of banana bubblegum permeated her nostrils, the aroma rotting with every second it wafted farther into her skull until it was a slight but sour stench.

Behind her, the ruffled blankets gathered until they came to a sturdy mass and rose. A light wind passed through the room and fluttered Simone's hair, just as it did in the picture.

The bed covers continued their leisurely ascent until the hanging fabric outlined a petite human frame.

In the photo, Simone spotted movement. She brought the photo closer to her face.

An arm raised through the sheet from the obscure covered shape floating over Aaliyah's bed. It reached for Simone as she pulled the photo so close it was only inches from her eyes.

Chapter 23

Again, in the photo, her hair flapped. Aaliyah's closet door slammed shut.

Simone gasped and spun around to find her daughter's sheets still lying disheveled but now across the bed instead of in a centered heap. Another muffled crackle pushed through the room, and Simone eyed a ceiling vent now dispensing heat. She burst into tears, only clearing the deluge of moisture from her eyes when they became too clouded for her to see the bedsheets she was straightening and tucking into Aaliyah's bed.

Shifting her weight from side to side, Simone listened to the phone ring multiple times through the receiver held against her ear before the she heard the familiar, *"Hello?"*

"Hey My, it's Simone. I was seeing if you wanted to come by for coffee tomorrow morning after I get the girls off to school?" Simone struggled to strip a soulful whine from infiltrating her voice. It was an invitation, she wasn't begging, she reminded herself.

"I would love to, but not sure tomorrow will work. Is everything okay?"

"Yeah, I'm fine. Just not feeling like myself lately." Simone dropped into a chair she had dragged from the breakfast table to underneath the wall phone.

"I'm down for coffee, but I think I have a good story, so I don't want to make a promise for tomorrow morning."

"Is that what all the police cars were about?"

"Yep. Have you heard?"

Even though Simone could not see her friend's face, she was sure it was brimming with investigative excitement like it always did in high school when she was onto good gossip.

"No."

"Dr. Duran. She was shot coming out of the grocery store," Myeisha said, the hint of enthusiasm bouncing along the syllables that was characteristic of journalists in response to such tragedies.

Simone jerked as if pelleted in the chest with a rock. "What! Is she okay?"

"In surgery, I hear, but they think she'll recover. He only got her in the arm, I think. Seems she put up a good fight. Right now, all I know is some guy tried to steal her purse. She wouldn't give it up so … he shot her. Not sure who the guy was. He wasn't from Black Water. It was lunchtime, so of course Sheriff Handow was there in the parking lot. He tried to stop the guy, but the guy raised his gun, and Handow shot him dead."

"That is awful. I hope Dr. Duran will be okay."

"Yep, so I gotta go, but I'll call you back on coffee."

"Sure," Simone agreed before hanging up.

Larry Barnum, the only homeless person in Black Water, stumbled from the police station just as Myeisha lodged her cellphone back into her purse. Larry wasn't actually homeless, just an alcoholic. His parents lived in a stately, white house on Orchid Court that donned an award-worthy lawn—it had, in fact, won several—with two oversized wooden rocking chairs in the center and colorful flower boxes on each of the street-facing windows. Sobriety was the only requirement his elderly parents had for his return—which was why he never did. Being that he constantly roamed the streets of Black Water, Larry had witnessed a variety of strange small-town happenings, including the shooting of Dr. Duran for which he had been sitting right outside the grocery store's sliding doors, holding out his paper cup for anyone who wanted to drop something inside.

"Hey, Larry. I bet they didn't feed you in there." Myeisha jogged across the street, holding up a paper bag from the OC diner.

Larry snarled, "I ain't hungry."

"Well, neither am I, Larry," she sang, slyly raising the pint of brown liquor from the bag for him to see.

"You know what I like," Larry crooned in a voice that was suddenly smooth and warm, like the whiskey he wanted.

The pair dipped into the next alley. Larry made himself comfortable on the cool concrete while Myeisha poured a swallow of the drink into a paper cup before handing the almost full bottle to Larry who immediately took a deep swig. Leaning against the brick wall, Myeisha moved the cup to her nose, shunning the offensively sweet smell before throwing it down her throat with a groan. Myeisha scrunched the paper cup into her pocket, then zipped her jacket. "Seems like it's cooling off early this summer."

"He wasn't grabbing for her purse." Larry, not one for social amenities—at least not until the elixir of his addiction had properly oiled all his systems—pushed to the point before turning the bottle upward once again.

"What do you mean?" Myeisha moved closer to Larry to hear him better.

"I *mean*, I didn't see him grab for no purse. He was waiting for her to come out and then"—Larry shrugged—"looked like he was just talking to her. Pissed as hell but just talking at first. Then, all the sudden, I see something shiny. She go pullin' back, and he shot. Then Handow shot. Bunch a shots." He sniffed.

"What was he saying? The guy."

"I couldn't hear too well. He was talking fast but quiet, you know? That's how I knew he was mad." Larry's voice rasped again as he finished the bottle.

"You had to have heard something, Larry."

He lifted himself and started back toward the street. "But I didn't," he grunted.

"That's hardly worth a to-go bottle." She pulled another small paper bag from her purse.

Larry held out his hands like a cup into which Myeisha tossed the bag-covered bottle. "I'm not sure, but I might have heard him say, *Amber.*"

"Amber? That's it? What is that? Is that a name?" Myeisha threw up her hands.

"How the fucks should I know?"

"Larry! Someone is dead."

"Someone's always dead around here, My," he reminded her as he disappeared into the odd collection of familiar faces crisscrossing the streets.

The kitchen faucet dripped. No matter how far Simone grinded the handle to the left, it refused to stop. She pulled open the cabinet doors under the sink as if her superficial inspection would lead her to some sensible conclusion about the mechanics to which she knew she was ignorant.

"But you can do anything you put your mind to," Simone whispered to herself. "Especially when you have the internet."

Through the window of the back door, she eyed the shed where Mack kept his tools. After pulling on a fluffy, lime cardigan that was snug around her belly, Simone headed across the yard, passing the bulky, plastic garbage cans. The worn hinges that held the distressed wood door to its depressed dwelling gave a rusty whine as it opened, as if she were hurting it. Damp darkness greeted her, and she coughed against the dust that attacked every orifice of her face. Inside was a landscape of ordinary findings, like a collection of broken rakes, 2x4s, bricks, and a shovel littered throughout over the years by renters passing through the house. But interspersed was a museum of remote roadside gas station oddities that included a kid-sized, carnival-like ticket booth painted red and a worn wall sign that read COOTIES across the top and farther down attempted to present a scientific explanation for the bogus condition; Simone couldn't be sure whether it was satirical.

On the far back wall, Simone noticed three rusted bikes. They didn't belong to the Mills family but made Simone think of how she and Ella loved riding bikes in the summer—a favorite pastime of most small-town child cliques. The older they got, the more they found solace outside the four walls of their home. Average preteen angst perhaps, but at a certain point, the older the children became, the more their family home seemed to close in around them. Shrinking in the shadows of parents' anxieties and insecurities disguised as rules and beliefs made the need for outside air much like that of the necessity for air itself. The cold of the shed's uninsulated walls and the foreignness of its contents made this disconnected compartment of her house that should have been mundane seem bizarre.

Looking to the main house, Simone appreciated how well she knew it. Every nook and corner were masterfully memorized from her and Ella's fervent games of hide and seek. As a child, she could quite comfortably squeeze under the kitchen sink and knew if she pressed just right against the wall of the upstairs linen closet, there was a space where no light touched no matter the time of day and made her almost impossible to find. As a child, it had all seemed too big, and when she first returned with her family, it was manageable in a way that relieved her. It hit her that it was growing overwhelming yet again in ways more abstract than the physical proportions of the floorplan. The sensation Simone felt raking through all the peculiar items gave her the sense of knowing something well and it still having disconnected and discombobulated dimensions to which there was little access.

Goosebumps pimpled her flesh as she moved a box nonspecifically marked *Decorations* to the side and spotted the bright red toolbox on a low shelf near the back. Carefully maneuvering her oversized front through the junk, she grabbed the heavy metal box. When she turned to exit, he was there. Physical pain exploded through her chest at the sudden and fiery pumping of her heart.

He stood right in front of her now, as if he had been waiting patiently all this time to reveal himself. His signature snarl gave Simone a glimpse of his ferocious teeth.

"You." Simone's voice was low but held the resolve of a captain going down with his ship as she spoke to him.

The Sandman.

The deafening clatter of the toolbox hitting the cement floor and launching its contents in multiple directions startled Simone. She stepped back in a jerky reaction, tripping on one of the 2x4s. Sailing backward with her arms flailing in front of her, she watched his face until the blackness, caused by her head hitting the pile of bricks, clouded fully across her vision.

Chapter 24

<hr>

A s routine now prescribed, Jada raced ahead of her sister as soon as they exited the school bus. If their mother wasn't waiting at the bus stop, she was usually on the porch which was why Aaliyah felt her stomach drop as she came around the bend of the gravel path and saw Jada sitting on the porch steps, her backpack at her feet. The fact that her mother's car sat out front probably should have made her feel better—it could have been that her mother got sidetracked with work—but Aaliyah's stomach sank further.

"What are you doing?" Aaliyah yelled.

"Waiting for Mommy! I knocked, but she's not answering."

Jogging now, once on the porch, Aaliyah jiggled the locked doorknob.

"I already tried that, genius," Jada quipped.

Rolling her eyes, Aaliyah knocked on the door while calling for their mother. The girls didn't have a key; they never needed one. When louder knocks on the door and windows failed to summon anyone, Aaliyah plopped next to her sister in a huff.

A chill blew across the porch, and the sisters locked eyes at the sudden banging.

"Stay here a sec," Aaliyah instructed before creeping around the side of the house toward the heavy thuds. A few yards away, she studied the forest and shivered at the thought of her mother and aunt as kids, dancing in and out of those ominous trees. As she approached the back corner of the house, the clanging continued. Peeping around, her mouth dropped at the sight of the screen door flapping in the wind against the hard frame.

"Mom!" Aaliyah called as she raced up the back steps and grabbed the door. Inside, she could hear the soft drawling of jazz music filtering through the rooms. At once, there was a presence at her back. With shallow breath, Aaliyah turned to see the shed door wide open, and her blood went cold.

"Mom?" As she tiptoed toward the shed and the dry grass crunched under her every footfall, her body prickled, as if little bolts of lightning simultaneously struck every part of her. A few inches from the door, she could see Simone sprawled across the dirt floor inside.

"*Mom!*"

After a short surgery, the nurses delivered a sleeping Dr. Duran to a sterile room. Pacing the shiny checkered hallway floor, Myeisha consumed cup after cup of steaming, black coffee, poking her head into the room every fifteen minutes or so.

"Dr. Duran?" Myeisha called softly at the notice of movement in the bed.

"Oh no, Myeisha. Not now," Dr. Duran spoke groggily.

Myeisha shrugged. "First, I just wanted to make sure that you were okay."

Dr. Duran met the reporter's darting glances with an authoritative skepticism.

Tilting her head, Myeisha relented, "Okay, and maybe ask you a couple questions."

"I'm fine. I was lucky. It's a minor injury. I'll be out of here in a couple days." Dr. Duran flattened the bunched material of her pickle-colored hospital gown.

"That's good news. Did you know the man who shot you?"

"I don't think so." Dr. Duran shook her head, her features sagged as if the terror of the event hit her at once. "He tried to take my purse. When I wouldn't give it to him, he shot me, and that's all. Nothing too fancy."

"Did he say anything to you?"

"No."

"Nothing at all?"

"Not that I can remember. Now please, I'm tired."

"Okay." Myeisha smiled as she tapped Dr. Duran's feet through the blankets and waltzed toward the door. "Get well. I'll be back."

Myeisha stopped at the nurses' station as Shay Davis, one of her many cousins in town and a nurse, nodded at her. "Your friend came in today."

"Who?" Myeisha asked, leaning against the large desk.

"The Parker girl, up in labor and delivery."

"What? I just talked to her, and she was fine."

"Babies come when they're ready."

Myeisha shuffled toward the elevator. "Thanks, Shay."

Simone woke in what could not be more accurately described than a fog— a labyrinth of blurred, moving shadows and distant chirps that could have been words.

"Baby? Can you hear me?"

Mack's stunningly symmetrical and full features drew together, allowing Simone to distinguish her husband from the abstract haze around him.

"Mack?" Simone whispered dryly. "The girls?"

"The girls are fine. Your friend, Myeisha, came by and offered to take them home. You fell and hit your head, and you're in the hospital."

As if confirming the safety of her children somehow now made space for her own sorrow, a vibrating pain thundered through her head while a searing agony swept across her abdomen. She grasped at her flattened belly, and the emptiness of it hallowed every other part of her instantly. "*The baby!*"

Mack's face now came into clear view. "The baby is fine, Simone. He's fine. A little early but a perfectly healthy baby boy."

Tears gathered in Simone's eyes, breaking the levies of her boundaries—physical and otherwise. "What?" Against the raging pain, she shot upright, searching the room.

"It's okay. He's in the NICU. His color was a little off, but the doctors say he will be fine."

"But I don't even remember it." She groaned as she lay back. Simone's gaze wandered to the white ceiling, and she saw the face of the baby boy as she imagined it. She wanted to see him, to ask for him, but it seemed more than she could handle. There was too much surprise, confusion, and gut-wrenching pain. She gently touched the bandages that covered the fresh cut across her lower belly as she emerged fully into the harsh reality of what was taken.

The nursery wasn't quite done. They didn't have any diapers. What about skin to skin? He needed to be put to the breast.

They had known Trace was coming for the previous eight months, this was her third child, yet she felt grossly unprepared.

"What about the birth plan, Mack?"

Stunned, Mack cleared his throat. "Baby, there wasn't any time for that. You were injured. Trace was in distress."

Like a flame to gasoline, the fluid mess of worry and anxiety sparked to anger in a wail. *"How could you?"*

It was not the birth for which she had been unprepared; it was the lack thereof. It was stolen. Her only son born without her even knowing, her stomach ripped open without her permission. Nesting somewhere deep inside was still a hint of reason dictating that she should be grateful for her own health and that of her baby, yet the bareness of her womb left her woefully vapid in the category of logic.

Her husband's face skewed. "What?"

"How could you let them take my baby?" she cried, her anger disintegrating as quickly as it had spun up as she dissolved into a shapeless mass in her husband's arms.

Over the next two days in the hospital, Simone slept most of the time. Pain medication provided some relief, but she suspected it also was partly to blame for Trace not being eager to take to her milk, a first in her three children. At Simone's request for the lactation consultant, her nurse replied simply that they didn't know she planned to breastfeed. Any other day, such a response would have invited, at least, a stern reply, but plainly put, Simone was too tired, and Mack, flipping through the television channels and gulping down her Jello without a spoon, had missed the microaggression.

It wasn't until day three when she felt normal again, if such a thing existed anymore, especially in the sickeningly sea-green color scheme of the bland, beeping hospital room that made her feel as if she were lost at sea, floating aimlessly with zero inclinations as to the direction of dry land.

Trace screamed through Dr. Penny's entire visit. Simone tried to listen while consoling her son, who she finally handed to Mack, where he started to calm. Mack, not her, had been the first parent to hold him skin to skin, so it made sense that his scent reassured their son, even if it hurt her feelings. After a brief physical exam, Dr. Penny informed her that she and Baby Trace were being discharged, news at which a dull excitement coursed through Simone, but the throbbing, narcotically untouchable pounding in her head made enthusiasm an impossible chore.

"Are you okay?" Dr. Penny asked.

"I'm fine besides the pain in my abdomen and the thrashing in my head." Simone rubbed her temples. Her eyes met Dr. Penny's before skewing to her husband who bounced the baby lightly while cooing.

"You appear to be healing fine. You shouldn't be in as much pain today—"

"But I am," Simone snapped.

"Simone," Mack inserted in the signature tone he used to reel her in.

"Mack!" she retorted, hardly in the mood to be lulled.

Dr. Penny lightly smacked her tongue. "I can take a look at your current dosage of pain medication and maybe make an increase."

"No," Simone growled. "I just want to go home."

Dr. Penny replied with a stale smile. "Simone, I know this situation was hard for you, but you're strong, and you will get through it. You imagined a different birth, but I want you to know how lucky you are to be healthy and have a healthy baby."

Mack's sweet gaze affirmed in such complete betrayal that Simone, even though she recognized a morsel of truth, had to press her palm to her throat to keep from vomiting.

"I know you're right, and it's fine. I'm fine." Simone nodded in agreement before reaching to her husband in demand of her child.

Chapter 25

<hr/>

To the cheers of their daughters who were anxious to meet the baby, Mack entered the house first, bags on one arm and a car seat on the other. Each plodded step up to the porch Simone calculated so as not to put any extra strain on the stiches that stabbed at her abdomen.

"Welcome home!" Myeisha greeted, coming out to help Simone into the house. "I just finished feeding the girls dinner, and yours and Mack's plates are on the stove."

"Thank you so much. I really appreciate you taking time to help us. You didn't have to."

"What are old BFFs for?" she quipped before turning a more serious tune. "I wanted to help."

Once settled in the living room, Simone watched as Mack gleefully hosted the girl's swoon session over his baby boy.

"No!" Simone shouted with her palm raised stiffly in the air as she noticed Jada coming to jump in her lap.

The girl's face dropped.

"Honey, Mommy's stomach was cut open, and it's still healing, so we have to be really careful, okay?"

First studying her mother's midsection as if it were now alien, Jada lifted her eyes to Simone's and nodded solemnly.

"Come here ... slowly." Simone patted the couch cushion to her side. Jada sat, and Simone squeezed her in a side hug.

"Myeisha, I appreciate you so much, but I don't want to keep you. I know you're probably backed up on your story. How is Dr. Duran, by the way?"

It was true, Simone knew her friend must be anxious to return to work, but more honestly, as much as she appreciated Myeisha stepping in to help, Simone was exhausted. Her body and head ached, and rest was her priority.

"She's home now," Myeisha confirmed. "Are you sure you don't need me to stay?"

"Aren't you ready to get back to work?"

Myeisha bit her lower lip. "I am, but I want to make sure you're okay too."

"I'm fine. Mack will handle the kids, and I'm going to bed," Simone responded as she struggled to lift herself from the couch.

After Myeisha's brief admiration of Baby Trace and goodbye to the girls and Mack, Simone hobbled after her to the door.

Myeisha turned to face her. "If you need anything at all, call me."

"I will," Simone assured her with a smile and a light hug. "Thank you."

None of the clothes in Simone's drawers felt comfortable. Either they bothered her bandaged belly, they weren't warm enough, the material felt scratchy, or some other minor irritation made them unwearable. Across the room, her mother's black, paint-splattered smock lay across the box she had pulled from the basement weeks earlier. An odd choice, but slipping into that soft, well-worn cotton felt intended.

When Simone woke, her cellphone face read 10:01 p.m. She didn't remember slipping into bed but was glad Mack had not woken her for any reason. Trace was her second thought, the dull ache in her stomach a close third. On her nightstand, Simone discerned the silhouette of the pill bottle but decided against another dose. In addition to making her feel like she was living life through some fuzzy photo filter, she wanted to ensure that nothing further hindered the feeding efforts of her breasts which, despite their heaviness, produced too little to fully nourish her newborn. As she shambled toward the nursery, she heard a noise downstairs. Descending the steps, she recognized the soft, static oozing from the living room television. Simone cringed at her pronounced gait as she waddled across the empty room.

In the same moment she clicked the television's tiny power button, she flinched at the unmistakable feeling that she was not alone. The gray reflection of the TV screen under the moonlight revealed movement behind her. Turning too swiftly, Simone groaned at the sharp awareness in her lower abdomen.

There was nothing. The recliner rocked at a leisurely pace. After bringing the slowing movement to a full stop with a firm grip on the back of the chair, Simone tried to bend to see if perhaps something under it had caused its movement, but her injury made ordinary range of mobility an impossibility. Simone scanned the room once more before rubbing her tired eyes and trudging toward the stairs.

One step, then two before she heard a familiar sound. The front door swung open. She stared at all the darkness just beyond its threshold, expecting it to rush in like a black tide overwhelming her before she could slam the door shut, but not a thing moved. Even more terrifying than something creeping about was the absolute stillness. Prey rarely saw a master predator upon them before it was too late. A cool breeze pushed into the door and through Simone, freezing every inch of her skin in one spectacular moment that filled her with a shrill panic.

She rushed forward, fumbled the door locks, and despite the pounding—not just in her chest but through her whole body, as if everything inside was clamoring to spew out—she got them properly in place. She peeked through the window at the side of the door to see nothing but Mack's truck and her minivan.

Simone wondered if she had forgotten to lock the door after Myeisha left, or perhaps Mack had gone outside for some reason. *How could Mack have been so irresponsible?* Black Water seemed to most like a place where people could leave their doors unlocked, and while they played along to stave off the collective sense of dread, the natives knew better. Much better.

Back upstairs, the door to the nursery creaked tenderly as she pressed it open. A scream caught in Simone's throat at the sight of his silhouette. In the corner, half covered by the window curtains, the Sandman stood watch over her son. With a blink, he was gone. Simone moved to the crib where Baby Trace slept soundly. In the next second, she was in the corner, trashing the curtains and blinking wildly to ensure he was gone. Through the window, something caught her eye.

"Aaliyah," she whispered as her daughter took confident strides across the darkened yard toward the huddle of garbage cans.

Simone scrambled down the stairs, completely ignoring the all-but-pulsating pain in her lower belly. The moment Simone opened the back door, her daughter stopped and turned to face her, locking eyes.

"Aaliyah!"

"He's out here," Aaliyah said. "But he wants to come inside."

Once Simone had ushered her child through the door and locked it, she took a breath. "Who wants to come inside?" Simone asked, a tremble in her voice.

Aaliyah was silent, offering only a blank stare.

"Who? The Sandman? I've already told you he's not real. He—"

"Not him. Charlie."

How could she have known about Charlie? Simone had *never* spoke on the details, especially not to her children. Simone opened her mouth to speak but stopped to lean back, trying to gather the thoughts shuffling through her head. As mothers did when their child brought up a subject for which they were unprepared or plain unwilling to discuss, Simone moved the conversation to safer territory. "I'll get you a glass of milk, okay? And then I want you back to bed."

In cooperation with her mother's overt censure, Aaliyah nodded before moving to the refrigerator, still bouncing somewhere on the peripheries of her entranced state.

Tugging at the door that still stuck, whispered curses burst from Simone after the door refused to open with her first two pulls. The third time, she yanked hard. It sprung open and collided with something in a thud.

"Ouch!" Aaliyah cried, her palm shooting to her face

Simone whipped the door shut and pulled her daughter's face closer for a frenzied inspection of the injury. "Why were you standing there!"

Even in the thin moonlight, Simone could tell it was already starting to bruise.

Aaliyah's faced dropped as sadness seeped into her features.

"Oh, honey, I'm so sorry. I'm not angry with you," Simone said with a sigh before grabbing a baggie from the pantry to construct an ice pack.

Faint but distinct screeching drifted from the nursery, and Simone realized the only thing she wanted in that second was sleep.

"Go to bed and put this on your eye. I'll bring up your milk." Simone placed the cold, clear bag in her daughter's hand and listened to her light footfalls fade up the stairs.

Looking over her shoulder, she noticed the faucet was quiet. Not a single drip. After turning it on and off once again, it remained perfectly sealed. On the counter were two yellow slips of paper with quotes for alarm systems. A smile crossed her lips.

A flash of light waved through the darkened kitchen. In the dining room, through the window, Simone watched an unfamiliar red car bump up the path toward their house. When it stopped, the inside lights flashed on, and Mack emerged from the passenger side. Next to him, Simone could decipher Nita giving some jovial farewell.

It was a dream. Simone pressed her eyes closed, willing herself to wake up. Her heart dropped at the clang of the keys in the door.

"What the hell is going on?" were the words that startled Mack as he shuffled through the door. Not drunk, she knew her husband well, but more than two beers, likely three.

"What?" Mack said, flicking on the foyer light as his wife emerged from the shadows of the dining room.

"Where in the hell have you been?" Simone asked in a cracked whisper. Noticing that Trace had soothed himself, she didn't want to disturb the kids' sleep.

"Nicco, Sam, and Nita wanted to take me out for a quick drink to celebrate the baby. You were sleep, the kids were sleep, and I was only gone for two hours. I timed it. I just needed to get out for a moment, and I didn't think you would mind." Mack removed his jacket with a slight sway before dropping it on a hook by the door.

"You didn't think I would *mind*? I was just injured and then gave birth, and you couldn't stay home for one night?"

Mack approached his wife and massaged her rigid shoulders. "I haven't been out since the day we moved here, and I didn't plan it. When Sam heard about the baby, he came by and wanted to buy me a beer. Honestly, I wanted to celebrate too. Celebrate that you and Trace were home and that everyone is happy and healthy."

"And so, you *celebrate* by drinking. Then you and your girlfriend come carousing in our front yard."

"My girlfriend …?" Mack's features twisted into thick knots. "Is that really what you think? Sam picked me up. I didn't have my truck, and he got too drunk to drive. She dropped both of us home. We dropped him before we got here. I'm barely even tipsy."

"You left the door unlocked too."

"The door?" Mack's face angled to the door "I didn't. When do I ever leave the door unlocked?"

"I can't believe you, Mack. Maybe if you were more concerned about me and the house, you would have fixed the sink before, and I wouldn't have fallen in the first place!" *Too far, Simone.* "Just now, I was getting Aaliyah some milk, and the fridge door handle hit her in the face because it was sticking, but no worries as long as you had a good time!" Simone turned and headed up the stairs.

"I fixed the door. I fixed everything," Mack mumbled, dropping his tired face into his hands.

Chapter 26

———◆—◆—◆———

The moon was high, the center of nights celestial worship; the branches of the trees reached upward like arms lifted in praise. He was crying again.

Aaliyah's eyes fluttered open, trying to solidify the waking haze of her vision into recognizable shapes. She jumped at her little sister's silhouette.

Jada stood at her bedside, staring out from the two dark holes of one of her quirky masks, a fox this time.

"Jada? What have I told you about those stupid masks?" Aaliyah whispered in the dark. Her teasing question evoked no response. Sitting upright, Aaliyah studied some unfamiliar features on her sister—Jada was taller. Aaliyah realized she had never seen these pajamas on Jada—who was not a fan of dinosaurs. Her gaze darted to the stranger's mask.

A shadow swept across the back of the room—a largely unrecognizable figure cloaked in black. The only things she could discern clearly were the pointed ears sitting atop its head and the irregularly long snout. At once, he jerked his arm upward, and as if it were invisibly tied to the girl's face—his own marionette—her mouth opened, unleashing a swarm of black butterflies that plummeted the room into the total darkness of their hoard.

Aaliyah sprang from her bed, sweat dripping down her face, her chest heaving. As her feet touched the floor, the darkness dropped like a released curtain, setting her back down in her uneventful room. Frantically, she spun in search of anything there only a second before, but it was her alone.

At her parents' bedroom door, Aaliyah raised her hand to knock after trying to twist the locked knob but reconsidered such resolution. It was a rare occasion that she slept with her parents, and she knew they would not object, but she had her period now. Sleeping with them because of a dream seemed immature and better left for children like Jada.

At her back, across the hallway, she heard the strain of the linen closet door opening. Aaliyah backed herself down the hallway and into Jada's room where she closed the door before releasing a *whoosh* of breath she didn't realize she had been holding in her chest.

Under the blanket, her sister's body pulsed with slow breaths.

Aaliyah removed the rosy-cheeked piggy mask Jada was wearing and placed it on the nightstand before climbing into bed with her and wished for one thing—peaceful sleep.

Sheriff Handow's brisk steps across the burgundy tile of the sheriff's department floor were meant to leave Myeisha behind, but she was on him. "My, I'm telling you, there is no story here, so just leave it alone. The details we have are in the report. It'll be public information soon enough, and you're welcome to it, but other than that, I have no comment."

Now in the center of the two-room station that consisted of Sheriff Handow's office separated by a glass wall and door and the front of the building where all of the other desks sat, Myeisha spun, as if speaking from a theatre in the round. "How is anyone supposed to report the news in this town if the sheriff's department is uncooperative?"

Turning back, Handow hissed from one side of his mouth, "My!"

"The good people of Black Water deserve to be informed."

Handow's stare went blank, as if Myeisha had sucked the last wisp of his energy.

"I'm the press, for god's sake. Can you at least tell me if he's the burglar you guys are looking for?"

"Well, he certainly could be, but I can't very well question him about that now, can I?" Sheriff Handow slammed his office door.

Turning in a huff, she noticed Kevin McKinney shuffle something under a piece of paper on his desk. While she and Kevin had dated briefly in high school, he had never forgiven her for wanting more than Black Water. Now that she had returned, their relationship edged on intimately awkward.

"What are you working on, Kevin?"

"Nothing." He sighed.

"What are you working on, Kevin?"

"No."

"Oh, c'mon! I'll get most of the information once you release the police report anyway. Give me a jump.

"I could lose my job," Deputy McKinney snorted, pretending to type.

In her peripheral vision, with no privacy screen, Myeisha could see he had closed whatever he was working on, and his keyboard taps made no changes to the monitor at which he glared.

"You could lose your job if I told Handow you still smoke weed."

Kevin cut his eyes at her. "You wouldn't!"

Myeisha's eyes rolled to look at the ceiling. "I wouldn't," she relented rapidly, "but gimme a jump on the story, anyway. Your name won't be in it at all. I promise."

"The report isn't finished yet." He moved a blank sheet of paper on his desk that revealed a second sheet with the photocopy of a license belonging to a young man, Michael King. "This is it, Myeisha!"

"This is all I need." She smiled as she snapped a shot with her cellphone.

After ringing Dr. Duran's doorbell a second time, Simone bent to peek through the white, ruffled curtains that decorated each window of the yellow Victorian that sat on the outskirts of town. Inside, Simone spotted a hearty woman marching toward the door.

"Hi, I'm Simone Parker, a friend of Dr. Duran's, and I was just coming to check on her and bring coffee." Simone held up the paper cups.

The hulking lady moved aside, then closed the door behind Simone. "Why, that is lovely. I'm Marlene, just helping her out around here a bit. I'll let her know you're here."

"Who is that, Marlene?" Dr. Duran called from a back room.

Simone cut in, "It's Simone Parker. I was just coming to bring you some coffee."

"Simone, come on in here," the age-worn voice sang through the hallway.

Marlene gave her a nod of approval, and Simone crept down the hallway, nursing the ache that still plagued her stomach.

In the back room, Dr. Duran was watching what must have been a recorded sermon as it wasn't Sunday. With a click of the soft remote button, Dr. Duran sent away the stiff, white-shirted preacher, allowing her to catch only a hint of his fire-and-brimstone raving.

"How are you?" Simone engaged in a half embrace that they both appreciated due to their injured conditions.

"For being shot, I'm doing all right, I suppose. Have a seat. How are you? This is just what I needed." Dr. Duran removed the plastic top from the cup and dressed her morning coffee with the creams and sugars from the brown paper bag. "I heard you had that baby boy. You are the one who should be resting, not coming over here worried about me."

"It's okay. I needed to get out anyway, and it's such a beautiful day."

"It is," Dr. Duran agreed, eyeing the windows that were filled with the morning light.

"What happened?"

It was clear from her disconsolate expression that she was downright tired of the question. She pushed up the sleeves on her thin, clover-colored sweater before she started casually, "Oh, some out-of-town vagrant trying to steal my purse. Not worth continuing to discuss. What about you? How are you doing? I have to admit, I've been a little worried about you in the house." Dr. Duran adjusted the over-the-shoulder sling on her arm.

"It's not too bad."

Dr. Duran's expression went skeptical.

Simone's shoulders fell. "Okay … okay. I am a little scared. I feel like someone is watching us."

"Who?"

"I don't know. Maybe watching isn't the best explanation, more like … not alone."

"Well, you're not alone. You have your family."

"More than them. I feel like others are there … lurking," Simone explained with a wince. "And now I have a migraine that just won't go away, which isn't helping."

"What does your doctor say? About the headache."

Shrugging, Simone pressed her fingertips into her eyes. "I talked to her this morning. She said lots of women have headaches after childbirth—change in hormones or something. It's normal. The headaches are normal. The not sleeping well is normal. 'You have a new baby,' she says."

"Do you think any part of it could be what you experienced in that house?"

At the mention, all the air in Simone's chest was snatched. "How do you mean?"

"I mean … the Sandman, Simone?" Dr. Duran asked.

It was hard to swallow now, as if Simone had a golf ball thrusted down her throat. Her body was moist from the thin layer of perspiration that now covered her. "What about him?"

"Is he there?" Dr. Duran leaned forward.

Pressing back in her chair, Simone's head tilted at a quizzical angle. "Of course not. He's not real. I know that now. I've known that for a long time."

"Then who killed your family? Did you see their face?"

"No, I didn't see his face," Simone lied.

"Let's try something. I usually do this downstairs in my office, but I am in no condition to get down there right now." Dr. Duran wrenched herself up from the couch.

Simone jumped to help her.

"Lay on that couch over there," Dr. Duran instructed as she closed the blinds.

Simone knew what was next. This part of her life was over; she did not want to be a patient anymore. "I'm not sure this is appropriate. I mean, I'm not a patient anymore. Besides, I told you, the insurance I have right now won't cover any of this."

"Just lay back and relax. This may help you relieve some of your stress. Let's not make it a production."

While Simone was not anxious to relive anything from her past, any occasion to lay down and close her eyes without the constant bumping and thumping of moving children was welcomed. "Fine."

"Picture yourself looking through a window into the night at a darkened forest. Everything is still and quiet. You are focused on a small black opening that will allow you into the trees. You are walking toward that black hole. You enter, and now you are inside. You go deeper until there is no light from the moon or the stars, just darkness all around." Dr. Duran's voice spoke in the soothing rhythm of a lullaby.

Simone's own deep breaths were the only thing she heard as she teetered on unconsciousness. From some alternate universe, Dr. Duran's voice seemed to rain on her through the trees guiding her thoughts, like a puppeteer masterful in their craft.

"Go back to the night Ella fell from the butterfly tree," her voice goaded, evoking a wounded whimper from Simone. "The full moon is high in the sky. Are you there, Simone?"

Simone woke. "I'm here."

"What's happening?"

"I'm in Ella's room. Charlie's crying. There are footsteps in his room. He stops crying. Now there are more footsteps down the stairs and out the back door. I hear the door slam. I hear the back door open again. Something is happening. There is a noise downstairs. I'm scared. Ella holds a single finger to her lips and whispers only one word, 'Hide.' I start to get under her bed, like I always do, but she says, 'No, not there. You always hide there.' There's Mr. Bobo. I take him and go to the corner of the linen closet. Ella is screaming and running down the hallway. Her cast is thumping the floor. My heart is beating so loud, I just know that whatever is chasing her will hear and come for me. Ella's door slams, and then there is banging and more banging. She must have locked her door, but it doesn't help much. She's screaming now." Tears course down Simone's temples and into her hairline. "Then she's quiet. Everything is so quiet. I slide out of the shadow and peek into the hallway. It's him. I see him. It's the Sandman. He's searching for me. The footsteps have stopped now. I'm even more scared to stay in the closet than I am of whatever may be waiting in the hallway. My steps are silent. I follow the light, muddy footprints he left behind. There he is, standing at the top of the stairs. I'm not afraid. I approach him as he turns slowly to greet me, his glitter in hand." As if the connection with this historical dimension dropped, Simone's story ended.

"What then?"

"I-I don't know," Simone said, those words revving the engine of tears that once again streamed from her closed eyes. Even in the alternate state, Simone felt her skin go cold as she approached the Sandman. Her head shook with the unconscious understanding that she had to get out of there.

"Focus, Simone. What is happening?"

"I don't know."

"You do. What is the Sandman doing?"

"*I don't know! I can't remember!*" Simone sobbed as he lowered himself so that they were face to face.

Marlene was knocking. "Is everything okay?"

"Okay, okay, Simone. I am going to count down from five, and when I finish, you will be back in my sitting room. Five, four, three, two, one."

Just as the Sandman started to speak, Simone's eyes popped open, transporting her back to the safety of Dr. Duran's couch.

Chapter 27

 — — ◆ — ◆ — ◆ — —

From the porch, Simone could hear the girls screaming inside.

"I can't believe you, you little brat!" Aaliyah yelled as she chased her sister up the last few steps and down the hallway.

By the time Simone reached Aaliyah's room, she had Jada cornered. "What is going on?"

"She destroyed my science project!" Aaliyah cried. "My solar system is ruined!"

"Mom, I didn't! It was the Sandman!"

Both Simone and Aaliyah stopped to focus on Jada, her chest heaving.

"He's angry."

"Hey! I'm trying to put Trace down. What is going on in here?" Mack appeared in the doorway, gently bouncing the baby boy.

"Aaliyah's science project," Simone explained before focusing on the purplish hue growing around Aaliyah's eye. "Your face," Simone whispered as she caressed her daughter's cheek.

"Honey, go take a nap. I got this." Mack shooed his wife from the room.

Closing her bedroom door, she shut out the last sounds of Mack scolding the girls in a hushed voice. It was hard to tell if Jada was getting in trouble or if Mack was trying to reason with Aaliyah, but Simone was too exhausted to figure it out. She removed her clothes and caught a glimpse of her naked body in the mirror over the dresser. Her stomach reminded her of a rippling pool with new creases displacing old skin. Stretch marks that hid in the tightness of her rounded belly during pregnancy now worked their way to full visibility. She lifted the white gauze strapped to her abdomen to study the crooked smile of a scar that was beginning to develop. As she slipped into the unmatched comfort of the painting smock, she noticed that her breasts at least still held some firmness from the milk that built furiously but refused to flow. Simone left the smock unzipped as she slipped into bed with the breast pump. No matter how hard she tried, it would inevitably mock the inadequacies of her lactation, leaving her chest weighted with hard breasts full of mother's milk. After filling one of Trace's tiny bottles to the midway point with the one side that had offered any cooperation, Simone popped two of the sleeping pills that Dr. Duran had prescribed and swore would not be harmful to her baby.

As the sinking sun saturated the sky with swirls of pink and purple, the girls chased each other through the swings and down the slides of the park, isolated in the intimate bubble of siblinghood. In Simone's arms, Trace lay content, his suckling jaws working overtime to fill himself. She smiled, her bright eyes sparkling after a whiff of what was keeping her son from drifting into a glutton's slumber. Like a magician yanking the cloth from a set table without disturbing the settings, Simone laid him in his stroller and flicked her wrists in a swift diaper change. Some maternal skills could never be lost.

Refocusing on the playground, Simone caught sight of her oldest daughter breeze past a group of smaller children on her dash to the top of the jungle gym. After scanning the brightly colored jackets that dotted the park, Simone called, "Jada." Her glare darted from one end of the playground to the other.

Aaliyah took notice of her mother's voice.

"Aaliyah, where is Jada?" Simone asked, approaching the playground.

The girl looked around, then shrugged. "She was here a second ago."

"*Jada!*" Simone yelled, even though it seemed she could not get enough air in her chest. Her breath went shallow.

From behind a tree, Jada emerged and returned to the spirited mob on the playground. Jada waved to her mother with a smile.

Simone smiled back before returning to the bench where she immediately noticed something missing. Her stroller. "*Trace!*" Simone screamed, frantically searching the entire park with a spin. He was gone. "*Trace!*" Simone cried again, hardly audible over the soundtrack of screeching laughter from the playing children.

At the entrance to a trail that led into a canopy of trees, she spotted the blue stroller. Running, she felt the stitches in her abdomen pulling and opening, sticking her shirt to her with her own blood. The energy that had filled her only moments before drained and dropped her into that sunken place of sheer exhaustion.

Panting, she cautiously approached the stroller. "Mommy's here," she cooed before her body contracted with terror at the sight of the thick blood that soaked the beige-colored cushions inside the stroller. She looked to where the trail entered the trees and saw the Sandman holding baby Trace in one arm wrapped in an initial emblazoned emerald-colored blanket while holding Jada's hand in the other. Aaliyah stood close behind him. "*No!*" Simone screamed.

Simone jerked upright to shrill ringing. "Hello?" she answered, her mouth dry. "Katherine? … No, it's no bother. … I'm fine. The baby is fine." Next, she responded to the news that Mack had informed Katherine of Simone's early delivery a few days before when she had called. "Oh, good. … Yes. He's great. I'm glad you liked it. … Yes, I can pull that information for you quickly."

Simone jerked up her bare feet from the carpet as soon as she placed them down, a reaction to the sensation of tiny, granular pieces of sand cutting into them. "Uh, yes, just give me a second to get to my office," Simone said, forgetting the floor as she shuffled into the hallway just as the baby began to cry. She passed Mack who was heading to Trace's room.

"Where you going?" he asked.

"I need to get something from the office." She pulled the phone from her face to speak out of its microphone's range.

His hand went to her stomach.

"I got it. Just get Trace." Simone said as she went down the steps and returned to Katherine's legal ramblings. By now, her stitches should be healing, but they felt almost as uncomfortable as they did the day she left the hospital.

Simone gulped as she opened the door to her office. All her neatly stacked research and notes were strewn across the room. Choking back tears, she gathered and reviewed the papers to find that no semblance of order remained. Her body was wracked with discomfort, and though she had only just opened her eyes a few minutes before, she felt a voracious need to lay down. "Katherine, I'll need a little longer, maybe a couple hours. I understand the deadline, and I can get it right; I just need a little time. … Katherine, please. No. It really isn't a prob— … Okay … okay." Simone lowered herself into the chair, still clutching a handful of documents. She pressed them to her face to dry the flowing tears. It wasn't as if she had been fired—not quite. It was more likely pity, a subdued yet more deprecating sentiment than frustration. *Poor, little mother just trying to keep it all together.* From frustrated whispers, there was hope for redemption, its nature hinted at a level of investment, but from the sluggish depths of pity, there was no return. There were no screams, admonishments, or a dramatic firing, but Simone doubted there would be any future projects. No matter how good the work, it was useless if preoccupations precluded it from getting done.

"Mom?" Jada called as she pressed through the office door. "Have you seen my bunny mask?" The girl stopped short, seemingly surprised by the messy display.

"What did you do?" Simone gurgled, unable to recognize her own voice. "Did you do this?"

"It wasn't me, Mom. I swear."

"You're lying!" Simone hissed.

Crying, Jada fled.

Simone flew from the chair, momentarily distancing herself from her own physical pain.

In the hallway, Jada ran into Mack and wrapped herself around his waist.

"What's going on?" he asked.

"My work. All of my research is turned upside down, and I'm pretty sure I just got fired." Simone sobbed.

"Upstairs, Jada," Mack instructed with a kiss.

As their daughter slunk up the stairs, Mack embraced his wife. "Fired? Why?"

"I wasn't exactly, but I might as well have been." Simone cried through shudders of her chest.

"But I spoke to Katherine, and I told her—"

"I know, but she needed more of my research, and ..." Simone's voice trailed off as Mack moved to her office.

"What the hell?" Mack exclaimed. "You think Jada did this?"

"Who else, Mack? If she messed up Aaliyah's science project, then ..."

"This isn't like her."

"I know. I don't think any of us are like ourselves lately."

"You'll hate me for saying this, but you don't need that job right now. We're fine."

"How can you say that?" Simone stepped backward. What irritated her most was that this was not a revelation. These words were a clear manifestation of Mack's thoughts developed over time. As her husband reached for her, Simone dashed into the guest bathroom across the hallway and slammed the door behind her to hide in the room's windowless darkness.

"Simone, please."

"I'm tired. My head is pounding, and I just need a minute," Simone lied, needing more than a minute—she would need thousands of them to ease herself. There it was again, the gritty texture under her feet. She flipped the light switch and lifted her foot to study the golden particles and droplets of blood that pushed to the surface where they had dug into her skin. "No," she whispered.

"What?" Mack called through the door.

"N-Nothing."

"Okay. I'm going to go and talk to Jada." His footsteps were on the stairs above her when her phone rang.

Unknown Caller was the title for which Simone rarely answered, but today, she felt compelled. "Hello?"

"Simone," the voice moaned.

"Who is this?"

There was a moment of silence before she was drowning in the whispers that exploded from the speaker.

wElcOme hoMe, SiMonE.

RemEmbEr mE?

CLose youR eyeS.

IT's oKAy. I'm HEre.

SImoNe, You'Re fiNe!

I'm ComiNg for YoU.

SlEEp!

The strange voices tumbling over one another in varied pitch, pace, and volume sounded like thunder.

"You're not real," Simone murmured as she pulled the phone from her ear to quell the noise, the words still bouncing through her skull. Even with the phone at an arm's length, the voices remained in surround sound, echoing through the bathroom until the walls shuddered with their resonance. Searching the tiny room, Simone eyed the toilet. She lifted the seat and threw the phone inside, its shell making a *kerplunk* as it splashed into the shallow water, finally quieting its taunts.

Chapter 28

———◆—◆—◆———

A child's desperate cry can wake even the most dormant mother. After some research on the prescribed sleeping pills which rendered a list of maddening potential effects that included dizziness, dry mouth, irregular heartbeat, irritability, confusion, and hallucinations without a full eight hours of sleep, Simone opted not to take anymore. She spent the better part of the day sweeping, mopping, and vacuuming every floor in the house while Mack watched with disapproval. Even under the lingering hallucinatory effects of sleep medication and the fact that she alone had felt it, she was sure the sand had been there.

Without the pills, utter enervation allowed her a few hours of sleep before she woke to Trace's adamant wailing. The house was cool and tinted with a ghoulish gray hue from the late-night moonlight. For a moment, she hesitated to place her feet on the carpet but was relieved to feel only smooth fluffs when she pressed them into it. Mack's light snore was evenly paced. He slept soundly. Still, Simone tried to be quiet as she pulled his blue robe from a hook on the bathroom door and slipped down the hallway and into the nursery. Her baby's cry was more pronounced now, as if being pumped into the room through speakers. Simone grabbed her head at the noise. In the crib, she found Trace swaddled and sleeping soundly. She caressed his face which was dry and as still as if he had taken a dose from Simone's pill bottle. She placed her hand on his chest to ensure the almost imperceptible rise and fall. Perking, Simone realized the sound was coming from outside the house.

"Whiskers ..." The commotion of the last few days had all but blocked the little feline from her mind. While not an animal lover, Simone guessed the cat had not received his daily ration of milk, and if not satisfied, may whine all night.

The season is starting to turn. Simone tightened her robe at the chill coming off the back door. She pushed aside the curtain and peeked out the window in search of the cat who had quieted by now. After unlocking the door, Simone called out in a whisper, "Here, kitty kitty."

The crying revved to a screeching start. As far as she could tell, the cat had gotten himself trapped in the garbage cans.

"Stupid cat," Simone muttered, stepping her bare feet onto the porch, then the ground in soft pats across the dirt. The moment Simone pulled the top from the garbage can, her body reeled backward. Decomposition made for the putrid aroma that filled her mouth and nostrils. Even in the dark of night, Simone recognized the only item tossed inside—an emerald green blanket with the letters CM embroidered at one corner in rich gold.

"Charlie." Simone's cracked sob barely left her mouth before its insides became moist with what little was in her stomach and started to push its way back up.

It was moving. The blanket pulsed gently, like some hibernating animal, and its deep green hues faded to black.

With better focus, she realized the huddled pulsing mass was an onyx kaleidoscope of butterflies. Lowering her face farther, she heard a hint of buzzing emitting from the mass of insects just before they advanced on her. It wasn't until they were whirring all around her that she discerned the bundle of insects were not butterflies at all but a swarm of flies fleeing into the air around her, bringing with them the stench of waste. Holding it was no longer an option, and she vomited a splash of bile into the receptacle from which the source of her disgust originated. Her mouth was sour now from its flavor, and she peered into the can again to confirm the only thing it held was the remnants of her stomach.

Admittedly, she may have imagined Charlie's blanket, but her skin prickled with the unmistakable intuition that someone was watching her. Whirling around, she laid eyes on him standing in the doorway of the shed where she now recalled seeing him just before hitting her head.

"You ..." Simone said, a greeting for an old friend more so than the accusation it was the first time she said it to the Sandman twenty-three years before.

Chapter 29

———◆—◆—◆———

Myeisha McDonald's body didn't contain a single religious bone, but that never stopped her from singing gospel songs in the car at the top of her lungs. As she sang, she took notice of the sky's remarkable clarity; it held only the sun while every other inch was unencumbered space. She had been on the road for about four hours when she finally met her exit. Another ten minutes passed, and she found herself turning into the Golden Oaks Apartments, the address on Michael King's license. Snaking through the inner roads, she studied the old but decently maintained buildings before pulling into a parking space she guessed was close to apartment 203. A chill swept through the breezeway where Myeisha stood, knocking for several minutes before a young woman with hair sitting sloppily to one side of her head and a twisted brown sweater yanked open the door.

"Hi, my name is Myeisha McDonald."

Unimpressed, the young woman stood firm, waiting for the punchline.

"I wanted to talk to you about Michael King."

"Are you a cop? For Christ's sake, he's dead. What more to do you want from him? I've already told you everything I know." The woman's voice trailed as she walked away from the open door and plopped onto a large couch with a color and condition matching her sweater.

"I'm not a cop at all." Myeisha entered and sat at the other end of the couch. "I'm a reporter from Black Water. I just have a few questions, that's it. What's your name?"

"Kayla," the woman who, under a particularly soft beam of sunlight from the window now appeared a girl, responded flatly. Her eyebrows lifted briefly before dropping to their routine state of spectacular boredom. "A reporter ... jeez. Listen. I've already told the police, I have no clue why he would try to rob some random, old lady. I mean, it's not like we're living like royals over here, but we didn't need to rob anyone." She scoffed, tears welling in her eyes. "Why'd they have to shoot him?"

Myeisha exhaled at the abrupt reveal of emotion. "I'm so sorry, Kayla. Was he your boyfriend?"

The girl huffed before turning her eyes to the ceiling to dry them. "I guess you could call him that. We'd been living together for about a year or so."

"And you have no clue why he would do this?"

"I already told you and everyone else, I don't."

"What about his family?"

"What about them?" Kayla waved her hand into the air. "They're kind of ... estranged or whatever. He's got some problems, so he didn't talk to them too much, but he *didn't* need to rob anyone."

"What kind of problems?"

"He was depressed." Kayla shrugged. "Aren't we all?"

"About what?"

"It doesn't have anything to do with this."

"Sure, but I'd like to know."

A few moments passed. The giddy screams of children who played on one of the apartment lawns floated through the half open window.

"His sister, he was close to her. She died a long time ago. He was obsessed over this professor at the university, Professor Cramer."

"The university I passed coming here? About two hours north?"

"Probably. It's the only one around here."

"Someone killed his sister?" Myeisha leaned toward Kayla to catch every word.

Kayla shook her head. "No, no one killed her. She killed herself. He found Amber hanging in her bedroom closet one Christmas break when she was home. He was just a kid."

Myeisha's head clicked away, and her eyes shifted, trying to locate a piece of information embedded in her mind. "Did you say *Amber?*"

"Yeah, Amber King."

From one shoulder, the blue robe hung limply, exposing Simone's left breast. Sitting in the nursery's rocking chair, she cradled Trace who was squealing in want of milk that he could not rely on to flow from his mother's breast, causing the infantile but instinctual distrust that made him shun any attempts at the breast altogether. So focused was Simone on some invisible object that allowed her the mental distance to block her son's deafening wails, she didn't notice Aaliyah had entered the room and pulled the robe up to cover her mother's chest. The caress of her collarbone at her child's hand caused Simone to blink back into the present.

"I made you your smoothie," Aaliyah said, proffering the plastic cup to her mother before setting it on the side table next to the rocking chair.

"Thank you," Simone responded with a slow grin as she rocked to calm Trace.

"You're welcome," Aaliyah whispered.

"Your eye …" Simone cupped her daughter's face in her hand. "It was an accident, baby girl. I'm so sorry. It's starting to heal."

"I know."

"Go and play with your sister. I'll put Trace down, then make you some lunch," Simone said as she watched her daughter tread toward the door, linger, then look back before disappearing down the hallway.

Simone's eyes narrowed at the orange-colored slushy-like substance in the glass as she brought it to her nose for a sniff before returning it to the table untouched.

Myeisha supposed the campus was a good size, though not as big as she expected. According to the oversized property maps behind lit glass partitions strategically placed at points where someone may ask themselves, *Where the hell am I,* there were a total of eight buildings. No one in the science building, which included medical, had heard of Amber King or a Professor Cramer. Now a young, wannabe journalist was turning her away from the university newspaper who she presumed was as sincere in his ignorance about Amber King as he was about anything that took place more than twenty years prior—a time when he was probably still lobbing action figures at one another to the tune of his onomatopoeia-saturated vocabulary.

Myeisha thought she could try the local police station, then remembered Amber had not died here but in her hometown. Maybe the local city newspaper, she thought to herself. As much as she hated it, all the answers weren't here. *At least there's coffee before I hit the road,* Myeisha thought as she stepped into the campus library that, according to the sign, also housed a coffee shop.

A petite, young woman with short and fluffy brown curls and thick, black-rimmed glasses took her order. "Large coffee. That's it?"

"Yup," Myeisha confirmed as she reached into her bag for her wallet.

As the girl pulled a paper cup from a neat stack, she spoke from a half turn. "You have your ID? Faculty get a ten percent discount."

"Wow, no mistaking me for a student at all, huh?"

"Are you a student?" the girl asked, already exasperated by the needless mystery.

"Neither. I'm a reporter."

"Something happen?"

"Not lately that I know of. I was trying to find some information about a girl who went to school here a long time ago. Her name was Amber King."

"The one who died by suicide?" The girl passed the hot cup over the counter and nodded toward a separate area that held the creams and sugars.

Myeisha's eyes cocked up to meet the young woman's face as she anxiously handed over her debit card. "You know something about her?"

"Her and Cramer? Sure do. Working here, we all have to take our turn in the coffee shop, but I'm studying to be a librarian. I read *a lot*." Her expression remained blank as she ran the card and returned it. "I'm Adrienne Cotts."

"I'm Myeisha McDonald. I'm a reporter for the *Black Water Observer*. Do you have a few minutes to talk? I'll buy you a coffee."

Adrienne scanned the empty tables. "Why not."

Disregarding her deep disdain for it, Aaliyah allowed her little sister to wear her fox mask while she read, "*We're all mad here. I'm mad. You're mad—*"

Aaliyah stopped at a rustling in her bedroom closet. In the hallway, the vacuum revved to yet another start, subjecting the girls to more of the cantankerous *vrooming* that originated from different rooms constantly throughout the day, regardless of how they woke the baby. She and Jada's eyes met.

"*Mom!*" Aaliyah yelled. Over the noise, she persisted, calling again, "*Mom!*"

A second later, the motor stopped, and Simone entered the room. "Can you not holler for me?"

Jada sat upright from the warm place she had created in her sister's side and pointed. "We heard something in the closet."

Blowing at a wisp of frizzed hair that had dropped over her eye, Simone shuffled across the room and placed her hand on the closet doorknob. Swallowing hard, she glanced at her girls before whipping open the door, then faced the deep and empty blackness. "See. Nothing here—" Just as she turned back, she screamed at the sight of Ella running full speed toward her. Before she could get out of the way, Ella evaporated into Simone's body, pushing through her to the other side and into the closet, piercing not only her body, but her soul as the two merged for only a second before she was gone. The closet door snapped closed just before the bedroom door creaked shut, but not before Simone saw the Sandman standing just outside it.

The girls yelped, Trace cried, and heat whistled through the ceiling vents.

Simone's voice shook as she spoke. "It … It's just the heat coming on." Simone pulled open the closet door again and yanked the string that brought light to the confined but ordinary little room filled with shoes and colorful clothes. "Finish your book," Simone instructed as she went for the bedroom door.

She tugged the staunch doorknob. It didn't move. It was locked. The heat could explain how the door closed but not how it locked. To not alarm her girls further, she quietly unlocked the knob and studied it before stepping into the hallway. As she suspected, he was gone, and she stood in the hallway alone. Pulling Aaliyah's door to a close, she listened as they muttered excitedly before returning to the wonderland from whence they came.

Downstairs, the phone rang, and Simone passed the soft cries of the nursery as she descended. "Hello?" she answered.

"Hello. May I speak with Simone Parker?"

"Speaking."

"This is Kimberly from Dr. Penny's office, and I am just reminding you of your follow-up appointment tomorrow morning."

Pressing her hand to her aching belly wound, Simone spun to face the refrigerator where she noticed, for the first time since she had come home from the hospital, her birth plan still tacked to it with a magnet. What had been the sum of her simple wishes for her son's birth was now left behind as carelessly as a grocery list.

… delivery is planned as unmedicated vaginal … the lights dimmed … as few interruptions as possible … I would like skin-to-skin contact immediately … no pacifier to be given to baby … I plan to breastfeed exclusively … exclusively … exclusively … The words repeated in her mind, fighting against the pounding in her head for space.

"Hello?" the woman on the other end called.

"I'm not coming," Simone declared before slamming the phone onto the hook.

Back upstairs, she covered her son's soft weeping and her daughters' chatter with the clatter of the vacuum cleaner as she powered it up and drove it over the hallway carpet.

Whips of steam lapped at Adrienne's face as she leaned into the corner table. "I spend a lot of my free time studying the school archives. I don't know why, but that kind of thing interests me. Always been a nerd like that. Honestly, there isn't much information on it. I tried to partner with one of the school reporters to do a story last semester, but the admin shut that down fast. They said it had already been done, but it's gone, and I think they just want it to stay that way. I don't blame them, though. Gotta keep the school name clean and all."

Through the window, Myeisha glanced at the sky that suddenly grayed and opened to rain. Refocusing on Adrienne, she pulled her phone from her bag. "Just for notes."

"Esther Cramer was working in the school's counseling office when Amber, who was a freshman at the time, began going in for sessions."

"So, she wasn't a professor?"

"No. I've heard the stories that spun it that way, but she was never a professor. Anyway, they got close to the point that Esther began talking to Amber outside of the office. After Amber hung herself, the rumors started. Some of Amber's friends, even her roommate, suspected that Esther wasn't helping her at all but doing the opposite. The Cramer family had a little money and influence. They got a lawyer up here to the school, and the accusations stopped, but Esther was never allowed to return to the counseling office. The Dean fired her, and she unenrolled shortly after. The office burned down about a month later."

"Wait, wait, wait ... *unenrolled?* She was a student?"

Adrienne's face lit up at the reaction to the plot twist. "Exactly. She wasn't a professor or a doctor or anything else I've heard in the rumors, just a psychology student who worked at the front desk at the counseling office. Anyway ..." Adrienne shrugged. "When it was all said and done, Esther Cramer disappeared and never turned up here again."

"Any ideas on what happened to her?"

"Not sure. I heard something about her having a son out of wedlock, and her religious family excommunicating her, but I don't know how true that is. They were some type of zealots who lived on a compound-type place in Beckstown a couple hours from here."

"The Church of All Saints?" Myeisha's face warped with childhood recollections of the cult like group's visits to Black Water.

"Sounds right." Adrienne nodded.

Myeisha drifted over her many memories of passing through Beckstown on one road trip or another, her mother droning on about their cult. *"A strange-looking red, brick house that's probably about ten thousand square feet, a little church, and a few other houses scattered on the grounds. It's all surrounded by tall, chain-linked fences. Craziest thing you ever saw. It's there, right by the elementary school at the north end."*

"I know exactly where that is," Myeisha said, emerging from her reflections.

"I have more research on my computer from when I was trying to get the story run, if I find anything else I think may be helpful. I'm off in a few minutes, but thanks for the coffee." Adrienne took Myeisha's number and returned to the backside of the counter.

"Thank you!" Myeisha said as she scuttled into the gold of dusk. If she hurried, she could get to that motel right outside of Beckstown before it got too late.

Chapter 30

————◆—◆—◆————

When Mack arrived home, his concern about his wife doing too much housework too soon was looming over their every interaction. That morning when he had left for the shop, she had been sweeping the hardwoods, and now she was plowing the carpet with the vacuum cleaner, but he thought better of mentioning it as commenting on how his wife passed the day—along with almost anything else that came out of his mouth—could be taken critically. The most venerable action was probably to assist without question.

"I'm going to order a pizza and wings. Do you want anything special?" Mack slipped his arm around his wife's waist and kissed her neck.

Jerking around, she slapped away his arm, her eyes bulging as if a stranger stood before her. "Mack, you scared me."

"You didn't hear me come in?"

"No," she snapped.

Mack sat his lunchbox on the foyer table before repeating himself, "I'm going to order pizza. Do you want anything special? Maybe a salad?"

His wife's gaze dashed to her belly, then to him as he moved to correct his catastrophic blunder. "I'm not saying you *need* a salad, it's just you usually get one when we order pizza."

Her body loosened, and she placed the broom against the wall. "No. I'm not too hungry. Trace is asleep, and the girls are bathing. I'm going to visit with Dr. Duran for a bit."

"Scared?" Dr. Duran asked. "Of what?"

The words caught in her throat as she could have dealt with almost anything except those four words being true. "The Sandman is real. It was him. He killed my family, and I tried to deny it, but I have to admit it's true now because ... because now he wants my husband and my children, and I can't allow that to happen. I know it sounds crazy. Trust me, I know, but you're the only one I can talk to about this. I must face him, like I did that night. He's inside."

"You're right," Dr. Duran admitted coolly, repositioning the mint green blanket that covered her legs on the couch.

"Wh ... what? You believe me?"

"Of course, I do, and you realized it just in time. The full moon is tomorrow. That's when he'll come for them."

"What?" Simone stammered, hardly able to grasp such validation.

"The Sandman *is* real, Simone. I became a doctor so I could help people like you. My job is to help you fight the demons no one else believes in before it's too late. Do you understand?"

"But why do you believe me now?"

"When he came the first time, he let you go. As a result, you let him go, but now he's back, you said so yourself. I have always believed you, but it was you who had to make the realization, and now you have to fight him with his own fire."

Slipping into the hallway in the middle of the night to skulk about checking on all her children, her head felt full of a fog that nothing besides the painful pulsing within it could penetrate. Simone wanted the children to sleep with them that evening. *"All of them?"* Mack had asked for clarification before disagreeing mildly. She knew she had to tell her husband, though she was sure he would not believe her until it was too late.

It's all my fault. Simone peeked over the crib railing to find Trace wrapped tightly, his soft features arching and shrinking in response to some dream of light and angels. *If I had never brought them here …* She pushed Jada's bedroom door to catch sight of her shape under a bundle of covers.

As she turned to head for Aaliyah's room, she heard the low wisps and hisses of whispers. In the dark living room, her father's recliner moved back and forth. Simone came around it at a wide angle and found her oldest daughter sitting, the sockets of her eyes appeared empty under the tricky moonlight shadows.

"Aaliyah?" Simone called.

The girl angled her face to her mother, casting it into a sickish purple-hued splice of moonlight.

"Who are you talking to?"

"Grandpa."

"Go to your room!" Simone growled.

"But why?"

"Go!" Simone instructed through clenched teeth.

A reluctant Aaliyah slunk to the top of the stairs where she squatted and watched her mother through the slats.

Facing what seemed a ghoulish yet invisible audience, Simone spoke with tightly clasped fists. "You are not my father! You are not any part of my family! You can't have them, and you can't have me!"

Aaliyah tiptoed down the hallway to her room where her mother appeared moments later.

Simone set her weary eyes to the task of studying her oldest daughter. "I don't want you to be afraid, okay? I'll take care of everything. I won't let anyone or anything hurt you or Jada or Trace or Daddy. I'm going to make it all right."

Aaliyah fixed her mother in her own meticulous sight without a word.

"I'm sorry I was harsh with you, but I want you to stay in your room at night, okay? Don't … leave … your … room."

Aaliyah was silent.

"*Okay?*" Simone's voice climbed, and Aaliyah nodded in agreement. "You hate me, don't you?" Simone's voice took on the heralding tremble of uncontrollable grief, then she fled into the hallway before Aaliyah could see her tears.

Chapter 31

Myeisha devoured a breakfast of pancakes, bacon, eggs, and two cups of coffee at the greasy motel's neighboring diner before hitting the road at full speed in the direction of Beckstown.

❖ ❖ ❖

Mack woke to the sound of his wife shoving the vacuum cleaner up and down the hallway. He hurried to open the bedroom door. His and Simone's eyes met.

"It's the sand." She pressed her socked toe into the red power button at the base of the appliance.

"Sand?" Mack's eyes examined the floor. "Baby, it's too early for this. The kids are still asleep."

Her expression choked into one of confusion as she looked around, as if she herself had not noticed the children were not engaged in their usual early morning play. Then another thought became evident as her features mutated in keen awareness. *They weren't asleep. They didn't sleep, none of 'em. They were pretending.*

"I will vacuum, okay? I just want you to get back into bed while I get you some coffee. As soon as the kids are up, I'll vacuum. I promise." He added the last part in response to his wife's distrustful stare. As of late, Simone seemed out of sorts, and while Mack knew a new baby always brought on some stress, he was starting to worry.

Climbing into bed with so much still to do was difficult, but she had to admit that sipping a hot cup of coffee under the covers in her mother's old smock was as comfortable as she had been since the baby was born. The flesh below her abdomen waved in pain. It was more than her incision. This discomfort was one that had plagued her monthly since the age of twelve. Her oncoming menstrual cycle was just another sign that she was failing at breastfeeding and all her other maternal and wifely duties.

As Mack made breakfast for the girls and tended to Trace, Simone sipped silently, trying to block out all the terrifying thoughts except one— how she would tell her husband that, tonight, the Sandman was coming.

Ghost town now seemed a more fitting name for Beckstown, Myeisha thought as she passed an abandoned building whose shape revealed its past life as a fast food favorite but now no longer even had the dignity of front doors, just a wide-open square that led into pitch blackness. Slowing her car as she reached the north end on the one road that led this way, she spotted the mammoth house off a side street to her left. As the compound came into full view, Myeisha surveyed the failing chain-linked fence and open black holes where no wood covered the squares that once held windows. She sighed when she spotted the padlocked chain around the gate entrance. Nonetheless, she parked crookedly on the curb, jumped out, and approached the grounds, readying her phone camera for a few snaps.

"They've been long gone." A pronounced but shaky voice startled Myeisha.

Whipping around, she saw a woman removing envelopes and crumpled papers from the mailbox that sat on the curb in front of a dilapidated trailer.

"You lookin' for the Cramer family, huh? We get about one of ya'll every few months."

"Actually, I'm looking for information on the daughter, Esther Cramer." Myeisha looked both ways, then crossed the street, something she hardly needed to do as she had barely counted three or four cars the entire time she'd been in *ghost town*. "I'm Myeisha McDonald. A reporter."

"I bet you are. Lori," the woman grumbled as she flipped through the envelopes. "Nutjob, that one. All of 'em, really, but that one … macadamia."

"How so?"

Lori rolled one eye—a special talent of the easily annoyed. "They was all strange, even for Jesus people, but her … she was *dangerous*, because she seemed so normal. Not like the others, she could blend right in wit' regular folks like you and me."

"But she wasn't," Myeisha inserted, noticing how Lori, as much as she'd like to come off as aggravated by the routine visits of the insatiable consumers of creepy curiosities, she enjoyed gatekeeping the urban legend of her neighbors. Now Myeisha doubted the coincidental midmorning mail check was coincidental at all.

Lori squinted, then raised a hand to shield her eyes from the sun that cast a harsh glaze on everything in its luminous trajectory. "Not at all. She was worse than the rest of 'em, even as a girl. Enjoyed hurting people, 'specially those weaker than her. She was closer to my little brother's age than mine, but I had her number. He ain't the brightest crayon in the box, so I watched them closely. One time, she tricked him into climbing into a well out back and pulled up the rope. Took us three hours to find James, *mmm-hmm*. Had we not found him before nightfall, no tellin' what could have happened. He wouldn't never tell on her. We ain't snitches like that, but I was wise to her. Finally convinced my mother not to let James play with her anymore. Probably only reason he's alive today with his RAGGEDY, UNEMPLOYED ASS PROPPED ON MY COUCH!" Lori yelled in the direction of the trailer's screen door. "Another little neighborhood girl, Nellie, who used to play with Esther, wasn't so lucky. They was playin' up around the overpass one day, and according to Esther, Nellie just ... fell over. Could be, but that didn't explain the cuts on the insides of Nellie's hand, like she was trying to hold on, and it certainly didn't explain the bruises on her knuckles as if someone was pounding on 'em. But no one, especially back then, would call a little girl a murderer. A *monster*. Just didn't make no sense."

Once in her car, Myeisha sat back and closed her eyes to try to give some form to all the information, but her phone chirped a text from Adrienne—*Esther Cramer*. Myeisha pulled the phone closer to her face in anticipation of the incoming photo. The downloaded message flashed to a fully formed image.

"Impossible," she mumbled before her jaw went limp in disbelief of how she could have missed the thread that threatened to draw together a web of motives and mendacities that spanned the Black Water community, herself included.

Chapter 32

———————◆◆◆◆◆———————

The face held no lines, the eyes were bright with the shine of invincible youth, and there in the cursory grin, something ominous lurked. It put Myeisha in the mind of those sickening black and white photos of the smiling, camping, marching League of German Girls who came home in the evening to dinner tables to lovingly break bread with fathers and brothers whose days were spent executing atrocities. In photographs, they appeared docile, but they were the devoted keepers of a house of vile violence; in real life, their faces often screwed in shouting masks of evil. Monsters, all of them.

But it was that beauty mark barely visible on her left cheek that merged the identities of Esther Cramer and Black Water's beloved Dr. Candace Duran. A second text from Adrienne buzzed. At first glance, the older man in the photo, dressed in a crisp, white collar shirt and khaki pants was familiar though not recognizable, but after reading the accompanying message, all the identities fused, telling part of an unbelievable story that smacked her back into the middle of her childhood.

Jonathan Cramer, founder of the Church of All Saints. Father of Esther Cramer.

After leaving a message with one of Simone's girls who informed Myeisha that her friend had been in bed all day not feeling well, she tried Simone's cellphone. It went straight to voicemail.

"Simone, this is Myeisha. I don't want to go into too much detail because I still don't know everything. I'm out of town right now, but I'm coming home tonight and coming over to talk. In the meantime, could you just not see Dr. Duran? Again, I don't want to alarm you, but just don't … see her, okay? I'll see you tonight."

All day, Simone's family had been catering to and creeping around her which she thought was for the better as she had been pouring over all the ways to explain to her husband what was unfolding. There was no good way. Simone was fingering the explosive green splatter of paint across the black smock she wore, the only thing that didn't bother her belly scar, when Mack came into the room with a cup of tea.

"How are you feeling?" he asked.

"I need to tell you something. Mack, I know this will be hard for you to believe. I didn't want to tell you, but now I have to. Because I want you all to be safe. It's the Sandman, he … he *is* real, and soon he will come for us." Already, Simone was sobbing, tears bulging from her eyes like hurricane induced waves.

Every line in Mack's face surfaced. It was a few seconds before he could form words. "Simone, what the hell are you talking about?"

Her gaze darted back and forth across the carpet. Without her feet even touching it, she knew the sand was there; she could see it.

"Simone!" Mack called her back from some remote place that existed only in her head.

"I figured it out, Mack. We just have to sleep. He's getting to them. He's getting inside our children. I think Aaliyah has been poisoning my smoothies. That's why they taste funny. He's been working on them since we got here, but I've figured out how to keep them safe." Simone's voice was hoarse.

"*What?*" Mack reeled back.

Simone sank. "I know it's hard to believe, Mack, and I am so sorry I brought you all here, but it's true."

"Did you tell Dr. Duran about this?"

"You don't believe me, but he's here. He's here right now." Simone turned and pulled something from beneath her pillow.

As Mack took what appeared to be the filthy head of a beast into his hands, he whispered, "What is this, Simone?"

"He's … real." Simone's eyelids fluttered to dam what seemed a never-ending stream of tears.

All of what was any anger at his wife's strange behavior dissolved as he held up the old mask designed in the way of a snarling, long-snouted wolf. Something was very wrong here, something that no amount of anger would resolve. Mack could see that now.

"He was in the shed. He was there the day I hit my head, the day I gave birth to Trace. He's been there. He's been here … all this time, and because I chose not to believe in him, he has only been getting stronger through our children."

"Baby, he's a fairy tale."

"*He's not!*"

In body language and words, Mack segued into compliance. "Okay, okay."

"You don't believe me."

"I do. I believe you." Mack spied the burnt-orange pill bottle on the nightstand. "Did Dr. Duran give you these? They're for sleep, right?"

"Yes."

"I want you to take one." Mack opened the bottle and removed a white oval-shaped pill.

Simone was swept by confusion. "But we all have to sleep. If we sleep, he won't come."

"I know. We will." He moved the pill closer to her face and placed the cup of tea in her hand.

"All of us. You, me, and the children."

"We will. I'll take care of it, just take the pill." He placed it against her lips.

Simone opened her mouth just enough for the pill to tumble onto her tongue, sparking a bitter flavor. She swallowed a gulp of tea, feeling every movement of the large pill in her throat as it went down. "Promise me, Mack. Promise."

"I promise. Now, lie down." He pulled back the covers so that she could get comfortable under them.

Downstairs, Mack grabbed the notepad paper from the fridge and dialed the number scribbled after *Dr. Duran's office*. He spoke in low tones as his wife settled into sleep in their room. "I need to speak to Dr. Duran. She's friends with my wife, Simone Parker." He listened. "No message. Just please have her call me as soon as possible. It's an emergency." He pounded the phone onto the hook.

Chapter 33

As soon as she passed the sign welcoming her to Black Water, Myeisha grabbed her phone and dialed. After three rings, a hospital operator answered.

"Is Dr. Duran on duty?"

"She is. I can have her paged. What's your name?"

"Uh … Clare," Myeisha said before the man left the line. Myeisha pressed End on her phone and turned onto the street where the yellow Victorian sat.

Parking halfway down the block, she sunk into her seat and watched the house and neighborhood. She turned off the car when she again noticed the gas light that had been glaring at her for at least the last thirty minutes. Once satisfied no one would see her, she silenced her phone, then slipped from her car, made brisk strides down the sidewalk, and scrambled around the side of the house to the back window that offered direct access to Dr. Duran's office.

"Hello?" Dr. Duran answered the phone. When no one replied, she looked to the receptionist. "Who was it?"

"Clare?" the receptionist said, shrugging. "You also have some messages your office passed along." He handed over the pink slips of paper that Dr. Duran reviewed with an eyeroll before shoving them into her white coat pocket.

She returned to the room of her favorite patient. "I'm sorry, Johnny boy." She pushed pills through his slanted lips. "It's time to take your medicine."

Of course, it was locked. Myeisha jiggled the handle to Dr. Duran's back door once more as if it would magically open on her third try. Under the mat was nothing but cold concrete. Myeisha noticed an axe buried in the stump of a tree next to a pile of firewood and was reminded that fall was coming fast. She shivered before kneeling by one of the ground windows where she could see clearly into the basement room that was Dr. Duran's home office. Boxes were stacked along the walls, and some of her file cabinets hung open.

"At some point, all great journalists had to break the rules," Myeisha encouraged herself as she crossed the back yard and grabbed the axe. The glass shattered with one strike. While she had never climbed through a broken window, she had seen it done in movies and thought she could manage. With her jacket wrapped around her forearm, she cleared the remaining glass from the window frame. It was tight, but she squeezed into the gray, dusty room.

The one window offered only a single stream of light, and Myeisha was forced to turn on the desk lamp which flooded the room with a depressing ruddiness. Boxes lined one of the walls from top to bottom, cluttering the room which otherwise housed only a rustic wooden desk and matching file cabinets whose height reached Myeisha's chest. In the drawers, she recognized some of the names on the ragged manila folders, but nothing stood out.

"What are you looking for, Myeisha?" she purred to herself as she turned from the file cabinet to the wall of boxes that resembled a game of Jenga nearing its end. Pouring over the jagged writing scribbled on their sides in black marker, she stopped at one that read, *Amber King.* Myeisha removed the box from the stack as precisely as one would cut the disarming wire on a bomb. Fortunately for her, the monument of boxes only took to a pathetic slump after she removed one of its non-load-bearing innards.

Turning back in search of a spot to review the box's contents, she tripped on another one right in front of her that read, *Dorothy Ann Mills.*

"No way." Myeisha set down Amber's box and opened Dorothy's as if she had just discovered lost treasure. Everyone knew Daniel Mills had hired what he thought was a young doctor to assist with his growing practice. Everyone assumed Esther and Dorothy had become good friends through this connection, but it was now clear that Dr. Duran was always meant to be more. Indeed, he had hired her to work with all his patients but especially his wife.

Myeisha pulled one of several cassette tapes from the box and held it to the light to better see Dorothy's name and a date jotted on the side. She went to the desk where she saw an old cassette player with the top popped open. A thin layer of dust covered almost everything in the office except the cassette player. Inside was another tape identified with Dorothy Ann Mills' name. Myeisha lowered herself into the desk chair, she closed the top of the cassette player, and then pressed Play.

Static erupted from the tiny holes before clearing the way for Dr. Duran's voice. *"Dorothy, do you understand why your husband wanted you to see me?"*

After a long silence, Dorothy responded, *"He … he doesn't think the Sandman is real … but he is. He lives on the dark side of the moon."* Dorothy laughed. *"I've always wanted to go there, somewhere, anywhere far, far away. Like the places I paint, like the moon."* Dorothy Ann spoke in a drawl. *"Just away."*

Myeisha returned to the box to retrieve the remainder of the tapes, then lined them up on the desk in chronological order. She fell into a concentrated state as she listened to bits and pieces of Dr. Duran's continued sessions with Dorothy Ann then, at intervals, flipped through excerpts from the papers in the manila folders tagged with her name.

"Tell me about your family," Dr. Duran said.

Dorothy scoffed. *"I never meant to get pregnant with Ella. I never expected Daniel to be more than a little small-town fun, but when I got pregnant, I had no choice. I had nothing, and he was going to be a doctor. I had to marry him. I couldn't raise a baby alone."*

"Do you love him?"

Dorothy seemed irritated. *"Maybe, in a way. He annoys me at times, but he's smart. I like that. Once I settled, then came Simone, then pregnant again."* Dorothy laughed hard, then stopped abruptly. *"Can you tell him that I'm getting better?"* She was sobbing now.

"I'm going to help you, Dorothy. I am, but I need for you to promise not to tell Dr. Mills about what we discuss here, okay? You understand, confidentiality and all."

"Okay," Dorothy muttered.

Three tapes later, Dorothy was growing paranoid.

"I feel like I'm being watched, like something is in my house, a monster." Dorothy Ann's voice trembled. *"Daniel doesn't believe me. I don't blame him. I wouldn't believe me either."*

"I believe you, Dorothy."

"You do?"

"Monsters can be real. But you can beat them."

"How?" Dorothy pleaded.

Myeisha could imagine the sheer desperation in Dorothy's eyes.

The tape clicked along several paces until Dr. Duran finally spoke. *"Embrace them. Manifest them. Once you make them real, they can be destroyed."*

With the phone at his ear, Mack leaned his forehead into his forearm which was already pressed into the wall. He sighed. "No, I don't want to leave a message. I've been leaving her messages all day in her office and on the hospital floor. But she's there, right? Yeah, you told me she's busy. If she won't call me back, I'll just go to her."

First, he left two messages with Myeisha to see if she could sit with Simone and the kids, but when she didn't answer, as upset as his wife might be if she woke while he was gone, he didn't have much choice.

He made another call. After two rings a familiar voice answered.

"Nita, it's Mack. I need a big favor."

Shadows shifted on the wall of the already gloomy room. Myeisha looked up from the files spread across the desk and noticed sunset had snuck up on her. A glance at her watch confirmed she had been there for hours. Esther could get home anytime; she had to get out of there. Before closing the files, she gave the last few documents a once over and noticed a term for the first time—*Psychosis.* Postpartum psychosis.

Her pupils spread like a pool of dark blood. Flipping through the previous pages, she reviewed the term she had seen multiple times—

postpartum depression—and while she had no intimate knowledge of the condition, she was at least familiar with it, but these words—this word, *psychosis*—tacked onto the end of it was new.

In her back pocket, she found her phone. She had two missed calls from Mack Parker. His voicemail asked if she could sit with Simone and the kids while he ran an errand. Little did he know, she was headed there next, but first, she opened her browser and typed.

Pages of results filled the tiny screen, and she scanned the text of several sites as Dorothy's voice droned on in the background. *"I love Charlie, I love all my children, but the Sandman keeps coming. He wants them, and I don't know how to protect them anymore. He's infected them, separated them from me. They hate me, and they show it. The noise, the messes, they're endless. I don't eat. I don't sleep. I am constantly watching and walking the hallways at night. I stand over their beds, studying their sweet, little faces. But they're not sleeping; they're pretending. When their eyes flutter, I just whisper, 'It's okay. Mommy's here'. I'm a mother, I know that, but I am not even sure who I am anymore. I'm a protector. Maybe I'm a guardian angel. God wants me to protect them from the Sandman. Maybe I'm a demon. The church says so."*

"The church?" Dr. Duran asked.

"The Church of All Saints. They were protesting us—well ... Daniel. They would stand just off our property with signs about how psychiatry is the Devil's work. It's for demons."

"I recall. They are actually a very insightful group."

"Maybe they're right. Maybe that's why the Sandman keeps coming. We opened the door to him. We gave him access to the children. They grow more mischievous by the day, especially my Ella. I gave her a necklace. I love you to the moon and back, *it said. She loves that necklace, but today, we got into an argument over her not*

doing her laundry. When I grabbed for her, she stepped backward which caused me to rip the necklace from her neck. It hit the floor and slid under the washing machine. I left a pattern of scratches on her chest." Dorothy Ann began to cry. "You hate me, don't you? *I asked. She does. She hates me. They all hate me, but it doesn't matter. I love her, and I have to protect her. I have to protect all of them."*

"Trust yourself, Dorothy. You're their mother, and you know what's best for them."

Dorothy Ann laughed. *"I hate to say this, Doctor, but you're looking a little round in the middle lately. Are you pregnant?"*

The tape clicked to an end, and Myeisha's attention shot in the direction of the hallway where she heard what may have been a footstep.

Chapter 34

U nder the radioactive radiance of the rectangular lights, Mack sat, one foot tapping in a rapid, repetitive beat that offered some relief of the anxiety that spread through him like a virus. Hospitals gave him the creeps. He could never understand what gruesome magic such a place held to smell overwhelmingly of urine and disinfectant at the same time. Simone wasn't a patient but being here to see someone for her loaded him to the gills with an aching sense of dread. If he was the foundation, she was the frame; lacking her stability, the family would easily collapse.

Don't think like that. She's fine. She'll be fine. She's fine.

The receptionist only agreed to page Dr. Duran after Mack had made it clear that he wasn't leaving until he spoke with her.

"Mr. Parker?" The woman seemed to be standing over him at once where she offered an awkward handshake since her better arm was still in a sling.

Mack stood to shake her hand before they both sat. "I'm sorry to just show up here, but I need to talk to you about my wife."

"Simone ..." Dr. Duran purred the name.

"Yes. I know she has visited with you a couple times, and I don't know what is going on with her, but she isn't doing so good."

"What do you mean?"

"Honestly, she's been a little different since we moved into the house, but since the baby, she's upset, breaking down a lot. At night, she paces the house. The only time she sleeps now is when she takes those pills that you gave her. She's constantly vacuuming non-existent sand. She thinks someone is after us—the Sandman." Panic rose in his voice with every word.

"Just a little baby blues. Nothing to be too worried about. Pregnancy and birth, though it is the most natural thing on earth, can be traumatic. All she needs is some time to recover. She'll be fine."

"*Baby blues?*" Mack spit the words like they were sour on his tongue. "She's had baby blues before when she had our daughters—a little crying and feeling down for a few weeks, but this is not that. Dr. Duran—"

The woman raised her hands in a relent marked with mocking. "If you really think it's something, I'll give her a call later this week and—"

"Does this look like baby blues to you?" Mack shoved a smelly mass of rubber and matted hair into Dr. Duran's good hand.

At the sight of the foreign article, she straightened at once, dangling it between her and Mack by a thin strip of hair—a wolf mask with two yellow-tinged, protruding eyes that undoubtedly glowed if one shut out the lights. Centered in the orbs were two cutouts for seeing from which the inner darkness of the disguise poured forth. A scowling maw revealed rows of whetted teeth and ears pointed straight up, all tangled in a mess of black fur.

"What is this?" Dr. Duran asked.

"According to Simone, it's the Sandman. She found it in our shed. What the hell does that even mean?" Mack studied every movement in the woman's face, trying desperately to gain insight into this mysterious creature that it seemed everyone in Black Water knew but him.

After waking in silence, Simone rolled over under the comforter and reached out, but the other side of the bed was vacant. Her head felt as if it were packed with drying cement, stiffening everything painfully in place. Now time seemed only an abstract concept that Simone floated above, bouncing down to tap her feet along its hard line only when she thought of it—which wasn't often. Through the window, Simone concluded this side of the world had only just stepped into the shadows of evening. Sand grated along the sensitive bottoms of her feet as she shuffled to the bathroom. She wouldn't clean it up anymore, realizing vacuuming what he left behind was futile, and the time for a face-to-face, as much as it terrified her, had come.

In the bathroom, she unzipped her mother's old painting jumper that had become uniform until the slide sat just below her waistline. The bandage over her belly was discolored, and the gruesome incision that lay under it gave off an odor of rot even with the covering. Fluttering her eyelids in a succession of rapid blinks, Simone tried to clear the movements that pulsed under the bandage from her sight. They remained as she scrapped at the strips of skin tape. Simone winced in pain as she lifted the bandage, revealing hundreds of tiny caterpillars slinking all over the blistering skin around her infected incision.

Closing her eyes, Simone wrestled back the vomit she felt churning at the base of her throat. She snapped them open again and rechecked the scar to see she had been mistaken. No, these little creatures were tiny, white maggots reveling in her reproductive decay. Doubling over, her face to the open toilet bowl, she submitted to the inevitable commencement of vomit. More bile—she could not recall the last time she had eaten. When she returned to her naked reflection, she was grateful to find the healing incision wickedly grinning back at her just above the clean bandage that hung from her abdomen. As she re-adhered the strips of tape to secure her dressing, the laughter of her girls filtered into the room and through her head, a deafening echo ricocheting the screeches against every inch of her skull's inner surface.

Movement drew Aaliyah's focus from the boardgame on the floor up over her babysitter's shoulder, and her mouth opened just enough to release a small whoosh of air as her mother lumbered into her room.

A mess of a barely bun sat atop her head, though much of her hair in the back had escaped the hair tie and was frozen in the position of a large wave headed for shore. Upon spotting Nita, her mother's dull eyes blazed in an indescribable emotion. Aaliyah's eyes blinked to Jada who clutched Bobo, her face fixed in what she assumed was an expression similar to her own, and while neither of them had any idea of what was about to happen, Aaliyah made a factual determination that it would not be good for the young woman who sat on the floor across from them, cradling their newborn brother.

The smile still set in her face from the laughter they had all shared just a moment before faded as she followed the girls' gaze backward toward the door. Nita gasped, dropping her game piece, and Aaliyah was stunned at how loud of a thud that little red plastic pawn made on the chipboard against the profound silence that saturated the room and seemed, likely to Aaliyah, to extend to the whole world.

Scarlet, vision-blurring anger exploded through Simone's chest from an emotional grenade detonated somewhere deep in her gut. *THIS BITCH WANTS MY HUSABAND AND MY CHILDREN!* The words flashed across the vacant backdrop of Simone's mind one at a time in hulking, cranberry-colored letters like the ones that had welcomed Simone on the rear of her home the day she and her family had arrived.

"Stay away, Sandman!" she heard a voice yell from a place so distant, the phrase was a whisper by the time it reached her.

"What are you doing in my house?" No one, not even Simone, recognized the growl of the words that came from her own gaping jaws.

Nita stuttered. "Uh … Mack called me and asked me if I would sit with the kids for a while so that he could run an errand."

"Why would he ask you to come into *my* home to watch *my* children when their *mother* is right here?"

"He … he said you needed rest."

"Mom," Aaliyah interjected.

Simone exhaled all the air from her lungs in an abrupt puff, her eyes ever trained on the intruder like tracking missiles. "Aaliyah, get your brother, and you and Jada go and get into my bed."

In response to most directives from her parents, Aaliyah was known for working in at least one rebuttal, but her tingling senses warned her to obey without utterance.

By the time the girls fled with Baby Trace and Simone started to speak, Nita was lifting herself from the floor on unsteady legs.

"Get out of my house."

Nita swallowed hard. "I'm sorry," the young woman croaked while angling around Simone and into the hallway. Before hitting the first step, Nita was already in a light jog.

In a pain-ridden shamble, Simone reached the top of the stairs just in time to see the girl grab her jacket and keys and slam the door behind her without looking back.

Myeisha tiptoed to the door and pressed her ear to the wood. Someone could be standing there, just waiting to bust her for her crime. What would she say? The window was broken. *Black Water Native and Observer Reporter Breaking and Entering.* She would be her own story, more interesting than anything else that had happened lately.

No turning back now, just go. She pulled on the knob and poked her head out the door. The dim light from the office bled into the shadowy hallway, giving only enough light to discern silhouettes of the boxes that lined parts of the walls in stacks. *Selma Dia … Toby Thompson …* She read just a few of the names of the Black Water natives she recognized that were scrawled on the boxes in black marker.

Nothing moved. *Hello?* Myeisha thought before any sound came from her mouth. No, she would not speak. They always did that in horror movies against the sage and screaming advice of everyone watching from the alternate universe of their home. It was dumb. If something was going to get her, it would have to do it without a greeting. Down the hallway, a mountain of boxes slouched against a wall, and she wondered if a spontaneous shift could have caused the faint shuffle that had drawn her attention. Before shutting herself back in the office, she scanned the corridor one last time and noticed a faint angle of orange light peeking through a crack in the barrier wall of boxes. Stepping out the door, she took a better look. It was not a wall behind the stack of boxes but a door.

Only once in Myeisha's adult life had she ever visited Dr. Duran's home office and only for a short time to discuss a community story in which she had minor involvement. *Had the door been hidden even then? Probably just didn't notice it because I wasn't looking for it?* Finding valuable things not sought was a rare luck.

One by one, Myeisha pulled down the boxes until she had a clear view of the door. Again, she pressed her ear to the surface before trying the locked knob. She removed a bobby pin from her high ponytail. This house, like all the others in Black Water, was filled with mostly standard-issue doorknobs—the same kind she had picked a million times in her own house when she was a kid after watching some savvy reporter movie. Popping the locks with a plastic card was more her expertise, but she didn't have one on her, so the pin would have to suffice.

She bent the top leg of the pin, studying it to ensure the perfect angle. She pressed it into the lock, wiggling it with precise pressure and slant, working feverishly to the soundtrack of Dorothy Ann and Dr. Duran's droning dialogue. Rusty in her childhood craft, it took two pins before she heard the familiar click that allowed her to then push open the door and flip the light switch inside.

"What the hell?" she murmured as she scanned the area.

The light from a small, blue lamp bathed the odd chamber in a golden glow. Musty wallpaper featuring endless prints of old-fashioned, red and navy-blue locomotive trains covered each wall. A large wooden crib, the sides of which were raised abnormally high, sat neatly against the far wall.

Myeisha's fingers swept the rail lines that crisscrossed the cream-colored bedding. Spinning, she beheld every corner of the nursery. *Did Dr. Duran have a son? How could she have a child no one knew about?* From the office, she heard Dorothy Ann explaining Baby Charlie's difficult birth, and despite having no children of her own, Myeisha could feel her frustration.

Though nothing in the nursery seemed out of place, Myeisha did notice something draped haphazardly across the rocking chair. Holding up the heavy, stained material, she made some unrecognizable sound at the realization that what she held was a small straitjacket—one for … a child.

On the dresser was one item, lying flat, face down—a picture frame. In the photo, a young Dr. Duran held a baby boy. It was obvious at first glance, even in a still photo, that he was different. Brown eyes, one noticeably larger than the other, filled the top half of his face, and his mouth sat crookedly to the left side. With her mouth, Dr. Duran smiled faintly, but her eyes offered no such cooperation. At once, Myeisha realized that just that morning, she had been planted in the same place where Dr. Duran stood in the photo. Beyond the fence behind her, the compound raised around the small, white building partly captured by the camera lens—The Church of All Saints. At the young mother's back, the place was bright and fresh, different than the dry, abandoned place that had met Myeisha earlier. She read aloud the engraved words at the bottom of the photo, "*Jonathan Cramer II.*" Just beneath the name was another line, *My Johnny Boy.*

Up above was a commotion of heavy feet pounding the floor. The family was home.

Myeisha scrambled back into the office, craned herself up through the broken window, and sprinted from the home without bothering to put anything back as she had found it. She folded herself into her car, jammed the startup button, and sped onto the dark road in what seemed like one powerful movement. After a few minutes, her gas light was no longer ignorable. When she pulled into a nearby gas station and parked next to a pump, she realized she was trembling. She shook out her hands and took a deep breath before dialing her friend.

As the phone rang, she struggled to calm the thoughts raging through her brain. *Dr. Duran was not Dr. Duran. She never was!*

The phone buzzed again.

She had a child? What happened to him?

Another ring.

She wasn't a doctor, so what the hell was she doing with Simone? Not helping her but making her worse, like she made Amber King worse, like she made everyone worse.

"Hello?" Simone answered stoically.

Myeisha exhaled in relief. "Simone? Are you okay?"

"Hello?" Simone called again, only hearing silence.

"Simone? Can you hear me?" Myeisha spoke louder.

Now that Simone could hear, she pulled the phone from her ear and stared at it, as if it were something she had never seen before, like a kid in the back yard examining some luminous thing that had just fallen from space. After securing the phone to her ear, yes, she could hear him clearly. "I can hear you," Simone confirmed flatly.

Static rose on Myeisha's side of the connection.

The Sandman snarled his words as Simone listened. "I have been waiting for you all this time."

"I won't let you hurt them."

"Hurt who?" Myeisha asked, plugging her free ear to hear Simone better through the intensifying white noise.

"I won't let you take them with you to the dark side of the moon," Simone stated firmly as tears filled her eyes, making her whole face heavy. "I will save them."

"But they're already mine," he hissed before Simone ripped the receiving cord from the phone base and returned to the methodic preparation of her children's cookies and milk.

"What?" Myeisha cried out. "Hello? Hello?" The line was dead. *The moon, Simone had clearly said the dark side of the moon.* Myeisha knew the legend as did everyone in Black Water. The Sandman had returned.

Chapter 35

———◆—◆—◆———

When Mack's phone rang, he thought it was Nita again. She had been so frantic that he could hardly understand her when they spoke just a few moments before. It wasn't Nita, but it was a Black Water area code and a number he recognized.

"Hello?"

"Mack? Thank god you answered. It's Myeisha. I have to talk to you. Are you with Simone?"

"No. I'm on my way home to her and the kids. What's this about?" He kept his eyes focused straight ahead as he hurried through the crowded streets.

"It's Dr. Duran, Mack. Simone has been seeing her, right? I don't think she's a doctor at all."

"What are you talking about? I was just at the hospital meeting with her."

"Meeting with her? About what?"

Mack hesitated to discuss his wife's condition.

"I'm her oldest friend, Mack. Please!"

He cleared his throat. "She's—"

"She's sick, isn't she? But there's more. I'm on my way, but Dr. Duran isn't who she says she is. Her real name is Esther Cramer. Her father was a man named Jonathan Cramer. When we were kids, he founded an organization called The Church of All Saints. At one point, he wanted to destroy Simone's father and his practice. I don't have all the answers yet, but I think she pretended to be a doctor to infiltrate the Parker family, but it wasn't the first time. When she was in college, she pushed a troubled girl to commit suicide. The man who shot Dr. Duran was the younger brother of that girl. She takes advantage of people who need help and makes them do awful things."

"What? Why?"

"I'm not sure. When she first met Simone's mother, I think she was working with her father, Jonathan, but I don't think she has any connection with her family anymore. I've never heard her speak of them, and I've never seen them around. The Church of All Saints hated a lot of things, including psychiatry and anyone who sought psychiatric help. They thought it was the Devil's work and that anyone who needed it was not sick but evil. I don't know, maybe she thought pretending to be a psychiatrist was a way to gain access to these people and punish them. She's punishing Simone and trying to push her like she pushed Simone's mother to do what she did."

"Her mother? What did Simone's mother do?" Mack asked, though the dread that flooded him was an indication that it had all come together for him in that moment. "It was her. Her mother murdered them, didn't she?" Mack's voice shook.

"Yes. Back then, Dr. Duran told the police Dorothy had started thinking she was this Sandman character after she found a wolf mask that belonged to one of Dr. Mills' patients in his office. When she wore it, she would assume this Sandman identity. Soon, she could no longer tell the difference between reality and fairy tale, and that night she killed all of them except Simone who had hidden. We all just thought she went nutty, but I don't think she did. I think she was suffering from something called postpartum psychosis."

Mack's sight blurred the charcoal colors of the road with those of the bright streetlights, and he could hardly find any clarity in the circus of shapes before him as his head swirled. His body jerk to a halt as he slammed on his brakes before almost plowing into the back of a truck. A horn honked from somewhere at his rear. His heart pounded so ferociously, he felt the beat pulsating in his eyes.

"Mack? Are you okay?" a faraway voice asked through his cellphone.

"How come no one told me this?" Mack asked breathlessly as he blinked the road in front of him back into focus and pressed through the light, weaving speedily through the cars that lined the street.

"We assumed you knew. No one wanted to bring it up again. Everyone thought that by moving back into the house, she was ready to put it all behind her."

Mack's voice faltered. "No, no, no, she never told me. She said it was one of her father's patients and that he was locked up, Marcus Sandon or Sand—"

"Marcus Sanden *was* a patient, but he didn't kill the Mills family— Dorothy did."

"But I thought she was killed that night too? Wasn't she?"

The phone went silent.

"Hello?" Myeisha asked. "Hello?" She was yelling now. Looking at the screen, she witnessed the last of its desperate buffering before it blanked to the flat blackness of phone death. After searching frantically for the tip of the charger and plunging into the phone, Myeisha popped her gas cover, hopped from the car, and plugged the pump into the mouth of her tank. Through the passenger window, she fumbled with removing a credit a card from her purse and slipped it into the reader attached to the pump. Even after banging on the grade selection button several times, the nozzle's lever was still limp in her hand. *See attendant,* the pump's screen read. A shriek burst from her as she ran full speed toward the gas station's store. She tugged at the door, but it didn't budge.

"Hey!" She slapped the glass, her eyes crisscrossing the store for any signs of life. Taking a step backward, she noticed a handmade sign taped to the door—*Back in 15.*

"Shit," she whispered as she ran around the side of the gas station to see if the cashier may have been occupying a bathroom. The filthy restrooms were empty, but just a few yards behind the gas station was a lit house and likely the home of the owners. She ran for it.

Repeatedly, Mack dialed, hung up, and then redialed. His wife's cellphone went straight to voicemail, and the house phone belched a dull, busy signal before it ever rang. Something like he hadn't experienced since childhood washed over him. The unease puffed itself into a bubbling, hot frustration that reached his hand, causing him to pitch his phone across the front seat. It hit the passenger window with a crack, then clattered to the shadowy underworld of his truck's floorboard.

Chapter 36

"*L ittle pig, little pig, let me come in,*" Simone read with a soft growl.

Aaliyah was asleep midway through the tale, and as Simone read the last words, Jada's eyes fluttered.

"You can stay in bed with your sister tonight," Simone whispered as she pulled the metal string on Aaliyah's lamp and tucked the covers around her precious girls.

"But, Mommy ..." Jada whined, "you always make us brush our teeth after bedtime milk and cookies."

"Not tonight. Now sleep," Simone said, her voice as soothing as a lullaby as she stared into the eyes of her baby girl.

Once all her children were sleeping safe and sound, Simone went to the kitchen where she made a steaming cup of lavender tea. Through the foyer, Simone passed Dorothy Ann's painting of the dazed woman that still sat on the floor where Simone had left it after bringing it up from the basement. In the living room, she sat sipping. The wireless speaker croaked to phantom life with the thumping, dragging melody of her mother's favorite version of "Gloomy Sunday." Somewhere buried deep in the murky fog that was Simone's sorrow-filled mind was the awareness that her waterlogged cellphone was no longer functional and the fact that the speaker was not connected to anything and therefore could not be playing, but there was no questioning Billie Holiday's mellow vocals as they poured through her as loud and clear as anything she had ever heard.

Mack burst through the door; his eyes zipped over the entryway, then stalled on his wife lounging on the living room couch. "Simone, are you okay? Where are the children?" he asked breathlessly.

Simone answered with prosaic tone. "I'm fine. The children are sleeping. What's wrong?"

Onto the couch next to her, he nearly collapsed with the relief that his wife was not in some psychotic rage as he had imagined repeatedly on his bolt home. With the first word from his mouth, tears crowded his sight. "I-I-I ..." Mack took a breath and steadied himself before he tried a second time. "I was just worried about you. I talked to Myeisha. She told me everything about your mother, about the Sandman. I think you may be sick, hon ... hon ... hon. I think you need some help," he finally spit, quelling his stutter.

Simone caressed her husband's face. "I'm getting help. I've been seeing Dr. Duran."

"No, not her! Not her! She is not who she says she is," Mack said halfheartedly as he couldn't be sure who to trust anymore.

"What do you mean?"

"Sh-sh ..." Angry at his body, Mack took a moment to will his mouth to the words. "She's the daughter of that preacher who stalked your father. She is trying to hurt you. Myeisha will have to explain."

"Myeisha? You're talking to Myeisha? About me?"

"It's not like that, S-Simone."

"I've known Dr. Duran since I was a child. She *knows* the Sandman is real."

Mack dropped his head before slowly raising it again, along with his voice. "He is *not real!*"

"It sounds crazy. I know, Mack, but he is real. He is after us, all of us, but I've figured out how to beat him."

Pushing the gas pedal to the floor, Myeisha dialed as she steered her car into Black Water as fast as it would go. It took three rings before anyone answered.

"Black Water Sheriff's Department."

Myeisha recognized the voice immediately. "Kevin, it's Myeisha. I need to talk to Handow."

"He's out patrolling, Summer Closing picnic tonight. It's crazy."

"Can you contact him? It's an emergency."

"What's the emergency?"

She sighed, trying to think of the best way to articulate something she didn't know. "I don't know."

"You don't know?"

Myeisha could picture his face with that same infuriating and incredulous smirk that he donned every time she told him she was getting out of Black Water. "I'm not sure, but I think there may be a problem at the Mills house."

"Why do you think there's a problem?"

Myeisha grew anxious as her car got closer to town. "I can't explain it all right now, Kevin."

"Well, you'll have to tell me something. We're already busy tonight, and—"

"Fine! A welfare check. Can you do that? I am officially requesting a welfare check for Simone Parker at the old Mills house immediately. Please!"

Mack's sympathetic stare settled on his wife, her dull eyes, and the dark circles of skin beneath them. "It was your mother, Simone. Your mother killed your family."

As Mack droned on, Simone retreated, pulling herself back from the outer walls of flesh and skin that encapsulated her. She knew the rumors about her mother, but they weren't true. It was only what *he* wanted everyone to believe.

Mack stopped as his mind found a fact that had escaped him previously. "Isn't it early for all the kids to be asleep?"

"I was always scared to look at him, but tonight I will. I will face him. I'm the one who got away, but I know what he wants."

"Simone …"

"My eyes. He wants my eyes," Simone whispered enthusiastically as the house went dark. "He's here."

Chapter 37

———◆—◆—◆———

The Sandman peered through the backdoor's window into the darkened house, his heavy breathing marked by the expansion and contraction of his huge chest. Bundles of matted, ebony fur encircled his permanently curled mouth and crumpled snout. One heavy swing and his axe shattered the glass.

Mack leapt from the couch. "What the hell was that?"

Simone stood behind him, then placed her teacup on the end table without a word. Her face set in a genuine grin.

As Mack scrambled to the bat that leaned dutifully against one of the entry walls, the backdoor knob rattled.

"Get the kids and stay with them until I call for you." He grabbed and guided his sluggish wife up the stairs before steadying his back against the wall at the landing and gripped the bat in anticipation for whatever was coming around the corner.

The Sandman barreled into the foyer, wild and clumsy, just as Mack reeled back and swung, striking the monster in the side.

The axe slid across the floor as the wolf-faced animal grunted.

Again, Mack drew back his weapon but not before the Sandman took hold of his neck. He strained to breathe as the pressure from the gargantuan hands around his throat intensified. The bat dropped to the floor as Mack used both his hands to paw at the pounds of pressure on his neck that ignited little pinpricks of red in his eyes. Objects in Mack's sight blurred, including the face of the familiar creature in front of him. He focused on the cavernous black points that sat perfectly center in their bulbous, milky orbs. A mental fog rolled over Mack, narrowing his sight further, until a deafening series of crackles erupted all around them.

The Sandman's grip loosened, allowing Mack to suck in a load of air and land a punch in the monster's throat. The throat of a stout, wild animal it was not; it was soft and malleable. Erupting in a viscous growl, the Sandman grabbed at its own neck.

Across the floor, Mack spotted the axe. Like a snake, he slithered along until it was firmly in his grip. Just as another blast of what Mack then recognized as fireworks boomed and illuminated the sky, Mack swung and planted the axe in the creature's leg.

The Sandman sailed to the floor with a howl. As Mack went to lift himself, the monster kicked his functioning leg into Mack's jaw, sending him down again.

Warm, salty liquid pooled in Mack's cheek. Colors flashed against the walls as the pyrotechnics continued to boom. Blinking, Mack searched for a weapon, and in the corner, he saw a shadowy figure watching and waiting. Before he could fully decipher the silhouette, it seemed to move under the shadows toward the kitchen. Mack's heart was intent on pushing through his chest when he noticed the Sandman pulling himself up along the wall. By now, Mack had only enough strength to reach up and yank the axe from the beast's leg, causing him to collapse into the frail foyer table.

It shattered under his weight. Rolling on the floor, he tried to cover the gaping wound with his hand, but blood rushed through his fingers and onto the hardwood.

"Mama …" Mack heard the beast whimper during a lull in the festival fireworks as drawers rattled somewhere in the kitchen. Mack pulled himself across the floor, and once close enough, saddled the beast and punched repeatedly, his grotesque face contorting under the power of Mack's fists. Only once the face was twisted unnaturally sideways did Mack see it wasn't a face at all. Self-imposed mind tricks in hand with the deception of darkness and the shadow shifting caused by the fireworks' beguiling illumination had made him see a monster where there was only a mask—the same leathery material and look of the one he left at the hospital in the hands of Dr. Duran. Lifting it, he found himself staring into the sad eyes of a child—eyes, one noticeably larger than the other, in the face of a troubled man.

"Who"—Mack inhaled and exhaled hard before he had the air to finish his sentence—"the hell are you?"

Another burst of fireworks filtered into the sky, sparking one after the other as what little air Mack had escaped his body in one swoosh as something plunged into his side. Yelling wasn't an option—one needed oxygen for such a thing—the only sound he could manage was a strained squeak. Reaching down, he felt the handle of a butcher knife he didn't have the strength to remove protruding from his lower back. Looking back, he saw Dr. Duran standing over him, the sparkling rage in her eyes highlighted by the last of the brilliant fireworks. Mack sunk to the floor in a wordless motion.

Simone bellowed a deafening scream as she lunged toward Dr. Duran and cracked her temple with the bat.

"Mama," the man along the wall sputtered, blood stringing down from one side of his lopsided mouth.

With a whipping change in direction, Simone was beating the man with the bat. It came down continually, thudding into the man's chest and head, splattering the walls with his blood.

"Please, no." Dr. Duran's voice was weak as she wafted back into consciousness. "My boy."

Simone stopped. "Your boy? Who are you?"

Dr. Duran crawled toward the man.

"Why did you bring him here?" Simone screamed, lifting the bat over the head of the sputtering man again in threat.

Lifting her hand into the air for mercy, Dr. Duran folded over her crumpled son in a heap of tears. "My family banished me when they discovered I was carrying him unwed. They said I could not come home unless I got rid of him. When he was born, they said he was sick because of my sin. My mother wouldn't even hold him, just nodded in obedient agreement with my father. They turned me away, but I tried. I have repented by continuing their work, ridding the world of *pathetic psychos* like you and your mother," Dr. Duran spat. "I gave up everything for my baby, but it still wasn't good enough. You know how it is; you're a mother." She spoke through sobs while kissing her boy's blood-soaked flesh and took no notice of Simone lifting the bat as she turned her son's fractured face upward so she could see his brown eyes. "I love you," Dr. Duran whispered a second before the bat slammed into her head, jerking it to an angle that ensured it was no longer properly connected to the rest of her body.

Jonathan blubbered a cry as his mother's lifeless body slumped to his side in a permanent and final pose.

"Simone, no!" Mack wheezed, but it was too late.

Harnessing his last remaining spark of energy, Jonathan threw himself onto Simone's lower body and pulled her to the floor.

Her head banged against the bottom step as she fell.

Mack fought the pain that surged through every inch of him and crawled across the floor where he wrenched Jonathan from his wife. Mack didn't have much left, but he banged the man's already broken face into the hardwood one good time before rolling helplessly onto his side and closing his tired eyes.

Simone gave her head one forceful shake, then squeezed her eyes closed to clear the haze.

Jonathan mewled but was no longer moving.

When Mack opened his eyes, Simone was standing over the man with the axe raised. "Simone, stop!" Mack called with only enough time to lift his forearm as the axe sliced down.

One last pathetic sound slipped from Jonathan's upturned lips as the blade sunk into his back. Johnathan's blood pooled underneath him. Mack gagged at its warm smoothness when the spread reached him.

He heard the sickening sloshing of Simone trying to wrench the weapon from Jonathan's tissue.

Once out, she raised the axe and let it fall again and again until the man was nothing more than a lifeless mound of bloody flesh.

Powerless, Mack resolved himself to the unconsciousness that had long been threatening to whisk him away. The moment he closed his eyes, a moving vision of his family on the day they had arrived at the home craned to life. *His wife smiled with both her hands pressed protectively to her bulging belly. The girls bounced playfully onto the porch and into the shadows just beyond the threshold.* Mack's eyelids popped open. "The kids."

Now would have been a good time to ask his wife to call someone—the police, Myeisha, or that Sheriff Handow—but his now hysterical thoughts returned over and over to his children. A knowing sorrow engulfed his face as he looked up the stairs. Neither the fight nor the fireworks had brought them down.

"Simone? Are the children okay?" Mack asked the woman whose face he hardly recognized under the full cover of Jonathan's blood.

She spoke tenderly, "Of course, they are. You didn't keep your promise, Mack, but I told you I would protect them, and I have."

For a moment, Mack was sure the axe had plunged into his chest instead of Jonathan's back as a crippling heartache coursed through its broad frame, leaving no inch of it free from agony. "What did you do to them, Simone?"

"I made them sleep. But that was only part of the problem. He's still here."

Hoisting his body up the steps, he called out, "Aaliyah!" His tears came in uncontrollable waves. "Jada! Trace!" Mack whimpered.

Stepping over Jonathan, Simone went to the Sandman. She took the face into her hands, then stretched it over her head. As she moved toward the foyer mirror, she wiped the blood from the mask on the painting smock she still wore, some of the red smearing across the massive, green paint splatter on the front. By pulling the mask over her face, his power now belonged to her. The reflection brought forth a barrage of memories.

Simone's child-age voice spoke to Dr. Duran weeks after the accident. "Mom was already stressed, then she had Baby Charlie. We thought he would make it better, but it got worse. Ella falling from the butterfly tree and having to go to the hospital was just too much, I guess."

Simone shifted her face in the mirror, studying the Sandman from all angles.

"If you live to be one hundred, I hope to live to be one hundred minus one day, so I never have to live without you," Jada's voice sang.

The last days of her pregnancy with Trace sprang to mind.

Simone sat in the nursery for hours while the girls were in school, staring at the walls. "There's no place like home," she repeated, reminding herself this was her home, not his.

Another flash.

Simone peeked into her father's office to spy on her mother who watched out the window as the members of the Church of All Saints chanted just along the tree line. There on Daniel Mills' desk lay the ferocious wolf mask her father had confiscated from his patient.

"Anything can happen, child. Anything can be," she stated squarely into the mirror.

The dry dust of the basement filled Simone's nose, and as clear as if she were there again, she watched from the steps as her mother ripped the necklace from Ella's neck.

"The greatest secrets are always hidden in the most unlikely places," Myeisha's voice echoed. "Doctors don't know if it's nature or nurture."

Simone sat in front of the mirror in Jada's room with both her girls just after braiding Jada's hair on the first evening of school. An eyeless Ella whispered in her ear, "You look just like Mommy."

The thud of the fridge door hitting Aaliyah in the face struck Simone. "I'll eat you up, I love you so."

Simone revisited herself in the hour just before Mack returned home that night.

Carefully, she crushed the sleeping pills prescribed by Dr. Duran and poured their contents into the bottle of formula and two glasses of milk.

Last was her final memory from the night Ella fell from the butterfly tree.

Chapter 38

———◆—◆—◆———

*J*ust a child, snug in her dinosaur pajamas, Simone crept toward the Sandman
who stood at the top of the stairs, waiting. As she got close, he turned. The
Sandman knelt, extending one arm. His hand—she knew that hand.
Everything in her told to run, to hide. He had hurt her sister, she knew, but something
stronger compelled Simone. She remembered feeling the soft fabric of the painting smock
against her face as she fell into the Sandman's loving but one-armed embrace.

"It's okay. Mommy's here," he said. In the hand of the arm folded behind her
back was the glitter of a blade.

As the Sandman released her, Simone searched his face, the sharp teeth showing
from under the grimacing nose. Then into his eyes she fell, reaching beyond the small
circular cutouts to the recognizable brown irises just beneath them.

"You," Simone whispered just before she shoved.

Down the stairs, the Sandman clattered head over feet, then head again until
her skull hit the last step with a crash. From beneath her oddly sprawled body, blood
ran from the wound where the butcher knife had stabbed Dorothy in her belly.

At last, Simone was back in the foyer, staring down her beastly
image in the mirror. A montage of faces reflected: those of the Sandman,
her mother, her daughters', and finally, her own.

"It's okay. Mommy's here." Simone's voice sloped mid-phrase to
an abnormally low key.

Turning in the direction of her husband's futile calls, she saw he was
already up the stairs, dragging himself down the hallway along the floor.

She grabbed the axe handle and dragged it; every thump of its butt hitting the steps beneath her feet gave Mack real-time proximity warning. As Simone centered herself in the hallway at the top of the stairs, Mack was halfway into Aaliyah's room where his holler mutated to a ghastly wail.

Mack could feel Simone over him now. He rolled over and peered up at the beast standing over him. "*Why?*"

"You can't wake them, Mack. I won't let you." She raised the axe high over her head before bringing it down, deep into the center of his middle.

Chapter 39

———◆—◆—◆———

I t was a bad sign. Myeisha's body trembled as she turned her car off Maple Road and navigated the short trail that led to Simone's home. The only thing giving her any relief as she passed the miserable seconds in a state so ridden with anxiety that she was in physical pain was that Sheriff Handow's patrol car had pulled onto the dirt path from the opposite direction a second before her and was bumping along just ahead.

"Please, please, please," she whispered to herself as she made the curve that put the Mills home into full view.

There was no light or movement inside. The full moon seemed to hover directly over it as if the two were affixed to one another in some bizarre fusing of cosmos and earth. Its intense shine through the leftover smoke from the fireworks display trapped the home in a dizzying turquoise-colored fog, distorting the sight of the house and making it more a delusion of nightmares than a family home.

A sickness crept into Myeisha's belly as she took notice of Mack's truck. *Why wasn't there a single light on when I had just spoken to him and told him I was on my way?*

As she shifted into Park and jumped out, the front door of the house swung open.

With a startled noise, Handow, who had barely emerged from his vehicle, drew his weapon.

"No, Simone!" Myeisha cried. Centered in the doorway, Myeisha recognized her friend, even in a mask.

"Holy shit," Handow whispered as his eyes grew to the size of the moon above them. When McKinney had radioed him to perform a welfare check here, not once had he suspected he would find anything more than a woman in bed, too sick to take or return the phone calls of a friend always in need of a story. The only thing that disturbed him more than what stood before him was that it wasn't the first time he had seen the results of this same monster making a visit on the family in this home, and to that, he mournfully shook his head.

Removing the mask, Simone sucked down a gulp of the crisp night air and tilted her head backward, basking in the headlights of Handow's patrol car as a series of smooth horns made the introduction for her sister's namesake to gush the lyrics of "Summertime" from the speaker that still played, even if only in her head. When she opened her eyes, she was eased by the sight of Myeisha and Sheriff Handow who stood still like scarecrows poking up from her front yard.

The Sandman was gone. She had won and help had arrived. At once, tears flushed powerful rivers down her cheeks as she looked down and nuzzled Baby Trace wrapped tightly in the green blanket with gold letters. She firmed her grasp on Jada's little hand.

The girl eyed her mother—her mouth curled in her signature joy, her eyes hidden beneath the bunny mask—as they descended the porch steps. Simone turned back to ensure Aaliyah was still following close behind.

"Myeisha ..." Simone said. "He was here. The Sandman. He tried to take us, but I figured it out. I faced him." Cold hair, damp with the drying blood that covered her, stuck to the side of her face, and she felt her own blood staining her inner thighs as she staggered forward.

Myeisha had trouble finding her words, and her legs shook as she stepped forward. "Are … Are you okay?"

Simone erupted in a polite cry. "I'm fine." She forced a pitiful smile. "We're fine. Everything is fine."

"Where is Mack?" Sheriff Handow asked, his weapon still trained on Simone.

At once, she seemed confused. "Uh, in the house, I think."

"And the children?" Myeisha's voice broke.

"The children? They're right here." Simone looked to the bloody, blue quilt that felt peculiarly light. She blinked multiple times, trying to find Trace somewhere in that little quilted mass. To her left, she searched for Jada who, just a moment ago, was griping her hand. Simone's head snapped backward in search of her eldest child. "Aaliyah!" she screamed at the empty space. They were gone. Simone's eyes flashed up to Aaliyah's bedroom window.

Inside, Jada lay across the floor on her belly, Aaliyah was neatly in bed, and Trace tucked in his crib; all cold and breathless.

"What have you done, Simone?" Myeisha cried. "*What have you done!*"

The words blew through her like the breath of a wolf demolishing houses made of straw and sticks. One last time, Simone eyed her bloody arms in search of the beautiful children they had once embraced, and again—and in finality—they were gone.

"Simone, I need you to lay on your stomach and put your hands behind your back," Sheriff Handow instructed before he grabbed his squawking radio to request assistance.

"He's done it again, Myeisha," Simone stated as she dropped to the ground. "He tricked me, and he won't stop until he gets what he wants."

"Simone!" Myeisha called.

"Simone, *get on your stomach!*" Handow shouted.

"*No!*" Myeisha screamed as Simone reached for her own face.

It was too late.

Her fingers were already deep in her own skull, grasping through the blood that gushed from the sockets. She ripped, feeling the soft balls break free of the nerves that attached them to her brain. She felt no pain but could hear her own screams pounding into her ears.

"Christ," Sheriff Handow whispered as he lowered his gun from the grisly sight of Simone holding her gory offering to the full, silvery, silent orb in the sky.

One Week Later

A herd of rubber-bottom shoes padded along the hospital's linoleum-floored hallway as a group of young people cloaked in offensively white coats followed behind an older doctor whose face was permanently streaked with the lines of stress. They passed room 329 where golden sunlight from the window drenched the space inside. Not that Simone could see it, but she could *feel* it. She felt the patches of gauze that covered her eye sockets. She also felt the thick, rubber restraints that held her arms by her side and her legs together, strapped to the bed.

"Give me my babies!" she screamed at them aimlessly. "I gave you want you wanted!"

They are alive, she often thought in her ongoing medical-induced hazes, but on other occasions when the nurses were running behind on her dosing, in that terrifying, unmedicated limbo where reality was permitted to pound at the door of her psyche, she knew they were dead.

Either way, it was the Sandman. He tricked me, just like he tricked my mother.

Simone couldn't think of Mack, not ever. Thoughts of him sometimes got close before she thrashed them from her mind in fear that if she ever formed his beautiful features fully in her mind's eye again, she would slip to an even more abysmal place of darkness from which return could never be an option. When she wasn't screaming for her children, she thought of her father, brother, sister, and mother. There had been good times, countless in their occurrence, and memories of intimate moments with her mother was the closest thing to divine. As she remembered how her mother would hold her and sing that lullaby she had been trying desperately to remember for her girls, it came to her slowly but in full. Simone hummed, then sang,

"Twinkle, twinkle, you are my little star.

I'll rock you and put you to bed, my house is made of gingerbread

And candy.

What can be wrong with me?

I love you to the core; it pulls me to the floor.

I fall, I stumble, and I crawl for you.

Hush, little baby, don't you cry.

Here comes the Sandman, close … your … EYES."

Epilogue

Myeisha slurred her request for *another*. That afternoon, she had promised herself she would visit Simone in the hospital, but her car had somehow driven her to a bar where she had spent the last several hours. As the bartender neatly placed the fourth, fresh rum and Coke in front of her on a napkin, she peered into the long mirror behind the bar, and for a single second, the startling reflection was that of her mother.

If you enjoyed this book

Take two minutes and leave a review. Reviews are imperative to the success and visibility of authors, especially independent ones.

Grab the first two books in this series to continue your descent into Black Water today!

Black Water Tales: The Unwanted

Black Water Tales: The Secret Keepers

Go to http://eepurl.com/bUiLp9 to join my email network and be the first to get FREE short stories, news on beta reading opportunities, availability of new ARCs, and much more.

Things to Think About

1. Pregnancy-related deaths are two to three times higher for Black, American Indian, and Alaska Native (AI/AN) women than they are for white women. (A:https://www.cdc.gov/media/releases/2019/p0905-racial-ethnic-disparities-pregnancy-deaths.html)

2. Women of color and low-income mothers are more likely to suffer from postpartum mental illness. For a variety of reasons, they are less likely to talk about it and receive treatment.

    a. Black women fear state-sanctioned organizations will remove their children from their care. National studies have found Black mothers are deemed unfit by child welfare workers at higher rates than white mothers (B:https://khn.org/news/black-mothers-get-less-treatment-for-postpartum-depression-than-other-moms/).

    b. Cost of doctor visits, medication, and therapy. (B)

    c. Cultural stigmas associated with Black women identifying themselves as struggling with a mental illness.

        i. Mental illness can be perceived as a sign of weakness within the community (C:https://digitalcommons.brockport.edu/cgi/viewcontent.cgi?article=1171&context=edc_theses) which flies in the face of the comfortable archetype of Strong Black Woman/Mammy.

        ii. Due to inaccurate portrayals as drug users and addicts, Black women fear being identified as medication seeking.

3. Because minorities commonly experience mental illness as physical symptoms (headaches, stomach issues, anxiety, etc.), it is less likely to be recognized by themselves or by doctors, as historically, most women included in postpartum mental health studies are white women who are able to identify their illness more directly. (B)

What's Next

Be on the lookout for the first release in my new dark thriller series, *Lies in the Water* (Summer 2021).

Dahlia Dixon's life is finally moving in a positive direction. After marrying her rich and handsome boss, she is whisked away to his beautiful lake house. The problem? His previous wife, who drowned in that lake, is still hauntingly present. After a mysterious car runs Dahlia off the road and she learns that yet another woman disappeared on the lake, she realizes that she is in someone's crosshair. Can she uncover what secrets dwell in the water before she herself is dragged beneath its glassy surface?

About the Author

Jean Nicole is a National Black Book Festival award-winning novelist. She has also garnered awards for her short screenplay, *If I Die*, from multiple film festivals, including the Shivers International Film Festival (Canada).

In 2016, she launched the only Black-woman-owned creative writing software, <u>Simply Stylus</u>, and she teaches an online beginner writing course titled, <u>Simply Writing: An Aspiring Author's Guide to Developing A Solid Writing Process and FINALLY Writing Their Novel</u>.

She writes because she loves words; she writes because she loves stories; she writes because she has a story to tell.

- *www.jeannicolerivers.com*
- *www.facebook.com/JNicoleRivers/*
- *@JeanNicole19 (Instagram and Twitter)*
- *@JeanNicole19 (Instagram and Twitter)*
- *www.goodreads.com/author/show/5582487.Jean_Nicole_Rivers*
- *https://www.youtube.com/channel/UCOU4nXpJy5vMTkWOhjuS5yQ*

Suggested Discussion Questions

1. What was Simone thinking when she first moved her family into her childhood home? Was she emotionally reliable at that point?

2. Mack learned more about Simone and her family after moving into the house. Did he just not know her well, or is it normal to hide darker parts of your past from your spouse?

3. Did Simone make a mistake in not seeking a new doctor after her initial visits with Dr. Penny?

4. Have you ever felt unheard by your medical professional during pregnancy, birth and/or early motherhood?

5. Simone felt the need to always be "fine." Why is that, and what toll does this expectation take on Black women?

6. Was Mack complicit or at least negligent in his wife's downward spiral?

7. Can maternal love and instinct alone overcome severe mental health issues?

8. Is being a mother the most difficult job in the world? Why or why not?

9. Was Simone justified in her last action against her mother the night Ella fell from the butterfly tree?

10. Was Simone a good mother?

Resources for support

*Valid at the time of publication

https://www.blackwomenbirthingjustice.org/

http://www.abpsi.org/

https://blacktherapistnetwork.com/

https://www.facebook.com/sobproject/

TRIGGER WARNING

This book contains depictions of child murder.

To the Moon and Back. Copyright @ 2021 by JNR Publishing. All rights reserved. Printed in the United States of America. No parts of this book may be used, recreated, or reproduced in any manner without written permission from the publisher except in the case of short quotes for marketing, promotions, and reviews.

Library of Congress Cataloging-in-Publication Data Black Water Tales: To the Moon and Back

ISBN 978-1-7364756-0-7